SUMMER FATE

EMMA NICHOLS

Britain's Next
BESTSELLER

First published in 2019 by:

Britain's Next Bestseller
An imprint of Live It Publishing
27 Old Gloucester Road
London, United Kingdom.
WC1N 3AX

www.bnbsbooks.co.uk

ISBN: 9781072597346

Also available in digital format.

Other books by Emma Nichols

To keep in touch with the latest news from Emma Nichols
and her writing please visit:

www.emmanicholsauthor.com
www.facebook.com/EmmaNicholsAuthor
www.twitter.com/ENichols_Author

Thanks

Without the assistance, advice, support and love of the following people, this book would not have been possible.

Bev. It's a good job one of us is funny, eh? Thank you for painstakingly going through the chapters again and again. I think we got there in the end, chicky.

Valden. Thank you for your supportive feedback. I'm delighted you enjoyed the book more than you thought you would.

Mu. Thank you for your on-going support, creative ideas and nailing another brilliant cover. Thank you, my love.

To my wonderful readers and avid followers. Thank you for continuing to read the stories I write. I have really enjoyed writing this romcom and I hope you enjoy the light-hearted humour, quirky – and of course – edgy summer romance.

With love, Emma x

Dedication

To Mum. It's been eight years now.
This book would have made you laugh x

1.

'Right everyone!' Doris Akeman said, her voice carrying across the small committee room and grabbing the attention of those present. 'The first planning meeting for this year's Summer Fete committee will be next Friday at 6 pm. I expect we will all be here,' she added, her tone leaving no room for question, as she squinted over the top of her glasses at the nodding heads. 'Good! So, on that note, we can close tonight's meeting.' She studied the face of the delicate gold watch hanging loosely over her bony wrist then looked up, removed her spectacles, placed them carefully into a case that she snapped shut and dropped them into her handbag. 'Unless someone has any other business they wish to raise?' she added, fastening the handbag with a sharp click of the clasp.

Jenny Haversham's chair scraped the wooden floor as she sat up. 'I have,' she said. Her warm smile wasn't returned, and she waited for permission to continue.

No one ever raised any other business. This must be serious.

Doris addressed Jenny with a glare and a flurry of wrinkles appeared to take over her face with the frown that narrowed her eyes. 'Right,' she said, placing her handbag on the floor and clasping her hands together. She rested them on the table in front of her and indicated for Jenny to continue.

Sheila Goldsworth looked up from the notes she had been taking. 'Is that the meeting closed, Mrs Akeman?' she said, pen poised, addressing Doris. She had been the local school secretary for more than forty years, during Doris's tenure as headmistress, and always deferred to the now parish committee chairwoman as if she still held the prestigious position.

Doris raised her hand in response and pointed to Jenny, whose hand was also hovering in the air, to draw Sheila's attention to her.

'Oh right.' Sheila flustered, picked up the ruler at the side of the pad and drew a line through what she had written. She stared at Jenny, returning her smile. 'I'm ready,' she said.

All eyes were on Jenny Haversham.

Jenny scanned the group as she took in a deep breath. 'Well, I'm speaking on behalf of Vera as well, of course,' she said. 'As you know, Vera went on a cruise yesterday.' She cleared her throat. 'She will be away for a month,' she said looking down and avoiding eye contact.

'I'm surprised you let her loose for that long,' Doug Pettigrew quipped.

Jenny ignored his facetious comment and went to continue with her point only to be interrupted by Delia Harrison.

'Oh, how lovely,' Delia piped up, from across the table.

'Yes, thank you, Delia,' Jenny said and smiled at her old friend.

'Isn't that a bit dangerous?' Esther said, looking quite shocked.

Jenny frowned.

'She's not on the bloody *Titanic*,' her husband, Doug retorted.

'Oh, I did love that movie,' Delia said, with a sigh.

'Uh-oh, here we go,' Doug muttered.

'We will pray for her safety,' Elvis said, directing a reassuring smile towards Esther.

Esther visibly relaxed. 'Thank you, Vicar,' she said.

'I do love Tom Cruise,' Delia said.

She had drifted into a world of her own making and Doug was gazing at her shaking his head.

'Tom Cruise wasn't in the *Titanic*, he was in *Top Gun*,' Doug said, rolling his eyes. He slouched back in his seat and crossed his arms.

'Meg Ryan was incredible too,' Delia added. She was on a roll now.

'That was *Sleepless in Seattle*, with Tom Hanks,' Doug corrected.

'I think Daniel Craig is the hottest of all though. Don't you, Jenny?' Delia said.

She was heading completely off-piste now and if Doris didn't interject soon, they'd never get to the end of the meeting.

'Bloody hell,' Doug said and held his head in his hands.

Doris elevated herself in her chair and cleared her throat. 'If we could get back to the point, please ladies. Thank you for your contribution, Doug.'

Jenny held back a chuckle. Committee meetings were always like this and she had learned over the years to just go with the flow. You couldn't be in a rush to do something else, and for some attendees, this was the height of their social life.

'Thank you, Doris,' Doug said in earnest, his face a shade darker than a few moments earlier. He studied his watch. 'Pub's open in a minute, Vicar.'

Elvis fiddled with his dog collar as if to loosen the shackle, sweat beaded across his forehead. 'Not as long as I'm here,' he said.

Sheila, pen poised, looked at Doris. 'Sorry, Mrs Akeman, was there a decision I need to note?' she asked.

Elvis placed a soft plump hand on hers and smiled. 'I don't think we're at that point yet, Sheila,' he said.

'Can we get to the bloody point?' Doug said, his cheeks now bordering on cerise. The purple tinges spidering across his skin were as much a result of his years frequenting the pub, as his frustration and added something qualitatively intangible to his otherwise handsome features.

'Vera's niece, Grace, is arriving this afternoon. She will be with us until Vera gets back.' Longer, if things go to plan, she thought. 'She's agreed to dog sit at the house,' Jenny said.

'I thought your Harriet was dog sitting for Vera?' Delia said.

'Yes, that was the original plan, and then, it all.' She hesitated. 'It all happened very last minute. Grace decided to take some time out from her busy work schedule and wants to spend it with us.' The latter was an extension of the truth, but sometimes less was more at committee meetings, and especially when it came down to the finer details.

'I thought Grace was a workaholic?' Doug said.

'She is; she was. But an opportunity came up and she has decided to take the summer off. Vera and I suggested she come here for a break and.' Jenny paused again, aware that all eyes were on her; except Sheila's whose eyes were on the sheet of paper in front of her, pen scribbling diligently. 'Well, Vera and I thought it might be an opportunity for Harriet too.'

'Sounds like Vera's Grace has stolen the opportunity to me,' Doug said, 'Since she's no longer needed for dog sitting duties.' He laughed.

Jenny interjected quickly. 'An opportunity to get them both together, Doug.'

'The dogs already live together,' Doug and Esther chorused.

'No, get Grace and Harriet together.'

'Not another bloody plan,' Doug said, reminded of a long list of plans the women had previously tried to engineer. He rolled his eyes, turned to Elvis and pointed to his watch as if to say, can we get the pub open?

'Ooh, that sounds fun,' Delia said, rubbing her hands together. 'Close encounters, eh?'

'Bloody *Fatal Attraction*,' Doug said, still shaking his head.

'Isn't that the one where she boiled the rabbit?' Esther said.

'Enough!' Doris said, raising her voice, and frantically tapping the table, having little effect on stemming the laughter around the room.

'We know Grace. It's totally different,' she insisted.

Elvis cleared his throat, his deeper tone bringing the room to order.

'If we could move along, please Jenny,' Doris said, and a tight smile wrinkled her lips.

'Bravo, Doris,' Doug chirped and lounged back in his seat.

'Bryan's picking up Grace as we speak, and we need a plan,' Jenny said with a greater sense of urgency, aware that Doug had reached his limit and Elvis needed to get back to open the pub.

'What, a *Mission Impossible*, plan?' Delia said, excitedly.

'Well, hopefully, a mission possible plan,' Jenny responded. 'We all need to support the plan though,' she added, gazing from one member of the group to the next. 'Are we all in? We all need to encourage the two girls to spend time together, and then keep our fingers crossed that chemistry works its magic'.

'*Operation Interfering Set-Up*,' Doug said, tucking his chair under the table.

'*Operation Purple Heart*,' Delia said with a dazed look. 'I've seen it in the cards, already. I told you all last month, I'd seen Hilda on the prowl again.'

'That'll be the homebrew, Delia,' Doug said.

Delia glared at him.

'Anyway, Purple Heart's a bloody military decoration for an act of bravery,' Doug said. 'I think Kev needed that, after the scare you lot gave him.' He laughed.

5

Delia ignored him and suddenly focused. 'We need a code word,' she said, excitedly.

'For what?' Doug said, scratching his full head of hair with vigour.

'If we need to warn each other or let each other know one of the girls is around, or something, so we can watch what we say?'

'That'll be the day,' Doug quipped, minded of the inability of any one of them around the room to be able to keep a secret for more than five minutes. 'How about *Operation I'm Going Home*?' he suggested. 'The 'G' stands for Grace and the 'H' for Harriet. Better still, *I'm Going to the Pub*,' he said.

'That's brilliant,' Delia said, nodding furiously.

He hadn't been serious.

'I'm not sure what we need a password for,' Esther piped up.

'Come on Vicar,' Doug said.

Elvis nodded to Doris who nodded back.

Sheila looked up from the paper. 'Was there a decision to note, Mrs Akeman?' she said. The pen quivered in her arthritic grip as she waited for instruction. She looked to Elvis as he squeezed her shoulder.

'I think the meeting's about closed,' he said softly. '*Operation I'm Going to The Pub* has just begun,' he added and smiled.

'Oh right,' Sheila said and scribbled a note. 'Is there a password, Vicar?'

'It'll be the same, Sheila,' Elvis said not wanting to confuse matters any further.

'Oh right,' Sheila said and wrote, I'm going to the pub, again.

*

6

Grace gazed out from the train at the passing landscape. The urban view had long since been replaced with rolling countryside, cows and sheep; mere dots that disappeared in an instant, and the odd smattering of houses distanced from each other by winding roads, and, more greenery. So much green! Of course, they had the parks in London, and she had visited Devon, and the moors, to see her mother, but that didn't compare to this. With each transition deeper into what felt like the wilderness, her heart weighed heavily and already she was questioning her decision to head up this way for a break. The feeling of isolation seemed to sit somewhere between her throat and stomach, and it was difficult to discern how much of the sensation was down to taking the trip and how much of it was down to the current situation at work.

She hadn't intended to tell her mother that she was taking a break from the job but after the first month off work, and with infinite time on her hands, she had confessed. I'm taking a sabbatical, she had said. She hated lying but didn't have the energy to try to explain the circumstances of the company's enforced leave. After a brief silence, Nell had insisted that she visit Devon, and Grace had conceded. Devon, though, had quickly driven her insane and she had returned to her flat in London.

Two weeks later, her mother had turned up on her doorstep, knowing full well that it would be harder for her to refuse a proposition face-to-face. Dog sit for your aunt Vera while she takes a holiday, she had said. Everyone's very friendly and welcoming in the Lakes, and there are more people your age. It will be fun.

And now, here she was, sat on a train heading north. She gazed at the passing scenery. More greenery! The gigantic, white turbines dominating the skyline had a mesmerising effect and she found her eyes closing and her mind drifting.

How did she get to this point? As founder and CEO of Events for Life, her own life had been consumed by making the right decisions, and she was bloody good at it. She was known for her sound judgement. It was what her reputation had been founded on – she was respected for the choices she had made that had led to the company's quick rise to success: the right events, at the right time, in the right location. Duplication had paid off big time, and global expansion had been effortless. It was this fact that made the incongruence of one flash decision, taken in the heat of the moment, even more incomprehensible. She had replayed the past weeks again and again and still couldn't work out how she had misread the situation. Had she? Deep down, she didn't think she had, but convincing the Board of her innocence was proving more challenging than she could have conceived.

Her eyes flashed open, but the reflections continued. Yes, she had been incensed when the Board asked her to take paid leave while they considered their options, and then enraged. Now, a hollow feeling had adopted her, and it didn't bring with it any sense of reassurance, just a boding sense of nothingness; a boundary-less world devoid of purpose and meaning. It sucked. Sandra fucking Floss sucked!

Nell was right about the need to take a break from London. Being at home with nothing to occupy her mind and too close to work hadn't given her any space from the situation, but whether Duckton-by-Dale was the right choice she wasn't yet convinced. Let alone dog sitting. She had never owned a dog, let alone two. At least she could maintain her privacy up here. No one knew her. There would be no one seeking her out to ask more damn questions about the events of the past weeks. No one in this small village needed to know about Sandra fucking Floss. And, how she wanted to forget that name. God, how she rued the day she had set eyes on the woman, with her encouraging smile and intense dark eyes. How could she have been so foolish? So, fucking naïve. Fuck it!

She released a long breath hoping to ease the tightness, gathered herself and directed her attention back to the rolling countryside. Then, her eyes shut again. Fuck, fuck, fuck! The burning sensation brought a tear that escaped from the corner of her eye and she wiped it gently and released another sigh. Sandra fucking Floss! She drifted with the rocking of the carriage, absorbing herself in the rhythmic clatter. Ten more minutes, and she could lose herself for a month in the inanity of village life. Quiet, peaceful, and private. She could keep herself to herself, walk the dogs, and escape to the hills. She nodded in affirmation of her thoughts. Yes, she would enjoy the rest, and the distraction would help her gain some perspective on her life.

2.

Grace opened her eyes to the sign *Duckton-by-Dale* and noted the duck footprints stencilled on either side of the words. She rose from the seat just as the train lurched to a final stop. She moved towards the door, lifted her suitcase from the baggage rack and waited for the green light to open the door. She strained to lift the case out of the carriage and stood on the platform. Alone. Locating the exit, which wasn't overly challenging given the one gate in and out of the small station, she crossed the track via the footbridge and strode out onto a cobbled pathway. The entrance to the station was set back from a single-track road, surrounded by fields, and had parking spaces for three cars. The place was isolated, and there wasn't a person in sight. A twinge of anxiety pricked her, and she challenged it with a resolution to enjoy the quiet life. She pulled her mobile from her jacket pocket.

'Shit, one bar,' she said and then that dropped out and she moaned as she put the phone back into her pocket.

She reached into the other pocket and pulled out the note from her aunt. *Bryan will pick you up from the station. It's only a short ride to the house.* Maybe she should start walking; she could do with stretching her legs, but which direction? And then, there was the not so small issue of high heels on cobbles and an oversized suitcase to drag. She looked down at her feet sitting off-balance on the uneven stones then looked towards the road. Not a bloody signpost in sight.

She registered the white-haired lady, in a purple, plastic raincoat, crossing the entrance to the station at the top of the road, walking a dog, and she went to call out to her. Then her brain struggled to reconcile the image. Something seemed amiss. What was that? The woman had passed already, and Grace tried to make sense of the residual memory. It was, without doubt, the strangest looking poodle she had ever seen. Not that she was a dog connoisseur but with its fluffy white trimmed coat, and puffballs at its ankles and a pink ribbon pulled in a bow around the puffs on its head, it certainly looked like a poodle. A show dog, maybe? Blimey! Something odd though! She racked her brain. Tail? Don't poodle's have a tail, usually with a puffball on top? Wait, paws… dogs have paws, not… Grace blinked towards the road, hoping the image would return. She shook her head. No, seriously. Was that a sheep? On a lead! She rubbed her eyes, gazed across the fields that surrounded her. Nope. She must be imagining things. She really did need this break.

A sense of relief passed through her as a black Land Rover turned into the entrance and drew up beside her. This must be Bryan.

Bryan Haversham leapt out of the vehicle with more energy than Grace expected to see for a man of his age and a broad smile that conveyed pure pleasure. Close shaven, short snowy white hair and ruddy cheeks that glowed, he looked the epitome of health and vitality. He bounded towards her; his hand outstretched.

'Hello, you must be Grace.'

She took his hand and in a split-second found herself pulled into a full body hug that stopped an ounce short of squeezing the life out of her. Released equally as fervently, she felt his absence as a shock wave down to the Jimmy Choo heels that slipped into a crevasse between the stones. Taken aback, she tottered towards him and he reached for her hand.

'Sorry, I'm under strict instructions to make you feel welcome,' he added, then started to chuckle. 'Did I overdo it a bit?'

Grace steadied herself. His hand was warm and soft against hers, comforting and strong. 'No, I'm good, thank you. I feel very welcomed,' she said, and he guffawed; a noise that caused Grace's jaw to relax and her lips to twitch.

'Good. You will be sure to tell Jenny when you see her.'

'Jenny?'

'My ex-wife. She still gives me instructions. Thinks I don't know how to behave,' he said with a wink, his eyes sparkling like a cheeky toddler.

Jenny, Grace repeated silently, reminded of the name her mother had mentioned. Jenny is Vera's closest friend, Nell had said. Jenny's daughter, Harriet, lives next door to Vera. Harriet has a smallholding, with horses, is a keen photographer, and gardener. I'm sure you'll like her, she had said. By all accounts, Harriet seemed to be good at most things according to Vera and would be able to help with anything she should need, and then Jenny would be in contact with Vera should there be any real issues to do with the house. Not that any were expected, but Vera seemed to have all angles covered.

'Right, let's get you home,' Bryan said, reaching for the large Luis Vuitton suitcase, lifting it effortlessly and throwing it unceremoniously into the back of the vehicle.

Grace gasped, her hand moving reactively to try to stop him, watching in horror as the case landed on what looked like half a ploughed field in the back of the Land Rover. 'Please, be careful with the...' Her words drifted as Bryan slammed the boot door shut, oblivious to her plea, let alone the state in which her suitcase would appear by the time they reached the house.

He opened the passenger door and a strong, acrid, lemon scent drifted into Grace's awareness, turning her nose.

He noticed her reaction and chuckled. 'Don't tell anyone, but it's to hide the smell of smoke,' he said. 'I sneak the odd one now and again.' He wandered to the driver's side and got in.

Grace's mind shifted from the state of her suitcase in the boot to the Burberry red and white check, short skirt that now revealed her long, bare legs as she eased into a seat that appeared to be in a similar state of hygiene as the boot.

She took in a deep breath and released it slowly, recalling her commitment to go with the flow of country life, to relax in peace and quiet, and wondered what had possessed her to dress for a city function? The sun had at least warmed the leather and that went some way to soften the tension in her shoulders and compensate for the adjustment needed to cope with the strong lemon aroma. The subtle hint of stale tobacco didn't offend her, though it normally would, but she couldn't help but grab the antibacterial spray from her pocket and squirt it into her hands. Bryan chuckled and she smiled. There was something about his demeanour that was endearing. He turned the engine, crunched the gears and slammed his foot on the accelerator.

'So, how was the journey?' he said, his voice carrying above the old vehicle's rattling noises.

'It was fine,' she shouted.

'How's London these days?'

Grace jolted, an involuntary visceral response that betrayed her deep desire to keep her private life private, and a frown followed her concerned thoughts. What did he know? Tension seemed to sit in her jaw and she sensed it in her inability to raise a smile. 'London's London,' she said and looked out the side window hoping Bryan wasn't paying her any attention.

'Good idea taking a break,' he said. 'Life's too short.'

Maybe.

He seemed to fidget in the silence that lingered between them.

Grace turned to look out of the front window, slowly, hesitantly, gripping the seat beneath her. Bryan was taking the narrow road at great speed and she was feeling hopelessly out of control. She wanted to ask him to slow down but didn't want to appear rude so bit down on her lip.

'Well, everyone is very excited to see you. We've all been expecting you,' Bryan said chirpily, looking at her while twisting the vehicle around the next bend.

'Shit!' Grace screamed and slammed her body back into the seat, her foot searching for the brake. 'Sheep!'

Bryan guffawed at her reaction. 'You're safe Grace,' he said. He had already started braking and slowed to a stop well short of the herd crossing the road. He leaned out of his window and gave a cheery wave. 'Ah-right, Kev!' he shouted.

The man herding the sheep waved back. 'Ah-right Bry.' He was walking towards the vehicle, whistled to his dog, which seemed to take control, and then leant through the window to address Grace. 'Hello, Grace. Got here safe and sound, then?'

Not yet, Grace thought. 'Yes, thank you,' she said, aware that her heart was trying to escape her chest, meanwhile the sheep meandered nonchalantly across the road, and Bryan chuckled chirpily.

'You look pale,' Kev said, addressing Grace with genuine concern.

'I'm good, thanks.'

'Country air 'll sort that out,' Kev said.

He whistled again and shouted, 'Rex back,' and the Border Collie returned to the rear of the herd. 'Right, I'll see you in about an hour,' he said, addressing Bryan and tapped on the door before heading towards the field.

'Right-oh.' Bryan waved as Kev disappeared into the field followed by the remaining sheep, and his trusted dog. Another man, a lot younger than Kev, shut the first gate, crossed the road and shut the second. Bryan waved again, 'Ah-right Luke.'

Luke waved back. Bryan crunched the Land Rover into gear and set off again. 'That's Kev. He's our local farmer, and Luke Harrison's his right-hand man. Luke is Delia's son. Delia's daughter is Kelly, and she's our Jarid's better half. She's our local vet and he's the village GP. You'll get to meet them all soon enough. Delia's a bit of a psychic, well known around these parts. He chuckled to himself, mumbling something.

Grace was only aware of the incessant noise – names she had no interest in – invading her right ear as she drifted into nowhere, her heart trying to settle, her mind working hard to take stock of her new surroundings. Maybe it was a poodle she had seen earlier. It didn't look like those sheep. People seemed friendly. Too friendly? Who was the vet? She might need a vet if the dogs fell ill. Did he really say psychic? She was sure Bryan meant well, but the last thing she needed was a list of who's who, let alone the detail of what they did and why. Peace and quiet were all she asked for and she couldn't wait to get to the house. Suddenly, the thought of the dogs as her only company sounded appealing. She leaned her head back and inhaled the lemon essence. There was already a comforting familiarity about the strange scent.

Within a short time, the road seemed to straighten and after passing a small number of large detached properties, she was back to watching the passing shades of green. Green fields yielding to green trees yielding to green hedgerows and then, beyond, more green fields. Her eyes narrowed at the sight of the sandstone buildings as they passed the sign for Duckton-by-Dale.

A series of houses spanned a narrow street then a small central square with a coffee shop, a convenience store, and a pub; The Crooked Billet, she noted. Aptly named given its uneven, sloping, walls and bowed roof. The chimney looked decidedly unsafe, given the angle at which it perched. The building must have dated back to the early nineteen-hundreds, perhaps earlier. A few people milled around, and an elderly couple sat on the bench in the centre of the square.

'This is your local,' Bryan said as they passed the pub. 'If you need anything urgently, you'll find someone in there who can help you. It's owned by our Vicar, so you'll find him there when he's not running a service up at the church. I work at the pub too, most days,' he added.

Grace frowned. 'A vicar who's the landlord,' she said, confirming she wasn't completely losing the plot in such a short space of time.

'That's right. He's only a part-time Vicar though. There's more call for the pub round here than the church,' he said.

Grace craned her neck as they drove past. 'Right,' she said in a whisper. The pub did look quaint, the sign looked recently painted, bold red lettering stood out in the sunlight, but she wasn't really a pub-goer and the chances of needing anything in a hurry would be slim. Anyway, apparently, she had Harriet and Jenny to go to in the first instance.

'Vera's is just a stone's throw away,' he said, and a short way outside the village he turned the car up a lane that opened into a double-width driveway.

Grace didn't remember the place; it had been too long. Vague recollection of a large house and out-buildings, but nothing concrete had come to mind. She pondered. It must be thirty years since she had last visited; she would have been five. She couldn't remember why she hadn't visited again since. Probably because this place was in the middle of nowhere and by the time her parents had settled in the UK, she was heading to uni.

The crunching of tyres on the dirt track drew her from her thoughts and she stared at the large, cream coloured stone building, with natural wood-framed windows and ivy clinging at its sides and running across the top of the upper windows. Bryan pulled the vehicle to a stop. The name *Duckton House* was carved into the solid oak door and several, variously coloured, ceramic pots with flowers in an array of colours, shapes, and sizes took pride of place on the extensive slate-tiled porch area that ran along the front of the house. An open-sided porch framed the door itself, which would afford little protection from any prevailing weather, but it looked pretty. The place had a majestic understated appeal to it if that were even possible.

'Here we are then,' Bryan announced, yanking the handbrake into position. 'That's our Harriet's,' he said, pointing to the quaint cottage sitting to the right of the big house and the other side of the shared driveway.

Grace smiled, glancing briefly at the cottage. The two buildings couldn't be any more dissimilar. She tried to open the car door, but it wouldn't budge.

'Hang on, it can be a bit sticky,' he said. He jumped out and jogged around to Grace's side. He opened the door then went to the back and pulled out her case. 'Door key will be under the pot,' he said. He carried the case to the porch and set it on the slate.

Grace frowned. She had a printed version of the email her aunt had sent her, but did everyone know where the front door key was? He was grinning at her and she couldn't help but smile. 'Thanks, Bryan.'

He nodded and made a quiet grunting sound. 'Maybe we'll see you in the pub later?' he said. 'Dogs are allowed.' He lingered at the porch.

'Maybe,' she said, knowing full well she wouldn't be going anywhere near the pub but not wishing to offend him, not that he looked like he would be offended.

'Right, I'll be off then,' he said, still hesitant to leave. He stepped away slowly and climbed into the car.

She waved at the vehicle as it rattled back down the driveway, then turned towards the house and sighed.

She studied the sandstone structure, the large wood framed windows looked newly renovated, as did the heavy oak door. It was truly majestic and impressive; she hadn't remembered this at all. And... there was the pot. The instructions said clearly, the rustic-red pot. She recognised the small, white, bell-shaped flowers of the Mayflower protected by its large green leaves. She tilted the pot and frowned. She rocked it back and forth, searching every centimetre of the space beneath, then stood back and gazed at the front door. She huffed loudly, tried the door handle, cursed, and banged on the door. Perhaps there was someone in, not that she was expecting that to be the case. But she wasn't expecting to not find the key, either. She got the feeling Bryan would have told her if there had been someone waiting for her. She pulled out the letter and reread it. *Key is under the rustic-red flowerpot on the doorstep.* Christ, even Bryan knew the key was there. Well, there was only one flowerpot of that colour and there was no key underneath it. The car had long since disappeared and the sound of birds chirping was the only interference for her irritated thoughts. Were peace and quiet that difficult to find? She sighed, dusted the straw and loose mud off the side of her suitcase and sat on top of it, checking her phone. No messages. No bloody signal.

'No! Flo, stop!'

Grace heard the shout immediately before her body achieved a moment of levitation. Her legs and the suitcase were swept from beneath her and a shoe flew from her foot into the air. She landed with a thud, immediately descended upon by a wet tongue licking at her face, preventing her groan escaping, and a whining, squealing sound piercing her left ear. That's not a dog; it's a bloody Shetland pony!

'Flo, off! Flo!'

The frantic command didn't seem to influence the lively black and white Great Dane one iota, whose front paws had Grace pinned in the prone position, and whose muzzle assessed her neck with great enthusiasm.

'Flo!'

The sudden escalation in volume had Grace jumping, and even the dog looked up towards the source of the instruction, before noticing the errant shoe and diving straight for it.

'No, Flo,' the shout came again, the woman running towards her, two dogs on leads. The Dachshund looked barely able to keep up and the miniature Poodle couldn't run fast enough.

'My Jimmy Choo,' Grace shouted.

'Off, Flo!' the shout came again.

'It's chewing my...' Grace's words were stalled by the sight of the dog's teeth firmly wrapped around the heel of the shoe, it's paws, trapping the shoe to the ground. She threw her hands to her head. 'Oh my God!'

'Off!' the woman said. Grace watched, dumbfounded as the woman in wellies, jeans, and bright yellow raincoat tackled the Great Dane. She took the shoe from the dog and studied it carefully, before holding it out to Grace. 'I am so sorry. I think it's okay, more slobber than damage,' she said. 'I really am so dreadfully sorry, she's not normally that excitable with complete strangers.'

The Great Dane stood, wagging its tail in an unapologetic fashion.

Grace eased herself up to sit, rubbing at her elbow, aware of the assessing gaze that she thought had lingered on her exposed legs before moving up her body and then making eye contact with her. She studied the damp shoe with a grimace and took it reluctantly between the tip of her index-finger and thumb and put it on the ground. She reached into her pocket and pulled out the antibacterial spray and squirted it on her hands and then on the shoe.

The woman was blushing but there was a glint in her eye that gave her a youthful, innocent appearance.

'I am so sorry. Flo, come here,' she said, in a stern tone.

Grace winced at the pain in her hip as she started to rise.

19

'I am so sorry,' the woman said again, clipping a lead to the lively Great Dane.

Grace tensed as the darkest eyes she had ever seen rested on her. She stood staring and words wouldn't come, her hand immobilised on her sore buttock.

'You must be Grace. I'm Harriet.' Harriet had Flo under control and settled at her side. 'She's still a puppy really, and I didn't think you'd be here yet. I must have lost track of time,' she said.

'You don't wear a watch?' Grace said and then wished the words hadn't landed quite as aggressively.

'No,' Harriet said, her voice softly apologetic.

Grace felt the wave of guilt flush her face. 'I'm sorry, I didn't mean.'

'It's okay,' Harriet interrupted. 'I should have kept a track of time,' she said, nodding her head. 'Are you hurt?'

'Nothing that won't mend.' Grace studied Harriet, the line of her jaw, the wavy hair that danced lightly at her shoulders as she moved, the kindness in her dark eyes.

'I hope the shoe is okay. I'll pay for any damage,' Harriet said, aware of Grace's apparent discomfort.

Grace released a sigh, held the concerned gaze and smiled. 'It's okay. I think I might have missed the memo regarding the dress-code here,' she said, pointing to her inappropriate attire, which was either covered in dust from the driveway or slobber from the dog.

Harriet took out a tissue from her pocket and handed it to Grace.

'Thank you,' Grace said, squirted the spray onto the cloth and wiped her neck.

Harriet shifted eye contact and directed her attention to the offending Great Dane who was sat perfectly at her feet. 'I'm glad you arrived safely,' she said.

Grace wasn't sure she qualified for the term *safe arrival*, yet. She hadn't made it into the house without injury and there was still a short distance between her and the front door. Anything could happen. She smiled.

'This is Winnie. She's the old lady,' Harriet continued.

Harriet's smile held affection for the elderly Dachshund and Grace felt the warmth of the smile in a trail that ran down the back of her neck.

'And this is Archie.'

Grace stared at the dark-orange-looking miniature poodle for what felt like a very long time. She wondered if it had bared its teeth at her, or it always looked like that. The poodle she had seen earlier, at the station, didn't resemble this one. This one wasn't puff-balled up like the other one, but there was more to it than that. It had an obvious tail that the other one was lacking and paws. Maybe, it had been a sheep on a lead after all? She cleared her throat and righted her suitcase.

'Archie's my boy,' Harriet added.

Thank fuck! 'Right,' Grace said. She didn't like the look of the poodle, and the brief thought that she might be responsible for it was terrifying.

'I have the key,' Harriet said. She went to the door, opened it and then stepped back.

'Do people always leave their keys in such an obvious place?' Grace said.

Harriet tilted her head back and forth. 'There's a lot of older people live around here,' she said.

Grace frowned. There were a lot of old people in London, but they wouldn't leave a key outside their house, under a flowerpot, and then let everyone know about it.

'It's in case… you know.' She was pulling a strange face, scrunching her nose oddly, and Grace's frown deepened. 'In case they die,' Harriet said. 'So, we can get in and sort them out before they decay too much.'

21

Grace's mouth opened and her eyes widened.

'Only kidding,' Harriet said with a shrug. 'The crime rates here are about zero. Do you need a hand with the case? I'll just put the dogs in the hunting room.'

Hunting room? Grace stood, open-mouthed, still processing the humour that she couldn't quite grasp and watching Harriet scoot into the house with the dogs. She dragged the suitcase into the hallway, which was the size of her large, ground floor flat in London, and stopped. There was the scent of polished leather and a musty smell, wood, and something she couldn't define, and then the sweet, gentle aroma of fresh-cut flowers came to her. She located the vase on a small round table in the middle of the large landing area at the point at which the central staircase divided, one staircase leading to the left the other to the right. A large arched window threw light from the landing into the foyer and Grace thought it must have afforded spectacular views across the fields and hills to the rear of the house.

'Right, let me help you with that?' Harriet said, jolting Grace from her musings.

Before Grace could refuse, Harriet grabbed the case by its handle and lifted it with ease. She was heading up the stairs and Grace still hadn't moved. 'I promised Vera that I would make sure you were settled. I'll show you to your room if you like?' she said.

'Oh, right, yes, thank you,' Grace said and started up the stairs. She glanced through the window on the landing as she passed. Spectacular indeed. Yes, there were more green fields bordered by hedgerows, and forestation to the left and a slither of what looked like it might be water higher up and you could see for miles across the valley straight ahead and to the right too. A small paddock, close to the house, seemed to provide a boundary between the two properties, and to the right of the paddock and at the back of Harriet's cottage was a small garden and then a series of vegetable plots, several sheds, a small glass greenhouse and then several very large, tent-like greenhouses.

Grace reached the top of the stairs just as Harriet entered the second room down the corridor. The dual aspect room situated at the end of the building sat directly above the kitchen and hunting room. In addition to affording a similar aspect to the landing window, it also overlooked the side-garden which was bounded by mature rhododendron plants just coming into bloom. The red and purple plants added welcome colour, a break in the otherwise green outlook.

'That's Duckton Water you can just about see from here,' Harriet said, indicating to the spot Grace had noticed beyond the forest. 'And Ferndale is the town in the distance.' She pointed to the valley, a long way beyond the greenhouses and just short of the horizon. Grace squinted as she looked. Harriet turned to face Grace. 'Would you like a cup of tea?' She paused. 'Or shall I let you unpack? I'm so sorry about Flo. She's a gentle giant really. I had expected to be back before you arrived.'

Grace had forgotten about the dog and didn't need reminding of the tender spot on her elbow and hip that would be stiff and bruised by the morning. 'Honestly, it's fine; no harm done,' she said. She smiled, aware that Harriet was staring at her oddly.

'Shall I leave you to it then?'

Harriet appeared mildly uncomfortable.

'I'll leave you to it, then,' Harriet said again, suddenly seeming in a rush. 'I live next door of course if you should need anything? If there's anything urgent and I'm not here, you'll always find someone who can help...'

'At the pub,' Grace finished for her.

Harriet smiled. 'Yes, at the pub. Right, I'm off then.' She turned away and set off down the corridor.

Grace felt suddenly alone in a strange place and followed her. 'Wait,' she said. 'Would you like that cup of tea? Or maybe something stronger?'

3.

'You said what? Drew was stifling a laugh as she passed a frothy Cappuccino across the bar to Harriet.

'I know!' Harriet was struggling not to giggle. She slowly stirred two sugars into the drink and sipped. 'She'll think I'm completely incompetent, or barking mad,' she added.

'Your opening line is, we need access to get the dead people out before they decay?' Drew couldn't hold back the hysteria and tears starting to stream down her cheeks.

Harriet squirmed. 'I know. I felt completely stupid.' Then she looked at Drew and started to laugh.

'And, having one dog take her out and then make off with her expensive designer shoes is quite the entrance, but then having another introducing itself by baring its teeth, isn't quite the warm welcome she might have expected,' Drew said. She wiped her eyes and sipped at the Espresso she had made for herself. 'How did you redeem yourself after that?' she asked.

'I made her a G&T,' Harriet said, wiping at the tears that were rolling down her cheeks. 'Three in the end, though I left her to drink the third on her own.'

'One of your specials?'

'Good God no!'

Drew studied her best friend of thirty years. She had seen pretty much every facial expression Harriet possessed over that time – from love to heartache and back again – and she could see something about Grace had stirred Harriet's interest. 'You like her,' she said.

'No. It's not like that.'

'Is she good looking?'

Harriet pondered as she sipped at her coffee, mindful of the fact that she had broken eye contact to stem the feelings that had stirred at first sight of Grace. The dishevelled, bare legged, flailing pose that had panicked her in the very first instance came to mind and she felt herself flush at the memory. Then, there had been the feeling of devastation as she had watched Flo quite literally toss her into the air, and the embarrassment that followed, and then the sense of intrigue as they had sipped their drinks in relative silence, watching the sun go down behind the hills together. Honestly, she didn't know what she thought or felt about Grace. She hadn't felt entirely comfortable, but Grace had asked her to stay and while she had shown an interest, asking about Grace's work, and London, Grace's monosyllabic responses had sent a clear message that she didn't want to talk. She was left with the impression that Grace was lonely and that had caused her to feel quite sad.

Grace didn't seem to be into nature that much either. She had been reticent to touch the dogs and complained that they smelled, and then squirmed at the sight of the deer's head mounted on Vera's living room wall. She had washed the drinks glasses even though they had just been taken from the kitchen cupboard and sprayed her hands with some sort of disinfectant lotion with frequent regularity. Preoccupied and distant would have been a good way to describe Grace, and with no inclination to be anything else. Harriet had walked home with an overwhelming sense that Grace had only asked her to stay because she didn't want to be alone, not that she particularly wanted Harriet's or anyone's company. No, she really didn't know how she felt about Grace Pinkerton.

'I'll take your silence as a yes,' Drew said, breaking the spell that had trapped Harriet in thought.

'Yes, I suppose she is,' Harriet said, her tone reflective. She had noticed Grace's deep blue eyes and the perfectly bobbed hair that had looked quite dishevelled by the time she pulled herself up from the ground. Her skin tone was pale, and she bordered on looking unwell, and then she remembered long eyelashes that framed an intense gaze from time to time.

What had surprised her though, was that worrisome thoughts about Grace had kept her mind occupied long into the night. It had been a long time since someone had kept her awake. In fact, the last person had been Annabel and that was five years ago. She shivered, dismissed the memory, and brought her attention back to Drew.

'Ooh, good. Be nice to have some decent eye candy around here for a bit,' Drew said. She finished her drink and rinsed the cup.

'Seriously!' Harriet sparked. 'You're the worst tease, Drew Pettigrew.' She chuckled. She couldn't help but smile at her friend's bravado. For all her talk, Drew had never been with a woman, though Harriet suspected it was just a matter of time and opportunity.

They had had a moment once, a long time ago. It had been after a picnic at the lake and more wine than both could handle. They had talked for hours about what it might be like to kiss a girl and then Drew suddenly suggested they try it, together. The bolt of lightning that shot through Harriet at the idea had taken her breath away and before she could respond Drew's wet lips were pressed to her own. At the point Drew's tongue touched hers though, she was thrust out of the kiss by an intense sense of wrongness. It had nothing to do with the kiss and everything to do with the person behind the sensual expression. She just didn't see Drew in that way, maybe in part because of Drew's history with boys, coupled with some romantic notion that the intimacy of this special moment should be shared with another lesbian. Fortunately, Drew seemed to have forgotten the event by the next day and the kiss had never been spoken about since.

'You know I'm always up for a bit of eye candy,' Drew said, moving to the machine and loading up another coffee.

The café door opened and closed, as if on cue, and both women looked up.

27

'Hi, Dad.'

'Hi, Bryan.'

'Good morning ladies.' Bryan approached the bar and plonked *The Mirror* and *The Times* newspapers on the bar. He always said, he read one for fun and one to know what was really going on in the world, though he was never clear which paper achieved what. 'So, did our new guest settle in okay last night?' he said, addressing Harriet.

Drew sniggered as she banged the spent coffee grains into the waste bin.

'Long story, Dad! I'm sure Drew will fill you in. I gotta dash.' Harriet finished the last of her coffee, gave Drew the evil eye – who continued to snigger – and walked out of the café.

Harriet walked straight into the path of Sheila Goldsworth, who looked startled and began to fluster.

'I'm going to the pub,' Sheila blurted and scampered off, in the opposite direction to the Crooked Billet.

Harriet frowned, head shaking. She didn't need to look at the time to know it wasn't even close to opening hours. Elvis would still be doing mid-morning service up at the church. The old woman has finally lost it. She crossed the road and entered the shop. 'Morning Doug.'

Doug looked up from the paper he had been reading at the counter and over the top of his glasses. 'Ah-right, Harriet, how's our guest settling in?'

'Fine, just fine,' she said cheerily. She wasn't having that conversation again. She snuck down an aisle and spotted the sugar she needed and returned to the counter. 'And a bottle of Bombay, please,' she said, indicating to the blue bottle of gin behind the counter on the 'spirits only' shelf.

'That well settled then,' he remarked, referring to the need for more gin.

'I didn't realise Vera was low on gin. She normally has a couple of spares in the house' Harriet said.

'That she does,' he said, reaching for the bottle. 'Maybe she took them on the cruise with her,' he added. He was joking. 'I'll need to get more stock in if that's her tipple.'

'Actually, I'll grab a couple of bottles of tonic water too.' Harriet moved from the counter to find the mixer-drink and returned to find Doris presenting a full basket of shopping to Doug.

'Do you mind?' he said, addressing the question to Harriet.

'No, go ahead.' Harriet smiled. 'Good morning Mrs Akeman,' she said, chirpily.

Doris turned to Harriet with something resembling a scowl that eventually broke into a half-smile. There was a fine line between the two poses and her natural tendency towards formality that made it difficult to gauge how she really felt. 'Good morning Harriet, I trust this day finds you well?' she said.

'Very well, thank you. How was the meeting yesterday? I'm sorry I couldn't make it,' she said, though they both knew she never had any intention of attending.

'It was a very well attended meeting, thank you, Harriet.'

Doris could never stop herself making a point where she considered a point needed making. She had been Harriet's headmistress during secondary school and taken a vested interest in her academic achievements through to the time Harriet had bailed out of university education. Harriet would forever be a disappointment to Doris. But Harriet had a soft spot for the old woman none-the-less. 'I understand the summer fete meeting is this coming Friday?' Harriet said, trying to redeem herself.

'The first of many, I'm sure,' Doris remarked.

'Great. I'll be there,' Harriet said. 'Would you like me to see if Grace will join us? She has a very successful events company in London. Maybe she can offer some advice?'

29

Wrong thing to say!

Doris seemed to grow an inch and a half in stature with the sharp intake of breath that she struggled to form words from. The till pinged, a welcome moment of distraction.

'Fifteen pounds, twenty, please Doris.'

Doris dipped arthritic fingers in a purse that was too small to take them and managed to retrieve a twenty-pound note. 'Yes, I'm sure Grace will be an asset to our well-practised process,' she said, handing over the money.

'Great,' Harriet responded, even more chirpily and wondered what the hell a well-practised process was. Every year the fete organisation was a bugger's-muddle, and she had no reason to believe this year would be any different. Although, at least this year, with Grace's influence, they might stand half-a-chance of achieving some sense of order.

Doris took her change and the carrier bag of shopping and hurried out of the door, leaving Doug and Harriet in peals of laughter.

'You know that's a red rag to a bull, don't you?' he said.

'I'm sure a professional event organiser might have something to add to the well-practised process, don't you Doug?'

Doug laughed. 'If that event organiser can get a word in edgeways,' he said. 'Bloody torture last night,' he added. 'If I hear one more reference to bloody Tom Cruise or Meg Ryan from Delia Harrison, with her bloody crystal ball gazing, I'll be moving to Upper Duckton.'

'You know you won't,' Harriet said, taking the offered carrier bag and pressing her debit card to the reader.

'Ah, don't go busting an old man's dreams, Harriet.'

'Gotta keep it real, Doug.' Harriet laughed. 'You going to the quiz night on Wednesday?' she said, sure of the answer.

'Yep, there's no way we're letting Upper Duckton win the title, at least not until I'm living over there. Maybe we can get Grace involved?' he said, mindful of *Operation Set-Up*, or whatever the bloody plan was.

'Maybe?' Grace said, though she wasn't convinced that would be Grace's thing. 'Catch you later.'

'Unless God gets me first,' he retorted.

'Yeah, right.'

4.

Grace cupped a handful of water and splashed her face, for the second time in the past three hours.

She had woken suddenly with the vivid image of a dark-orange sheep above her head, pinning her to the ground with pincer-like paws and baring its long, dirty-brown, sharp teeth. Heart thumping, she had opened her eyes, and then registered the whining noise coming from the hunting room. It had been 6 am on the dot and at that point she had regretted insisting that Harriet pour her the third gin the previous evening. Damn, they were good gins though, and the escape had been exactly what she needed. She'd never stayed anywhere with so many strange noises though, and sleep when it had come had been fitful. She had staggered to the kitchen and let the dogs into the small enclosed side-garden, before searching frantically for the headache pills that had become a trusted companion in her daily life. Two pills and a long glass of water later and she had staggered back to bed, leaving the dogs to play together in the garden.

She splashed the cold water again and groaned although feeling a little better for the additional sleep. Looking in the bathroom mirror to assess the damage she moaned at the sight. Fucking hell, those bags would support a whole wardrobe of clothes, high heels included. She patted her face dry, dressed and descended the stairs.

Coffee set to brew, she picked up the instructions Vera had left and started to read. The first line caught her eye.

> *Please don't let Flo out into the garden without keeping an eye on her. She's liable to run off.*

'Fuck!'

Winnie barked at the sound of Grace's voice, jumped to her feet with as much finesse possible given her arthritic joints, and pottered into the garden – continuing to bark enthusiastically.

Grace looked through the kitchen window. No sign of Flo. 'Fuck!' She opened the door to the hunting room and headed into the garden. 'Fuck, fuck,' she mumbled, heading from bush to bush. So many fucking bushes! 'Flo,' she called. Nothing. Three times around the plot, still no sign of the Great Dane. How could you lose a bloody dog the size of a small pony? Winnie staggered towards her and dropped a tennis ball at her feet. 'I haven't got time to fucking play,' she shouted.

Winnie barked, tail wagging, and nuzzled the ball to her toes.

'Oh, fuck it.' Grace picked up the ball and launched it deep into the garden, perhaps unsurprisingly targeting a leafy bush. 'Flo, Flo,' she shouted. No sign of the black and white Great Dane.

Winnie waddled towards her with the ball between what few teeth she possessed and dropped it at her feet.

'Not now Flo, Winnie,' Grace corrected. 'Flo,' she shouted again.

Winnie barked.

Grace bent over to pick up the ball and launch it for the third time, but before she reached a standing position, the world spun on its axis and she landed on her back in the grass with a thud, staring at a grey cloudy sky. Her scream was silenced by the licking tongue and wet nose that had her, yet again, pinned to the ground. Flo nuzzled deeper into her neck until the fact registered in Grace's mind. The bloody dog was only after the ball. That explained the extreme pain between her shoulders. Winnie yapping in her right ear was simply added value she couldn't have predicted possible. She moved and Flo quickly stole the ball from under her and ran off, Winnie nipping at Flo's ankles and barking.

Grace lay back in the grass and moaned, her heart rate slowly calming. Oh my God. She hadn't been here twenty-four hours and already she felt more exhausted than before she had arrived. She turned on her side and watched the dogs playing, before rising to her feet and returning to the house, overwhelmed with relief.

The coffee tasted good. She leafed through the instructions. What was where in the kitchen, where the wood was stored for the fire, what she should do if the electric fuse trips – should she be concerned? She hadn't fed the dogs though, which was the next thing on the list. Food measured precisely, she carried the bowls to the hunting room to find two pairs of eager eyes, and salivating mouths, already waiting and staring intently at her. Both dogs sat obediently, though Flo tried to attack the bowl before it reached the ground.

'Wait,' she said, surprising herself, and the dog.

Flo backed off and waited, watching Grace with eagerness and a desire to please.

Grace placed the bowls on the floor and Flo continued to stare at her. Grace stared back. 'What are you waiting for?' she said.

The dog waited, tongue licking its chops.

Grace lifted a hand in dismissal and walked into the kitchen, and Flo sat, watching her. Grace poured another coffee and waited for the dog to start eating.

Flo stared at her across the room.

'You can eat,' she said.

At the first letter of the last word, Flo dived into the bowl and devoured the biscuits. Bowl empty; she looked briefly to Grace and made a snuffling noise.

Grace shook her head at the speed Flo had eaten and wondered if she hadn't given the dog the right quantity of food?

She checked the notes and by the time she looked up from the paper, Flo was back in the garden with the ball, leaving Winnie working tirelessly to finish her food. She chuckled. This could be fun, she thought and sipped from the mug. Really great coffee.

A knock at the front door diverted her attention from the dogs and she realised she had been gazing out the window for a while. She put down the empty cup and went to open the door.

'Hello.'

Harriet hovered under the porch, sporting the same blue jeans, muddy wellington boots and bright yellow raincoat, and held out a bottle of Bombay Sapphire gin, the sight of which caused Grace's stomach to be reminded of its earlier objection to her overindulgence the previous evening. The orange poodle, on a short lead, stood silently, as if under threat of something vile happening if he so much as twitched.

'I bought you this by way of an apology for yesterday's rather ungainly welcome,' Harriet said.

Grace took the bottle, giving her attention to the label she knew well. 'Thanks, but there's no need to apologise,' she said. She looked back at Harriet and her throat felt tighter than it had a moment earlier. 'I think I overdid it last night.' She stared at Harriet and then awkwardness struck her. 'Umm, sorry, would you like to come in?'

'I'm just about to take Archie for a walk,' Harriet said.

Grace nodded, and the tightness in her throat disappeared. 'Of course,' she said.

Harriet started to turn from the door and then stopped. 'Would you like to bring Flo? I think it will be too far for Winnie.'

Grace looked towards the kitchen and the hunting room. 'Winnie's been running around the garden since about six,' she said.

'Blimey, that'll be her done for the day!'

'I'm sure Flo will go another million miles,' Grace said. She smiled and noticed Harriet's cheeks darken. 'Looks like it will rain,' she said, noting the charcoal band of cloud that looked to be closing in on the white sky.'

'There's a raincoat on the peg in the hunting room. It'll be a bit big for you, but I doubt Vera would mind.'

Grace considered her moleskin jacket in the suitcase upstairs and then decided in the best interests of her not needing to purchase a whole new wardrobe after this trip to go with the raincoat option. She nodded. 'Might help with the hangover.'

Harriet laughed. 'The coat or the walk?'

Grace studied the fine lines that sprung to life and lit up Harriet's cheeks, the sparkle that gave Harriet's eyes the appearance of black marble with the sun reflected in it, and lips that revealed beautifully white, ever-so-slightly-uneven teeth. 'I'll go and get the coat,' she said.

'Flo's is the red lead,' Harriet shouted as Grace disappeared into the house.

Seconds later Grace returned empty-handed. 'Would you help me get Winnie in; she's playing hard to get?' Grace said.

'Have you tried the tennis ball?'

Grace winced. 'It's somewhere in the garden, I think. They've been playing with it.'

Harriet reached into her pocket and held out a tennis ball. 'Always carry a spare,' she said. 'Wave it in the air when you call her name. You'll have to shout; she's quite deaf.'

Grace looked from the ball to Harriet. 'Thanks,' she said and then walked through to the kitchen.

Harriet waited, her heart fluttering. She didn't normally feel this way when taking the dogs for a walk. 'Good boy,' she said to Archie. 'Good boy.' When she looked up, she tilted her head. The purple raincoat must have been about three sizes too big for Grace, but the bedraggled look held appeal and her cheeks started to burn. She cleared her throat. 'Ready?'

'Lead on,' Grace said to Harriet, and with that Flo, taking the words as some sort of doggy command, yanked her through the door and headed up the driveway. She tried to tug on the lead, shouting, 'Wait,' but the dog continued to race. Then a piercing whistle came, and Flo stopped instantly.

Harriet moved alongside her; Archie close to her heel. 'If you whistle Flo will stop and then call 'come' and she will come to you. At least most times, she does,' Harriet said. 'Wait, only works where food is concerned. Otherwise, its 'stay' that will get her to stay where she is.'

'Right. Thanks,' Grace said. She studied Harriet for the first few paces, enjoying her in profile. She'd forgotten the instructions before they reached the road. They crossed to the fields and climbed over a stile, and then Harriet let Archie off the lead.

'You can let Flo off now.'

Grace looked back to the road.

'She knows where we're going,' Harriet said, reassuringly.

Flo sat to attention, full of expectation, and Grace dutifully unhooked the lead.

'This path leads all the way to Upper Duckton,' Harriet said. 'Lower Duckton is in that direction,' she added, orientating Grace to their surroundings. 'We sit slap bang in the middle of the two. How far would you like to walk?'

'I don't know. Whatever you had planned, I guess.' Harriet gave Grace a look that she read as, are you sure? It was a cute look, nevertheless, so yes, for the moment she was sure, and she nodded.

They walked in silence, and then, in an instant, the dark clouds were directly above them and torrential rain descending.

The temperature dropped and white ice joined the fall from the heavens in a short sharp burst.

'Bloody hell,' Grace blurted, as hailstones pelted her.

'Here, put this on.' Harriet handed her a yellow plastic hat, with a floppy, narrow lip and she pulled it quickly over her head.

'Where's a tree when you need one?' Grace said.

Harriet pulled the collar of her coat up around her neck and increased the pace. 'Come on, it will pass in a few seconds.' As if on cue, the wind that had turned to gale force had moved the dark clouds along, and within seconds, exactly as predicted, it all died down. The clouds were now puffy white, surrounded by blue sky and sunshine.

'Is the weather always this random?' Grace said and looked at Harriet who still had flecks of ice in her wet hair. She felt the urge to flick them out but resisted, though she couldn't take her eyes off the trickle of water running from Harriet's hair down her temples, her rosy cheeks, and dark eyes that lingered with utmost sincerity. An involuntary shiver swept through her and she hoped Harriet hadn't noticed.

'We have our own very special microclimate here. You get used to it. Makes the weather more predictable in some ways.'

'Oh, right.' Grace looked to the sky; it was a good distraction. She rarely gave attention to the weather. The events she had put on were always indoors inside large purpose-built arenas, so it didn't matter what was happening on the outside unless it affected travel arrangements of course, which had only ever happened once in all her years in the industry.

'You've never been up this way?'

'No. At least not since I was five.'

'That's a shame. What kept you away?'

Grace shrugged. 'We moved around a lot, with Dad being in the Navy. Spent a lot of time abroad when I was younger, and then they settled in Portsmouth. I went to uni in Bristol, and they retired to Devon. I didn't know Vera, and this place has never been home to me. London is my home, I guess.'

'Do you see your parents much?'

'Not much. I call mum regularly. I went to Devon a bit when I finished work, but it's too?' She paused. 'It's too slow for me. Events management is really fast-paced, and it was like the world had ground to a halt. I managed a long weekend then went back to my flat. And now I'm here.'

Harriet frowned.

'I think mum thought it would be livelier here, and she thought you and I would have things in common.'

'What, our love of dogs?'

Grace laughed. 'Maybe not so much, eh! It's not that I don't like dogs. I've just never had one. I'm used to bossing people around,' she said, light-heartedly. 'Mum said there were more people of my age here. Everyone I met in Devon must have been over sixty-five.'

'Wait 'til you come to our committee meeting,' Harriet said in jest and chuckled. 'You don't have any brothers or sisters, do you?'

'No.'

'All my family is here,' Harriet said. 'Jarid, my brother. Mum; Jenny. My dad, Bryan – you met him of course – and little Luce. I don't know what it would be like without them.'

'Your dad mentioned Jarid. Isn't his wife the vet?'

'They're not married,' Harriet said. 'That's not Kelly's thing,' she said, shaking her head with a smile.

'Luce?'

'She's my half-sister. My dad's girlfriend is Ellena. Mum and dad divorced years ago.'

'And they both live in the village still?'

'Oh, yes, they all get on like a house on fire. Let me just say, mum and dad have always lived a very open lifestyle, even when they were married. Wouldn't be my thing, but it worked for them.'

'Oh!' Grace was intrigued but sensed Harriet didn't want to delve any further. 'Have you been to London?'

'No.'

'What about other places?'

'I've been to York and Chester. Oh, and I went to Manchester once too. Didn't like it. Too busy.'

Grace chuckled. 'You don't like busy and I don't like slow.'

Harriet was shaking her head and a look akin to disgust accompanied her reflections. 'I don't like cities,' she said. 'Too many people and commercialisation.'

'Commerce makes the world go around,' Grace said.

'Yes, but it doesn't need to be quite so vulgar.'

Ouch! Commerce had been Grace's world for as many years as she had worked. She'd never thought of it as vulgar. Essential for developing economic prosperity and wealth, from which great good could come; yes. Vulgar, never. 'I guess we come from different worlds,' she said.

'Don't you think there's too much greed? The levels of waste we produce, and yet there are still millions around the world suffering from malnutrition and abject poverty?'

'Yes, of course, but I guess that's a price to pay for the benefits that we do achieve; advances in medicine and technology, though clearly not the technology in this area – my mobile signal is lousy,' Grace said, and laughed.

'Maybe that's a sign,' Harriet said. 'Most people visit here to relax and walk in this beautiful countryside. We should ban Wi-Fi in the countryside.' She illustrated with her hand, the hills in the near distance, pockmarked with rock, and the expanse of water slightly more visible than it was from the house.

Grace sighed. 'It is pretty,' she said.

'Manchester was so built up. York is pretty with its sandstone and architecture.'

'You're a photographer,' Grace said.

'Of sorts. It's more a hobby than anything serious.'

'Mum said you're good.'

'Oh!'

'Vera sent mum some of your pictures. It was one of mum's selling points for me to come here. She has your picture of the lake and sunset on her mantle-piece,' Grace said. She observed Harriet's coy smile and felt the effect filter through her, warming her skin from the inside out. She unzipped the coat that was beginning to feel oppressive under the heat.

'Ah, yes, Vera does her best to keep my sales up. I sell them at the market stall, along with the produce I grow.'

'Vegetables?'

'And seasonal fruit. The pictures are of this area; mostly landscapes.'

'I'd like to see them sometime. Have you thought of setting up a website and selling your work online?'

'That's not my thing,' Harriet said.

'You could make more money,' Grace said. She studied Harriet's gaze.

'I don't do what I do for money, Grace. I do it because I love it,' Harriet said. Her tone was soft. 'I have all that I need, and I sell what I don't need. It's a simple life, I'm sure, compared to London and other city jobs, but I enjoy working with the land,' she said.

Grace nodded. She could see that in Harriet and found herself admiring the strength of the woman's conviction.

Harriet whistled to the dogs and they stopped until the two women caught up with them. After a moment in silence, Harriet said, 'What do you like about living in London?'

Grace considered the question.

'Sorry, I shouldn't pry.'

'No, it's fine. I was trying to work out what it is I like particularly. Mostly, I guess it's work. My life has been centred in London since I finished uni, so in many respects, it's what I'm familiar with,' and it suddenly dawned on her that perhaps her life hadn't been as full and expansive as she had thought. She had always positioned herself in this world as having lived and achieved success at an early age. She had travelled with work, but mostly with the same work crew, moving within the same networks, staying at the same hotels and eating at the same restaurants. Even drinking the same drinks. She'd only have to show up in the bar at the end of an event day, anywhere in the world, and the right drink would be lined up waiting for her. 'What about you? What do you like about living here?' she said.

'The random weather.' She laughed, and there was lightness in the tone. 'I love being with nature, and my animals; my horses, and Terence.'

'Terence?'

'He's the ginger tom you'll see wandering around at some point. I rescued him as a kitten and he comes home when he's had enough of fending for himself or needs his annual flu jab.'

'He comes back for his jabs?'

Harriet flushed. 'Sorry, I was joking,' she said.

Grace smiled.

'I must stop that; you might find we have a silly sense of humour around here,' she said.

Grace shrugged. She couldn't remember having any sense of humour, and especially not at work. There was something refreshing and uplifting about the light-hearted grounded nature of Harriet though. 'Please, don't stop on my account,' she said.

'The people here are wonderful, once you get to know them. Even old Mrs Akeman who chairs the village committee. She comes across as quite gruff, but she has a kind heart. I got teased at school when I came out, and she took me into her office and told me that if anyone gave me any trouble I was to go and see her immediately. She kept an eye out for me even after I left school.'

Grace stopped walking and Harriet turned to face her.

Grace held her gaze with curiosity and she couldn't stop herself from asking, 'How old were you when you came out?'

'Sixteen,' Harriet said.

Grace nodded.

'I realised when I was a lot younger, though,' Harriet added.

'How old?'

'Ten.'

'Fuck! Really?'

Harriet chuckled. 'Do you always swear a lot?'

Grace blushed. 'Yes, I suppose I do. I'll try and kerb my city ways,' she said, and smiled.

Harriet felt the warmth in Grace's smile. 'You don't need to change on anyone's account here, Grace. We tend to take people as they are,' she said.

They continued walking.

Flo bounded over and dropped a stick at Harriet's feet and she picked it up and threw it. 'How old were you?' she said.

'Nineteen, though I realised at about eighteen and three-quarters,' Grace said, and laughed.

Harriet studied Grace. 'You're teasing?'

'A little, the penny dropped when I was about seventeen, by which time I had kissed a few boys and knew I felt absolutely nothing, but I didn't do anything about it for a while,' Grace said. 'Kissing a girl sealed that particular deal, I can tell you.'

'Have you ever been with a man?'

'No. You?'

'No.'

They continued in silent reflection.

'Are you hungry?' Grace said, her stomach reminding her she had skipped breakfast in favour of Paracetamol.

'Starving. We can stop at the pub in Upper Duckton if you fancy? They do a great Ploughman's lunch.'

Grace's stomach growled at the idea of food, though she had never eaten a Ploughman's lunch in her life. The most she knew was that it involved cheese and pickle and a chunk of bread. Right now, she could eat a horse, though that might not go down well in Harriet's animal-loving world. 'Sounds great,' she said.

5.

Grace studied the quirky pub. A dual-aspect fireplace, set into a stone clad wall split the area, servicing two large spaces, each furnished with low tables and armchairs. Beyond these cosy areas, another stone clad wall hid from view what looked like a formal dining area. The place was warm, filled with the aroma of home-cooked food, and pictures and maps of local interest, littered the walls. Real ales seemed to be a key feature of the bar, a row of six competing brand labels — none of which Grace recognised - offering options to cater to the broadest of tastes. She'd heard of Speckled Hen as a brand, but not Freckled Duck!

A couple of ruddy-cheeked men with broad smiles and eyes that shone nodded at Harriet and she greeted them with a smile. Harriet selected the small table in front of the open fireplace.

The fire would be cosy in the winter with orange-red flames and crackling wood bathing the place in comforting warmth. Now the grate looked as empty as Grace felt. She slid into the armchair, while Harriet went to the bar. The dogs stayed alert until she returned and then settled quickly, close to Harriet's feet.

'How come you decided to take a break from work?' Harriet asked, handing over the half-pint of Freckled Duck that Grace had insisted on trying.

Grace felt the anxiety that had become a companion to her over the past weeks settle in her stomach. She didn't want to lie but couldn't possibly tell Harriet the truth. She hadn't even told her mother. At this point, there were two truth's playing out in London, and until the Board made their decision as to her future, why would anyone believe her version? All the evidence currently pointed in the wrong direction, but the investigation was ongoing and there was still hope of being able to quash the allegation against her. 'It seemed like a good idea at the time,' she said, trying to pass the answer off as a joke.

Harriet didn't laugh. She looked at Grace with intensity and Grace flushed. 'Sorry, I feel I'm prying again,' she said, her tone conveying remorse.

'No, I'm sorry. That was my poor attempt at humour,' Grace said. 'I was tired,' she said, and that much was true. 'Burnt out.'

Harriet nodded. She sipped at the beer in her hand, and Grace mirrored her movements.

'I hadn't thought about how I might take my foot off the gas though,' Grace continued. 'I guess I'm still learning how to do that.'

Harriet nodded. 'Balance is important,' she said. 'I think I'm lucky. I have my family and friends here, so we look out for each other.'

Grace sighed. Where were her friends when she had needed them? She twisted the glass in her hand and took a sip. 'Yes,' she said.

'Do you have a girlfriend?' Harriet said, staring into the fireplace.

Grace shook her head. 'I'm not very good at relationships,' she said.

'Two Ploughman's?' the barwoman announced, approaching them from behind.

'Yes, thanks Tilly,' Harriet responded and smiled as the woman put two large plates of food on the table. Flo's nose twitched and she lifted her head off the floor briefly before flopping back down again.

'I don't think relationships are my forte either,' Harriet said.

Grace chuckled. 'See, we have a lot in common.' Grace stared at the bulging plate of food. What looked like half a loaf

46

of crusty bread perched on the side of the plate, three huge chunks of different types of cheese, and two slices of freshly cut ham, sweet pickle, tomato, and salad stared back at her. 'This is a Ploughman's and a half,' she said, breaking off a chunk of bread and lathering it with butter.

Harriet was already tucking into her food. 'Hmm, it's good.'

They ate in silence, occasionally catching each other's eye and nodding in mutual approval of the hearty lunch, the hum of voices and occasional bursts of laughter around them.

Grace leaned back in her seat and finished the sandwich she had constructed. 'I needed that,' she said.

'Me too.' Harriet sat back and her pace of eating slowed.

Grace studied Harriet and it seemed impossible to think of her without a partner. She was so likeable; so easy to be around. 'So, you don't have a girlfriend?' she said.

Harriet finished chewing and swallowed. 'No.'

'I don't suppose there's much opportunity out here in the sticks.'

'You'd be surprised.'

'Oh?' Grace waited, watching Harriet in deep reflection.

Harriet's focus returned, and she sighed. 'There was someone, once, a few years ago now.'

'Were you in love with her?'

'Yes.'

Grace froze. She hadn't expected such a confident affirmation and for some odd reason felt challenged by Harriet's openness. 'I'm sorry it didn't work out for you,' she said.

Harriet's lips thinned as she bit down on them from the inside. 'I was too,' she said. She held a tight-lipped smile that eventually softened. 'Long story short, she met a man and they went on a round-the-world trip. She invited me to go, but I'd already got the message that she was more into him than me, and I'm not like my parents. I don't want an open relationship. I just want one woman who loves me. She hasn't returned since. I think they're settled in New Zealand now.'

'Damn.'

Harriet shrugged. 'That's life, I guess. Hearts break; hearts mend,' she said, and Grace gazed at her, unconvinced.

'Did she break yours?'

'Yes.'

Grace picked at a piece of cheese. She had never been very good at dealing with emotions in relationships, it was one of the reasons she was lousy at them, but she could see bravado clearly in Harriet's reaction to the conversation.

'We had plans,' Harriet said. 'Family, settling down, working the small-holding together.'

Grace nodded.

'She had itchy feet, though. Funnily enough, she thought the pace of life here was too slow too.'

Grace flushed at her admission about Devon and the pace of life there. 'I'm sorry.'

'Hey, it's not your fault.' Harriet held Grace in an assessing gaze and smiled. 'You seem quite different to Annabel.'

Grace released a deep breath and sipped at her drink.

Harriet put down her empty glass. 'Shall we get back?'

'Sure.' Grace made a move to stand up and groaned. 'God, I'm stiff.'

Harriet chuckled. 'You wait 'til the country air hits you. You'll sleep like a baby tonight.'

Grace would enjoy that. A good night's sleep had evaded her for as long as she could remember.

They ambled back from Upper Duckton and Grace felt the route pass more quickly than their journey out and when they reached the house, Grace stood on the slate porch, shifting from one foot to another, Harriet watching her with a warm smile.

'Thank you,' Grace said, holding out her hand to Harriet. It seemed an odd gesture, too formal she realised, given the relatively intimate nature of their conversation, and she withdrew just as Harriet went to take it.

There was a moment of awkwardness, and then Harriet leaned towards Grace and pulled her into a hug. Grace stiffened with the unexpected contact and Harriet released her, nodding by way of appreciation for the walk.

'A bath might help?' Harriet said, and smiled.

Grace gazed into the dark sparkling eyes feeling their warmth and, as she watched Harriet until she reached the cottage, she was left with a strong, unfamiliar sense of emptiness – the like that came from having something pleasurable for a short time and then not having it. It was very different from the feeling of loneliness she had arrived at Duckton with, and different again she now realised from the emotionally shallow world in which she had immersed herself in London. And then, for the first time that day, thoughts of Sandra fucking Floss struck her.

*

'Come in, come in,' Jenny said. She poked her head out the door and peered up and down the street several times then shut the door behind Delia and Esther. 'Just checking,' she said.

'Checking for what?' Delia said.

'You know who?

'Old Hilda Spencer?' Esther said.

'No. The girls of course.'

'Oh, that.' Esther waved her hand in the air dismissively.

'You're not taking this seriously, are you, Esther?' Jenny said.

'I do know old Hilda Spencer was seen the day before yesterday, walking these parts,' Esther said. She looked as if she

49

had a rotten smell underneath her curled up nose as she broke the news.

'Ooh, now that's interesting,' Delia said and reached into her handbag. 'I told you I'd seen her prowling last month, and my Jarid said Phyllis said there'd been a sighting in Lower Duckton in the last week too. Something's brewing,' She pulled out a pack of Tarot cards and started towards the rear of the house. 'Come on, we need to do a reading,' she said.

'What did she have with her?' Esther said.

'Phyllis?'

'No, Hilda. What did she have?'

'Jarid didn't know. It was Jerry who'd seen Hilda and told Phyllis and he's near blind as a bat and her memory's not what it was, but he recognised the purple raincoat and white hair, apparently, heading down this way across the field. He was taking a pee against the hedge. Reckon he'd just fallen out the pub, so it's all a bit vague. There's something in the air though, I can feel it in my waters and the cards never lie. What happened the day before yesterday?'

'Kev spotted her wandering the field, lead in hand, but no sign of Brambles,' Esther said.

'That's odd,' Delia said. 'Lead and no Brambles, very odd, I don't think that's been reported before.' Delia was frowning and shaking her head. Hilda Spencer had never been seen without Brambles on the lead. 'It's a sign!' she said.

Jenny rolled her eyes. Everything was a sign. 'Right, I need a drink,' she said.

'Can I have a cup of tea?' Esther said to Jenny.

'There's a brew on the table. Come on.'

Delia had the cards spread out before Esther had poured her tea. Jenny picked up the green unlabelled glass bottle from the centre of the table and poured two glasses of wine. 'You sure you don't want any?' she asked Esther. For as long as the women had been gathering at Jenny's, which was now the best part of twenty years, Esther had never sampled the home-brew Jenny offered. Though she was partial to the odd sherry and on very special occasions had been known to opt for a gin.

'No, thank you,' Esther said and sipped at the tea.

'The cards can wait,' Jenny said. 'Any news about the girls?'

Esther sat up stiffly, her nose wrinkling on cue. 'I know that Doug saw Harriet in the shop this morning,' she said.

'Harriet's in the shop most mornings, Esther,' Delia retorted.

'Buying gin,' Esther said, in a tone that suggested she was releasing a top secret.

'Good,' Jenny said. 'Nell said Grace was partial to gin, so Vera hid her spare bottles.'

Suddenly indignant, 'Why did she do that?' Esther said.

'So, Harriet would take more gin to her and give them an opportunity to connect.'

Esther frowned. 'How did she know Harriet would go and buy it and not Grace?'

'It was a sixth sense.'

Esther puffed dismissively. 'Ridiculous!'

'She knew Harriet would want to make Grace feel welcome, and you know how good the gins are she makes. And how helpful Harriet is. Anyway, no matter, it worked.'

Delia sipped at the wine and winced as she swallowed. 'That's good shit, Jenny,' she said, nodding. 'Anyway, is that it? Can we get to the cards now? We need to find out why old Hilda's on the prowl.'

'Doug saw them both at the Duckton Arms at lunchtime,' Esther said.

'What Hilda and Brambles in the Duckton Arms?' Jenny said, raising her eyebrows.

'No, the girls,' Esther said.

'That's good,' both women said in unison and stared at Esther waiting for more information.

Esther took in a deep breath.

'Come on woman, out with it,' Delia said and took a long sip of her wine.

'They had walked the dogs across the fields.'

'Of course, they had, otherwise how did they get there,' Delia said and sipped again with increased urgency.

Esther twitched her nose in Delia's direction. 'Apparently, they were in deep confession with each other.'

'Really,' Jenny said and leaned keenly towards Esther. 'That's quite a good sign, I think.'

'Yes. They were talking about love, life and the pursuit of happiness.'

Both women frowned at Esther.

'That's Doug's abbreviated version is it, Esther? Any specifics around that?' Delia said.

'Seems they've both suffered in love and Grace isn't in a relationship right now.'

'That's good,' Jenny interrupted. 'That she isn't with anyone, I mean.'

'Nor does she want to be,' Esther continued.

'That's not so good,' Jenny said, shaking her head.

'Apparently, Grace isn't very good at relationships, and neither is Harriet.'

Jenny felt heckles rise at the back of her neck. 'Our Harriet is very good at relationships,' she said, firmly. 'That other bloody woman was always bad news, and anyway, that's years back.'

'Seems Harriet still isn't over that piece of bad news though. I'm only repeating what the girls were saying,' Esther said. She looked down at the cup in her hand, then brought it carefully to her lips and sipped.

'Damn it.' Jenny blurted, then finished the glass of wine. 'What else?'

'There was something he didn't quite catch about trying burnt trout and learning how to cook on gas,' Esther said.

Delia and Jenny frowned.

'No idea what that means,' Jenny said.

'Maybe it's a code?'

Jenny rolled her eyes. 'Anything else?'

Esther hesitated. 'Doug didn't want to tell me this, but I forced it out of him.'

'What?' Delia said, becoming irritated with the pace of the extraction of information.

'Apparently, Harriet's thinking of moving to New Zealand because she has a broken heart and her friends and family aren't supporting her.'

Jenny jumped to her feet. 'What?' she yelled. 'Of course, we support her, we have always supported her.' She started pacing the room.

'All sounds a bit odd to me,' Delia said.

'I'm only saying what Doug said, and in fairness, he was behind the wall and it was noisy. Maybe he got the wrong end of the stick.'

'He'd better bloody have,' Jenny barked.

'Sit down Jen; you're making me dizzy. Everyone knows Harriet's got friends and family who love her. Doug 'd probably had a few jars before he earwigged,' Delia said.

'Oh, God! What if Harriet does feel like that?' Jenny said, taking her seat and slugging back her wine. She refilled the glass and finished it in a long swallow.

'Oh, and there was something about the girls needing to look out for each other, God's stiffy and the country flair getting to you,' Esther added.

'Oh, good Christ!' Jenny muttered and it wasn't clear to what or whom she was referring.

Delia took a swig of her wine. 'I'll do a reading for the girls?' Delia said. 'It'll be more reliable than Doug's bloody interpretation of any conversation.' She picked up the sprawled cards, sorted them into a neat pack, closed her eyes and started to shuffle.

Jenny drifted, deep in thought. That would explain why Harriet had shown no interest in other women. She had convinced herself it was because of her daughter's love of the land and desire for a quiet life that Harriet had kept herself to herself. Harriet wasn't like her brother Jarid, who was outgoing and sociable. Harriet reminded her of herself before she met Bryan. Bryan had brought her out of her shell, and she had thought Grace might do the same for Harriet. Damn the bloody strumpet of a woman who hurt her baby, and her gallivanting ways, disappearing with that arsehole of a man and leaving her beautiful Harriet with a broken heart. Good riddance to them both. They deserved each other. One thing was for sure, they had better not return to Duckton-by-Dale, or they would have her to contend with, and that wouldn't be pretty. But what if Harriet was thinking of leaving? With or without Grace, that certainly wasn't the plan. Harriet hadn't mentioned anything of the sort, but then she hadn't spoken to Harriet properly in a long time. She refilled her glass and sipped furiously. She needed to speak to Harriet, soon.

'Have you heard from Vera?' Delia said to Jenny.

'Only that she landed safely.'

'I thought she was on a boat?' Esther said.

'It's a figure of speech, Esther,' Delia said, rolling her eyes.

'Is the weather nice, where is she?' Esther said.

'She was starting from Plymouth, Esther, I believe, so I don't think she's at the warm end of the Med, yet,' Jenny said and looked evasive.

Delia looked at her curiously. It wasn't like Jenny to be vague. 'Is everything alright between you two?' she said.

Jenny flushed. 'Of course, it is,' she said.

'Why didn't you go with her?' Esther asked the one question the whole village had ruminated since knowing Vera had decided to take the trip.

'It's just not my thing,' she said, her cheeks burning. She took a sip of wine. 'Anyway, a short break between people never did any harm, and we don't exactly live in each other's pockets.'

'Separation didn't do much for you and Bryan,' Esther said, and Delia glared at her. 'What?'

'Bryan and I weren't separated,' Jenny corrected. 'We had an open relationship. That's very different. Neither of us expected him to hook up with the other woman, any more than I expected to get together with Vera. The point is, Bryan and I are both happy and we all get along very well, and Vera being away is no reflection of any problem in our relationship thank you very much. So, if that's what people think, then please do feel free to correct them, Esther.' She took a long sip of the wine, both women staring at her with mouths agape.

'Right,' Esther said. 'That's cleared that one up. Shall we get onto the cards?' She poured another cup of tea and sipped, gracefully.

Delia turned the first card.

Death.

'Oh, great!' Esther said.

'Death is a good card. It signifies change, the end of a cycle, new beginnings, that sort of thing,' Delia said.

'Oh, right,' Esther said.

Delia drew another card. The Justice card reversed.

'What does that mean?' Esther said.

Jenny studied Delia intently, over the top of the glass at her lips.

'Dishonesty,' Delia said.

'Oh, that's not good,' Esther said.

She turned another card and placed it next to the first two. 'Eight of cups means walking away,' Delia said.

'Fuck!' Jenny blurted. 'Sorry. This isn't looking good, is it?'

'Well, it's not always that simple, but it looks as though something unjust is going to happen and someone will need to leave. I'll turn another card, that represents the end state,' Delia said and turned the Wheel of Fortune. She placed the card on the table next to the others.

'Ooh, that looks better,' Esther said. When she looked up neither Jenny nor Delia was smiling. 'Oh!'

'It means, Inevitable Fate,' Jenny said. 'Shit, this really isn't looking good, is it?'

Delia shook her head, then finished the glass of wine and reshuffled the cards. 'I'll run another pattern,' she said.

'Right. So, what are we going to do about old Hilda then?' Jenny asked Esther.

Esther gazed at Jenny intently, clearly deeply engrossed in something distracting.

Delia rolled her eyes and turned over the Hierophant. 'Morality and ethics.'

'Don't look at me like that,' Jenny said to Esther, who had that look on her face again.

'One last card,' Delia said and turned the Two of Cups. She smiled.

'What?' Esther said.

'That's better,' Delia said, tapping the card with a sense of achievement. 'It means unity, partnership, and connection.

Jenny sipped at the wine. 'That sounds more like it,' she said.

6.

Grace wandered down the stairs, stopped at the landing window, and gazed out across the valley; Ferndale blanketed by the haze that rendered the distance in cloud-like grey, the tops of the hills lost in the same mist. It would lift when the sun warmed and the day would be transformed.

The handsome chestnut horse was trotting lazily towards the gate, where the smaller black and white pony stood. Harriet approached, opened the gate and stepped into the field. Grace felt something inside her shift at the sight. The familiar bright-yellow raincoat with riding boots to her knees and a woollen bobble-hat perched on her head. Maybe it was the confidence with which she approached the chestnut horse and ran her hand down the white strip that ran down its nose? She seemed to be talking to the horse; its ears flicking and head nodding as if responding, and then it nuzzled into her hand. Maybe it was the tenderness with which she stroked and patted its forequarters, inspected its front legs and then continued around its body; and the horse standing perfectly still, nodding its head as if approving of the contact. Harriet lifted the saddle from the fence and placed it on its back, tying the straps beneath its broad chest, then went through the same routine with the black and white pony.

Before Harriet had finished tying the second saddle, an estate car pulled up with the word Doctor in large white lettering down the side. The tall man appeared, together with a young girl wearing a riding cap, coat, and boots. The man raised his finger to his lips and the girl followed behind him as they crept up to Harriet. They came closer to the fence then both leapt out at Harriet causing her to jump. Neither horse reacted. Grace chuckled. Jarid, and what was the half-sister's name? Luce. Harriet slapped Jarid in the chest; a playful move - they were all laughing – and he pulled her into a full embrace and rocked her in his arms. Harriet wasn't short by any means, but Jarid towered above her. She released him, slapped him on the arm, and patted Luce on the top of her hat, before lifting her up and squeezing her. Grace felt warmth fill her and was transfixed by the family, despite a distant awareness of the dogs barking.

Jarid went back to the car, opened the boot and removed a box of what looked like small plants. Harriet indicated to him towards the back of the house and he duly carried the box to the glass-greenhouse next to the vegetable plot and returned empty handed. He returned to the car and removed another box, all the while chatting and laughing.

Harriet had placed a step on the ground at the side of the horse and was helping Luce onto the black and white pony. She held the strap guiding the bit and led the horse around the small field. Then she let go and Luce took control of the pony. Watching, Grace became aware that she too had as big a grin on her face as Luce had and the realisation caused her to feel oddly out of sorts. Then her heart raced as she observed Harriet mount the large chestnut horse with effortless ease and set off around the field, catching up with Luce and walking the horse alongside her. They were talking and smiling a lot, and Grace felt a strong current move through her.

Jarid removed a bag of soil, threw it onto his shoulder and took it to the greenhouse, then returned to the gate and leant on it, watching the riders, pointing and laughing.

After the third time around the field, Harriet dismounted, carefully removed the saddle and stood next to Jarid. He placed his arm around her, and she leant into his shoulder, and Grace felt a sharp sensation prickle her. Both stood, watching their sister. Then both looked briefly towards the house, the window Grace was stood at, and she ducked away, her heart close to stopping. Grace felt her mouth parch, and yet couldn't help but peek back out of the window and resume her position, her gaze firmly fixed on the family, and more specifically, Harriet.

The orange poodle appeared from the back of the house and sprinted towards Jarid, who released his sister and lowered himself to the dog's short height. He petted it and it ran off into the field.

Grace didn't see the black-and-white dog bounding into view. It was the turning of Jarid's and Harriet's heads that alerted her to the fact that Flo had somehow escaped the side garden and was heading across the field at a pace.

'Fuck!' Panic jolted Grace from the dreamy warm space she had drifted into. She caught Harriet and Jarid laughing and felt the tension ease a fraction. The dog running loose obviously wasn't of huge concern to them.

Harriet was whistling and Flo looked up. She started running towards the gate, then stopped and darted back to Archie and resumed the chase. All eyes were on the dogs playing, the pint-sized Archie jumping and barking, easily bowled over by Flo. Grace stood at the window, in two minds whether to rush out and get Flo back into the side garden. Harriet and Jarid looked at ease with the dog's antics. As Grace pondered her next move, the dogs ruff-and-tumbled, chased and barked and Luce broke into a trot, drawing her attention. That was until...

Archie seemed to become suddenly obsessed with Flo. Flo seemed to be moving in circles to keep him at bay, barking and batting him with a large paw. Grace wasn't sure both dogs were on the same page as far as the game was concerned. The bloody orange dog wouldn't give up, and in one swift move, Flo seemed to have lowered her back legs and Archie had mounted her.

'No!' Grace screamed, her hand clasping her mouth, momentarily paralysed by the sight. 'Fuck, fuck!'

Grace ran down the stairs, out the front door, and sprinted across to the gate, coming to a swift stop in front of Harriet and Jarid. Both looked at her, their smiles shifting to concern with the realisation that something must be seriously wrong.

'What's happened?' Harriet said, reaching out and placing a hand on Grace's shoulder.

Grace was puffing, her heart pounding. 'I saw the dogs, umm,' she said.

She looked paler than when she had arrived from London.

Jarid burst into a fit of laughter, and Harriet smiled at her with softness. Luce had stopped the pony and looked as if she was waiting for help to dismount.

'Oh!' Harriet said. Jarid was almost bent over double, laughing.

'Fuck!' Grace said, and then caught Luce's eye. 'Sorry.'

Jarid had managed to control himself and held out his hand. 'Sorry, I shouldn't laugh, but that was quite some entrance,' he said. He had a warm and engaging smile. 'Hi, I'm Jarid, Harriet's sister, but you'll know that already.'

'Grace,' Grace said and shook his hand. 'Will Flo be...' she couldn't bring herself to say the word, pregnant.

Harriet had already moved to help Luce off the horse and started to remove the saddle. 'They were just playing, Grace,' she said. 'It's just a dominance thing.'

Luce approached Grace. 'Are you the lady from London?' she said. 'I'm Luce.' She smiled and Grace saw the same ever so slightly wonky teeth as Harriet's.

'Hi Luce, I'm Grace.'

'Will Flo have babies?' Luce said, addressing Jarid.

'There's not much chance of that,' he said but Luce was distracted, fiddling with the strap at her throat.

'Archie's been neutered,' Harriet said, more for Grace's benefit.

Grace flushed and avoided eye contact with all three of them in some vain attempt to hide from the embarrassment of not having realised the dog had no balls. 'Oh, right,' she said, mild relief bringing her heart rate down.

Archie bounded towards them, tail wagging furiously, and Grace felt an overwhelming urge to strangle the bloody dog for putting her through the indignity. But then, Flo appeared and flattened him beneath her front paws and it made her feel a whole lot better.

'Flo!' Grace said, and the dog looked up at her. Grace stared at the dog, its wide eyes searching her and she was unsure what to do next.

Harriet reached out and petted Flo, who nuzzled her hand. 'Shall we get her back into the house?' she said.

Grace nodded.

'Right, I'll see you both later,' Jarid said. 'Come on Luce let's get you to church.'

'Flo, come,' Harriet said, and headed back to the house. 'She does get out from time to time,' she said to Grace.

'I feel sick,' Grace said. She'd never been responsible for anything other than a business in her life. Running a business was so much easier, and a lot less stressful than country life. This place certainly wasn't like Devon. Not at all.

Harriet shut Flo in the hunting room. 'She's a bit of a handful, but don't worry, everyone in the village knows Flo and we always look out for each other.'

Harriet squeezed Grace's arm, but it didn't stop her from shaking.

'Can I help?' Harriet held out her arms and Grace fell into the embrace.

Grace felt the warmth and strength of the hold and a genuine sense of compassion. The shaking eased and she pulled back. 'Would you like a coffee?' she said.

Harriet smiled and her gaze held tenderness. 'Yes, coffee would be great.'

Grace primed the machine and a noisy whirring sound filled the silence.

'Do you like baking?' Harriet said.

Grace grimaced. She had never cooked a cake in her life. The best she could manage was a microwave meal or a slice of toast. If she wanted anything substantial, she would always eat out or grab a take-away.

'I baked some biscuits; I'll go and lock Archie away and grab them.'

Grace nodded, just a small part of her thinking, of course, you did! She hated that competitive side of herself and it only came out when she was feeling at her most vulnerable, or when she cared about someone. Did Harriet really have a perfect life, the perfect family? A wave of something unpleasant moved through her and she wished she hadn't had the destructive thought. Harriet was a good person and undeserving of jealousy.

*

'Bryan Haversham, I need a word. Now.'

If the sound of the heavy wood and cast-iron door swinging open, which still echoed around the walls of stone, hadn't alerted the arrival of Jenny Haversham, then her bellowing into the bowels of the church certainly did. All six members of the congregation turned their heads and Elvis stopped just short of delivering his key message of the day, on the topic of maintaining family cohesion in a mobile world.

'Jenny, how lovely to see you at service this morning,' Elvis said.

Jenny approached the front of the church, targeting Bryan who sat two pews back from Elvis's stage. She raised her hand to the Vicar. 'I'm sorry Vicar, I'm not here for the service, something far more important has come up. Bryan, I need a word.'

Bryan looked up as she stood over him with her hands on her hips.

'We'll take a short break in the service, our Lord will be happy to wait,' Elvis announced, and everyone's eyes turned to Jenny.

'What's happened?' Bryan said. He was frowning and Ellena, his girlfriend, gripped his hand as if to comfort him for the news that was about to descend upon him.

'Did you know our Harriet's leaving for New Zealand?' she said.

Doug, sitting two seats across the aisle from Bryan, scowled at Esther. 'I told you not to say anything,' he whispered. He slunk down and buried his head in his hands.

'What?' Bryan sat up stiffly and Ellena squeezed his hand again.

'Did you know our daughter is planning to leave, that she doesn't feel loved by her family?' Jenny continued.

Bryan frowned. 'Of course not, I would have said if I'd heard such a thing. What are you talking about, woman?'

Chatter echoed around the church, 'ooh's and 'ah's and one utterance of, 'really?'

'We had a meeting last night,' she started.

Bryan rolled his eyes. 'You saw this in the bloody cards,' he said. 'Sorry, Vicar.'

Elvis acknowledged the apology.

'No, in fact, we did not,' Jenny snapped. 'Esther.'

Esther slunk down in her seat next to Doug.

63

'Esther reported that the girls were overheard talking together in The Duckton Arms yesterday, and Harriet's planning to move to Australia.'

'You said New Zealand,' Bryan corrected.

'The same thing, stop quibbling,' Jenny retorted, waving her hand dismissively. 'So, how come you didn't know?'

'No, it was definitely New Zealand,' Esther piped up, drawing all eyes to her, and receiving another glare from Doug who slunk even lower into the wooden seat.

Elvis cleared his throat.

'I'm sorry Vicar,' Jenny said. 'This is important.'

'Well, maybe it isn't true. Has anyone asked Harriet?' Bryan said.

'Of course not! I can't just go up and ask her, she'll think we've been gossiping behind her back and you know how she hates that. We need a plan, Bryan.'

'Bloody hell,' Doug murmured, and Esther dug her elbow into his ribs.

'I thought you already had a bloody plan?' Bryan said. 'Sorry Vicar.'

Elvis acknowledged the apology.

'That's a different plan,' Jenny corrected.

'So, the plan to get the girls together,' Bryan started.

The opening of the door hushed the room in a unified gasp.

'I'm going to the pub,' Sheila blurted, slicing through the silence with an echo that seemed to linger.

Jarid and Luce approached.

'Morning all,' Jarid said, assessing the scene with a quizzical gaze. 'What's going on here then?'

'Your mother thinks Harriet's about to up and run to New Zealand. I haven't worked out yet whether she thinks that's with or without Grace, as per the plan that is apparently not the plan, but hey, perhaps you can throw some light on the topic?' Bryan said and smiled at his son.

'Harriet, New Zealand, never,' Jarid said and started to chuckle.

Doug had turned a shade closer to puce and Esther wasn't too far behind him.

Elvis cleared his throat. 'Perhaps we should resume the service now?' he said.

'I thought you'd be finished already,' Jarid said, by way of apology for the interruption.

'Jenny had a few concerns she wanted to air with our Lord,' Elvis said.

'Are you sure she's not leaving?' Jenny said to Jarid.

'She seemed normal to me,' he said with a shrug. 'What do you think Luce?'

Luce shrugged. 'Is Flo going to have babies? Mummy, can we get a puppy?' she said, addressing Ellena.

Ellena's eyes widened. 'I don't know about that, honey.'

'Praise the Lord,' Elvis proclaimed, as he did with the announcement of new life coming into the world.

'That'll be your two of bloody cups,' Jenny said to Delia. 'The bloody dogs uniting! Sorry, Vicar.' She glared in the direction of Doug and Esther whose eyes were firmly set on the man at the front, wearing the dog collar, urging him to continue with the service.

Delia pondered. She didn't think Jenny's interpretation was accurate, but she knew better than to raise the issue when Jenny had her knickers in a twist, so decided to keep her interpretation to herself.

Jarid laughed. 'No Luce, Flo isn't going to have babies.'

Ellena visibly relaxed back into the bench seat with a sigh of relief, and Delia sat nodding her head at the affirmation of her analysis. The cards never lied.

'Would you like to join us for the rest of the service Jenny? We can pray for Harriet, and the dogs.' Elvis smiled.

Jenny felt all eyes on her and squeezed into a space next to Bryan. Jarid and Luce took the empty spaces a couple of rows behind them.

Bryan wrapped an arm around Jenny's shoulder and tucked her under his arm. 'It'll be alright you know,' he whispered.

No, she didn't. Then it occurred to her, she needed to raise the stakes on, *Operation I'm Going to The Pub*.

7.

Grace stared at Flo lazing on the floor of the hunting room, feeling a strange combination of relief and humiliation. It hadn't even occurred to her that Flo needed to be in season, let alone the not so small point that demon-dog had had the chop. She found she liked him a bit more for that fact, though. Apparently, a female dog won't let a male near her until she is ready to mate, Grace had learned. The whole process can go on for days; weeks even.

And that knowledge had had her thinking of Sandra fucking Floss. If only Grace had exercised the same level of restraint at the after-event party, then that bitch wouldn't have put her in this position. She hadn't even wanted Sandra fucking Floss, just the company, and in the heat of the moment, it had been easy – meaningless, and effortless. And Sandra fucking Floss had bated her, sought her out, and then delivered the fatal blow. Grace groaned.

Although her first weekend at Duckton-by-Dale had been more eventful than she could have imagined, and her stress levels had soared at times, it still didn't compare to the traumatic kind of stress that had led her to be here in the first instance. She wondered, for the first time since arriving, whether the Board might have decided, yet? The thought sent a blaze of fire to her stomach, which then exploded and flowed vibrations back through to her hands, and left her legs feeling weak under the shock. She would likely find out tomorrow if that were the case. She didn't want to look at her emails. Being out of contact with London felt good.

Winnie, oblivious to pretty much the world, snored loudly from her bed, drawing Grace's attention and causing Flo's ears to twitch. Grace's thoughts drifted to Harriet.

Harriet was lovely. So, reassuring, so understanding, and always calm, and, she even made great fucking biscuits. There was tenderness in the way Harriet's eyes settled on her whenever she spoke. Genuine tenderness, the quality of which she had never experienced before and that seemed to unravel her – expose her. And all she could come up with was projected jealousy. She groaned in self-disgust and Flo's nose twitched at another interruption.

Attracted by the blue bottle that hadn't yet made its way into a cupboard, she unscrewed its cap and poured herself a drink. She wandered through to the living room and slumped into the oversized sofa, which swallowed her in an instant. Scanning the room, her eyes settled on the deer. Or did its eyes settle on her? She stared at it. It stared back at her. She sipped at her drink and it continued to stare. It occurred to her; it was a majestic looking beast. Harriet had said it was a rare catch, a ten-point buck. Vera had shot it. Fine markings gave the appearance of perfect symmetry and would set this deer apart from its peers. That said; this was the one stuffed and perched on a wall in Vera's living room, rather than romping freely through the countryside. Harriet had said culling was necessary and always done with respect for the animals. She stared at the victim and he stared back at her. He didn't have a smile on his face, but his eyes had a definite sparkle and focus to them that she admired. She sipped the gin, emptying the glass, and eased up out of the seat.

She wandered through to the kitchen, noting the dogs both fast asleep, and reached for the blue bottle. Momentarily puzzled – she was sure she had left the gin on the surface next to the sink – she frowned. Searching, she found it on the shelf in the cupboard. She must have been mistaken, in a haze of distress over the Flo situation and put it away. She poured a second gin, a little stronger than the first, and walked back to the living room.

Reacquainted with the soft, comforting, seat, she raised a toast to the deer and sipped. Weird, did its eyes just move? She dismissed the notion as nonsense and allowed her head to settle back into the cushions and her eyes to close, the cold glass against her fingers.

Rustling noises alerted her and she opened her eyes abruptly and the woman in a purple raincoat, short silver-white hair and swinging a lead at her heels, walked straight past her and through the door, heading towards the kitchen. Ice flowed down her spine and she froze. Eventually, she blinked, but the image wouldn't go away. Her heart pounded and she couldn't breathe. Some time passed before she turned towards the door, to see if the woman was still there. She wasn't. And at that point, Grace inhaled. She slugged at the gin with shaking hands trying to reconcile the trick her mind had just played on her. It was the same woman she had seen two days ago, at the station. Without the dog, or sheep, or whatever the fuck it was. She drained the glass and tried to convince her body to move. It refused. The bloody deer looked like it was laughing. It wasn't. Jesus, is there something in the alcohol up here? She closed her eyes and took short, focused breaths until her heart settled and the tightness had shifted enough for the muscles in her legs to work. Opening her eyes, she stood.

Slowly she took small paces, one at a time pausing after each, to the living room door, peeked through to the foyer and towards the kitchen, and listened attentively. Nothing. She took in a deep breath and slowly stepped across the foyer. Just past halfway her heart started thumping and she stopped to listen without the noise of her moving body to distract her. Nothing. She took another step.

BANG! BANG! BANG!

'FUCK!' Grace screamed and ran towards the living room.

The dogs barked and Flo came bounding into the foyer, followed by a tottering Winnie who proceeded to bark at the fresh air above her head just as the front door flung open and Harriet ran towards Grace.

'Grace, Grace! What's happened?' Harriet flung her arms around the dumbfounded woman, who looked positively ashen. 'Grace, you were screaming, what happened?'

Grace couldn't focus. She was vaguely aware of being in the house, Flo nudging her leg, Winnie barking, her heart pounding through her chest, the pressure squeezing her head, the voice speaking to her. What was Harriet doing here? The front door! Christ, she'd nearly had a heart attack.

'Grace?'

Harriet was trying to get her attention. Her ears were ringing, and she couldn't feel her legs. And then her head was spinning. And, thud!

'Grace, Grace?'

Grace could feel the soft hand stroking her face, tucking her hair behind her ear. She blinked repeatedly and then slowly opened her eyes. She was back on the sofa; Harriet sat next to her.

'Oh, thank God,' Harriet said.

Harriet, hand to her chest, looked worried.

'What on earth happened?' Grace said.

'You fainted.'

Grace groaned.

'I heard you scream and I let myself in.'

'I think there's a ghost,' Grace said, feeling all shades of stupid hearing the words stutter from her lips.

Harriet released a long breath, and then she smiled sweetly.

'You think I'm kidding?' Grace said.

Harriet shook her head and sighed again, the colour returning to her cheeks. 'I thought something dreadful had happened,' she said.

Ghosts certainly fit Grace's category of dreadful.

'That will be old Hilda Spencer,' Harriet said. 'There've been rumours she's on the prowl. You're honoured to have seen her. I don't think she's ever been seen by a visitor.'

Honoured wasn't a word Grace would have used to describe the frightening experience.

'Hilda Spencer,' Grace repeated. 'Does she normally walk a dog?'

Harriet chuckled. 'Or a sheep, or something in between, depending on who's doing the seeing,' she said.

Grace frowned. 'I saw her at the station, walking a poodle. At least it looked like a poodle, though I thought it was a sheep at one point. Now, I'm just bloody confused.' She sat shaking her head and Harriet reached across and took her hand.

'There are some who think Hilda is just a rumour, but others take her showing up as a sign that something is coming,' Harriet said.

'What, like an apocalypse?'

Harriet chuckled. 'Not quite! Usually a wedding, funeral, or birth; someone coming into the village or leaving, that kind of thing.'

'Did she have a poodle when she was alive?' Grace said.

'And a sheep,' Harriet said.

Grace frowned.

'She had a poodle for a long time, which is pretty unique around here. It's not a common dog in this area, but she was different from most people. She became senile with age though and when Brambles died, the local farmer replaced him with a lamb. She nurtured that sheep as if it was Brambles.'

'She didn't notice?'

'If she did, she didn't let on. She was quite confused by then. Kept her going a couple of years though, and then she died.'

Grace's eyes widened. 'How do you know what's coming?'

'Some say if it's a dog that's seen it's a birth coming, or someone moving into the village, if it's a sheep it's a death or someone leaving, and if it's undecided which, then it's a union or marriage. That pretty much covers all the bases,' she said, and Grace couldn't quite tell if she was being sarcastic or not. 'Usually, too many months pass before anything happens making any causal link impossible to prove. The last time Hilda turned up around here, it was six months before something happened.'

'What happened?'

'Arthur Newbury died.'

'Oh!'

'He was ninety-six,' Harriet added. 'It's so tenuous, only the diehards take it all seriously,' she said, and she delivered that soft, tender smile again.

'What if it's a lead and neither dog nor sheep?' Grace said.

Harriet frowned. 'I don't think anyone's seen her without Brambles.'

Grace studied the shaking hands in her lap.

'What did you see?' Harriet said.

'At the station, I was undecided. Just now, there was only a lead.'

Harriet pursed her lips, head nodding. 'Crikey, that's confusing.'

Confusing was an understatement from Grace's perspective. She swallowed to release the vibration in her throat. 'Tell me, the deer in the living room. Do its eyes move?'

Harriet burst out laughing and Grace felt it soften her and settle with fuzzy warmth in her stomach.

'No, I don't think so.'

Grace sighed. 'Good!' Her heart had returned to normal and the softness of Harriet's hand on hers was a more than welcome distraction. 'Would you like a gin?' she said.

Harriet stood and helped Grace to her feet and when she let go of Grace's hand, Grace made a fist as if to keep hold of the contact.

'Good idea,' Harriet said and held Grace's gaze.

Grace studied the dark eyes. In truth, she needed Harriet to stay the night if she was going to get any sleep, but that would be pathetic. It was only a ghost, right? And a harmless one at that... if it even existed. She was having a hard time convincing herself that maybe it didn't. Seeing it once was a fluke. Twice, and a pattern was beginning to emerge. At least this Hilda ghost person hadn't spoken. That would have been beyond fucking freaky. 'Has she ever spoken to anyone?' Grace said.

'Hilda?'

Grace nodded.

'I don't know. This is the only house she frequents in the village though.'

Fucking great!

'It used to be her house. Her father built it. Hilda was an original Duckton. Spencer is her married name. Rumour has it she was angry with her husband who lost the house in a bet. It never went back to the Duckton family after that. She visits the house from time to time. Vera chats to her.'

The whites of Grace's eyes expanded.

'I don't think Hilda responds though,' Harriet said, reassuringly. 'And she wanders around the local villages. I wonder what she wants?' Harriet said.

And those five words sent another chill down Grace's spine. Harriet did believe in the tales.

They walked back to the kitchen and Grace felt the ice move down her spine again. Fuck! The gin had made its way back to the cupboard.

'Will you stay for a while?' Grace blurted.

Harriet studied Grace with a gentle frown. 'Would you rather come and stay with me? I have a spare room, and the dogs will be fine together.'

Grace released a deep sigh, overwhelmed by the sense of comfort that came with the idea.

'At least in the morning things will look a little different,' Harriet said.

Grace was nodding with every word. 'Would you mind?'

'Not at all,' Harriet said, chirpily. 'I have gin too. And hot water,' she added. 'Do you like beef and ale pie?'

Grace nodded. How could she not!

*

'You did what? Vera said.

Jenny pressed the phone to her ear and whispered loudly, not that there was anyone in the house to hear the conversation. She sipped at the glass of wine she had treated herself to, after returning from Vera's house. She started again. 'I moved the gin,' she said.

'We're trying to get the girls together, not scare the shit out of Grace,' Vera said.

'I wasn't planning to do it, just keep an eye on Grace for a bit, to check she was okay. She'd had a bit of a fright apparently, with Flo escaping. It was alright because Flo ran into the field with Archie, and Jarid and Harriet were there. I was going to pop in and speak to Harriet, just to check she's not thinking of moving to New Zealand, but then I got distracted by watching Grace – that cubby hole behind the living room wall is so bloody uncomfortable, and she kept staring at the deer as if she was staring straight at me. Gave me the willies, to be honest. Anyway, when I heard the scream and the dogs ran into the foyer to investigate, it was fate. So, I nipped in the back and moved the bottle back into the cupboard,' she said.

'Oh, my good God almighty!'

'What?'

'What scream, Jen?'

'Grace screamed, but when I got back to the cubby hole our Harriet was there comforting her and they were sat on the sofa together holding hands.'

Vera's tone softened. 'That sounds positive,' Vera said.

Jenny paused. 'Come to think of it, she didn't look all that well.'

'What do you mean?'

'White as a sheet; and shaking like a leaf.'

'You scared the shit out of her,' Vera said. 'What do you expect?'

'No, she definitely screamed after our Harriet knocked on the door.'

A moment of silence carried down the line. 'What's New Zealand got to do with anything?' Vera said.

'Doug thinks he overheard something in the pub, but Jarid seems to think Harriet's her normal self.'

'She's not moving, is she?' Vera said.

'I don't know, but it did get me thinking, what if they really like each other and then Grace drags Harriet to London to live, or bloody New Zealand?'

'Never going to happen,' Vera said with convincing certainty.

'Anyway, Grace went back to our Harriet's and then I came home.'

'Good. That's very good.'

Jenny sipped from her wine. 'Anyway, how's Nell?' she said.

'Nell's great. Devon sucks though. It's like the Marie Celeste here, full of old people and too bloody quiet,' Vera said.

Jenny laughed. 'Are you having a nice time though?' Jenny said.

'I'm not sure if I can last a month,' Vera said.

'Oh! Do we need to amend the plan?' Jenny said with excitement.

8.

Daylight and birdsong filtered into Grace's awareness. Her eyes refused to open and she lay motionless for a while, savouring the warmth, the softness of the bed cover against her skin, and the mattress that enveloped her in comfort. She turned onto her side, the light floral scent teasing her, and snuggled deeper into the pillow and inhaled. Heartened, she moaned in pleasure, thankful that she had had the good sense to refuse another drink the previous evening and instead given her attention to eating. The beef and ale pie had been the best she had ever had, the meat melting in her mouth; it was scrumptious. Nothing like the same dish in London, the meat was tastier and the puff pastry light and fluffy.

Harriet's house was a lot smaller than Vera's and cosier. With two bedrooms rather than the six next door she had felt more relaxed, safer, than at any time in the last two days living at her aunt's. The quaint living room had been warm even in the absence of a fire and the gentle background music had made for a convivial atmosphere, in which they had sat and chatted.

Apparently, Harriet had a darkroom in the small cellar, but it had been late and she had agreed to show Grace on another day. Some of Harriet's photographs sat on the mantlepiece and a large framed image hung on the living room wall. It was the same lake view she had seen at her mother's house, only much larger and in black and white. With the rolling hills behind the lake and what looked like the sun rising over the top of them. The interplay of light and shadow in the picture had captivated Grace's attention and then she had effortlessly become absorbed by Harriet's explanation of the science behind creating the image.

When Harriet had said she needed to go to bed, Grace had felt disappointment in a wave that swept through her.

There was something about Harriet's company that had settled her, and in the absence of it she had felt susceptible. Being with Harriet felt comforting, and subtly intimate, in the short time they had shared Grace had also discovered that she had the urge to protect and defend Harriet – not that Harriet seemed to need either protecting or defending. And yet, the impulse was strong and unrelenting.

Grace sighed, blinked her eyes open and checked her phone. No messages, but it was half-past-nine and the signal was no stronger than in Vera's house. She rubbed her eyes and stared at the screen again. Nope, still half-past nine. The sun penetrated the thin cotton curtains and when she pulled them open, she squinted into the bright light and out across the paddock. It looked like a glorious day. Harriet had said it would be. Temperatures were going to hit twenty-degrees, which after eleven degrees at the weekend, would be welcome.

Harriet came into view carrying a large bucket and tipped its contents into a trough. Grace watched the chestnut horse approach and nuzzle Harriet's hand before tucking into the feed, and Harriet rubbing its nose and patting its neck. The black and white pony walked towards them and she gave it the same attention, and then walked back into the cottage. Grace hadn't been aware of the fluttering in her chest and her racing heart until Harriet was out of sight and the urge to pull on some clothes and head downstairs shifted her into action.

'Morning,' Grace said, entering the kitchen as nonchalantly as she could manage, feeling her cheeks flush.

Flo bounded toward Grace and greeted her with a nudge and a wet kiss to the hand. Winnie barked, and Archie snuffed through his nose from his bed. Grace petted the dogs briefly then rubbed her hands down her jeans.

Harriet turned from the sink and picked up the towel. She studied Grace with a quizzical smile. 'Did you sleep well?'

'I can't remember the last time I woke this late in a day,' Grace said and returned the smile.

'You look better,' Harriet acknowledged. 'Would you like coffee? Toast, or something? I have Rice Crispies, Luce's favourite, for when she stays over,' Harriet said.

Grace thought Harriet was babbling, but it was endearing and she chuckled. 'Rice Crispies will be perfect, as long as Luce won't mind me stealing her breakfast?'

Harriet laughed. 'Please, sit.' She loaded the coffee machine and pulled out the cereal from the cupboard, placed a bowl, spoon, milk, and sugar on the table.

'Can I just?' Grace indicated towards the sink.

Harriet nodded. 'Of course.'

Grace washed her hands and then sat.

Harriet stared at her, looking as if she wanted to say something.

'The bed is very comfortable,' Grace said. 'Thank you for letting me stay. The beef pie was the best and I haven't slept that well in as long as I can remember.'

Harriet smiled. 'I'm glad you feel better,' she said.

'It's been a bit of a roller-coaster since I arrived,' Grace admitted.

Harriet chuckled. 'I was wondering, would you like to go to the lake today? We could take a picnic. It's going to be warm.' She poured two cups of coffee and took them to the table.

'Thanks,' Grace said. She added milk and two sugars, stirred and then sipped. 'Don't you have work to do?' she said.

'I can take my camera. There should be some good views down into Ferndale later in the day.'

Grace smiled and nodded. A picnic at the lake sounded a lot more relaxing than chasing after a wayward dog or avoiding freaky ghosts. 'Sounds good,' she said.

Harriet beamed and seemed to fill with energy. She turned to the fridge and pulled out bits and bobs and started to make up the picnic.

Grace tipped the cereal into the bowl added a splash of milk and started to eat; the snap, crackle, and pop tickling her tongue and echoing in her mouth. Harriet continued to gather things together for the picnic and Grace watched her in awe, fascinated by the way she moved with focus and elegance around the kitchen, the way she seemed to caress the food as she prepared it. Harriet assessed, selected, and packed small containers with various fruit and vegetable combinations and stacked them on the kitchen surface. The silence didn't seem at all quiet. On the contrary, it was filled with vibrant energy and anticipation that filtered through Grace. She finished the cereal, picked up the crockery and washed it in the sink. 'I'll go and get washed and changed,' she said.

'You can leave the dogs here if you like?' Harriet said.

Grace smiled, grateful for not having to move them from one building to another. 'Thanks.'

'I'll come and get you. What, half-an-hour?'

Reluctant to leave, Grace nodded. 'Sure,' she said. She crossed the driveway and stopped short of the large oak front door. She studied it, needing a moment to adjust to her new knowledge about the place. Haunted house eh! She took a deep breath and released it slowly, her heart thumping in her chest. She stepped closer and peered through a downstairs window into the foyer. There was nothing to see, except sunlight streaming from the landing window. Taking another deep breath, she opened the door and entered. In many respects, it looked just as it had done when she arrived, but the memory of the previous evening and the sound of her own screaming sent a shiver down her spine.

'Come on, you can do this.' Talking aloud made her feel as if she had company. It helped. 'Hi Hilda, it's only me,' she said.

She wandered into the living room. The deer looked exactly as it had done – majestic, stuffed, and mounted. She wandered into the kitchen. She must have been mistaken, confused, last night. The gin was on the worktop next to the sink. She picked it up and placed it in the cupboard, poured herself a glass of water and made her way up the stairs. The view from the landing window looked even more glorious in full sunlight. Feeling reassured, she went to her bedroom, showered, and dressed.

She glanced at the laptop on the bedside table, the habitual temptation to look through her emails quashed by the feeling of anxiety that leapt into her stomach. Stephanie, the chair of her Board, would text her if there were any update from their investigations. She turned away and went back down the stairs, more eager to escape to the lake than she might wish to admit.

Grace opened the front door.

Harriet looked up at her and smiled.

A large rucksack was pinned to her back and she had abandoned the raincoat for a red and black checked shirt over the top of a white t-shirt, jeans and hiking boots. A vintage camera hung around her neck and Grace spotted a pair of binoculars tucked into the side of the rucksack. Three leads hung from her right hand; all dogs sitting perfectly still and gazing up at Grace. Harriet looked adorable, and even the dogs looked likeable.

'Are you ready?' Harriet said.

Grace searched the track leading to the main road. 'How are we getting to the lake?' she said. She could see the edge of lake from the house, in the distance. 'Where's the car?'

Harriet chuckled. 'We're walking; we can take the path through the woods from behind the house.'

Grace's eyes widened and she gazed down at the sandals on her feet. 'Right, I'd better change these then?' she said.

'We need to lock Winnie in, it's too far for her to walk,' Harriet said, handing over the lead.

'How far is the lake?'

'About seven miles each way.' Harriet said, chirpily.

Grace suddenly empathised with the old dog. She walked Winnie through to the hunting room and then ran up the stairs, returning with more suitable footwear.

Harriet studied the Burberry check-cotton sneakers and grinned.

Grace looked down at the footwear. 'I bought these specifically for the trip,' she said. 'Are they okay?'

Harriet pursed her lips, head on a tilt. 'They're pretty,' she said then she looked directly into Grace's eyes. 'Might get a bit scuffed,' she added and smiled.

Grace felt naked under the intensity in the gaze and heat flushed her cheeks. 'Oh, well,' she said and shrugged, and then it occurred to her that she couldn't remember walking seven miles, let alone seven miles each way. 'How far was the pub we went to?' she said, trying to gauge the difference.

'A couple of miles give or take.'

Fuck. So much for a relaxing day! Her legs had only just recovered from their hike to the Duckton Arms.

'There's no rush,' Harriet said as if reading Grace's thoughts. 'We can stop as many times as we like.'

Grace nodded. 'Okay,' she said, and Harriet handed her Flo's lead. 'I feel quite... light,' she said.

'You can carry the rucksack on the way back if you insist,' Harriet said and set off towards the rear of the house, Grace running to keep up.

Harriet shortened her pace until Grace walked alongside her. 'Sorry, I put a rucksack on my back and get into hiking mode,' she said.

'Do you do a lot of hiking?' Grace said.

'It's walking territory around here. I was brought up on it.'

Grace couldn't remember going on walks as a child. She couldn't remember spending time with her parents either. She could remember being confined to a military base somewhere in the world and finding ways of entertaining herself, usually by working out what could be traded and setting up a black market within local communities for things like sweets and books and writing implements that were of interest to the local children who didn't have access to things that she did. Her parents enjoyed an ex-pat lifestyle; she learned how to negotiate, source and sell. She had made a tidy sum of money by the time she reached early teens, and at that point had also learned the power of outsourcing the menial tasks such as supplying and selling to others. All that stopped though when they returned to the UK, and she had had to knuckle down and catch up on her education.

'There's nothing better than walking in nature,' Harriet continued. 'There's so much to see.'

Grace admired her passion, though her attention was firmly fixed on her own feet avoiding the roots of trees that cut across the path in front of them.

'We can let the dogs off now,' Harriet said, and unclipped Archie, who immediately ran to the nearest bush and cocked his leg, Flo bounding past him.

Harriet suddenly stopped walking and looked up. 'Listen,' she said.

Grace listened. The repetitive tapping noise echoed around the treetops. Then stopped. Then it came again. 'Woodpecker?' Grace said.

'Yes. Can you see him?'

Grace couldn't.

'Up there, just short of the third branch from the top,' Harriet whispered. 'You can just about see him from here.' She pointed.

Grace leaned closer to Harriet and squinted at the tree.

Harriet took a closer look through the binoculars then handed them to Grace.

'It's a great spotted woodpecker.'

The tapping noise came again and then a loud call that focused her attention. Grace zeroed in on the black and white blackbird-sized-bird with its long distinctively black beak and cream coloured chest feathers.

'You see the red patch on the back of its head?' Harriet whispered.

Grace nodded, acutely aware of Harriet's breath close to her ear.

'That's how you know it's the male of the species.'

Grace nodded, trying not to make a sound, her insides reeling from the tingling that flowed down from her neck.

Harriet lifted the camera to her eye, adjusted the focus, and clicked the shutter. She wound the film on, repeated the process a couple of times, and then let the camera hang freely again.

The bird flew off, and Grace took in a deep breath and handed back the binoculars.

'That was lucky,' Harriet said. 'They usually keep themselves to themselves and can be hard to spot.'

Grace studied Harriet, her throat dry, her stomach in bits.

Harriet set off again and Grace found that she needed to jog a couple of paces to catch up before they got back into step. They walked in silence and Grace became aware of the cacophony that surrounded them. Birds chorused loudly and a light breeze rustled the leaves above their heads. The earth had a hollow sound at their feet, and crunching noises emanated from the foliage inside the wood. The scent of blossom and young buds coming to bloom drifted on the air from time to time and then an earthy damp aroma that emerged from the wooded undergrowth.

'If we're lucky we might see a red squirrel,' Harriet said.

Grace swallowed. 'I've only ever seen grey ones,' she said, but it wasn't a vision of a squirrel in her mind's eye.

Harriet smiled. 'The red ones are native to this area and a few other parts of the UK. I doubt you'd see one in London,' she said. 'Come on, there's a stream a short way up here. We can take a break.'

The trickling noise became louder and then the stream came into view. Further up the craggy rock face, water gushed from what looked like a hole in the rock. Where they stood, crystal clear, bubbling water danced across variously sized stones and pebbles perfectly smoothed by its erosive powers. The water was shallow enough to walk across, though Grace jumped to avoid wetting her trainers. Flo chased down the stream and back up again, nuzzling and lapping at the water. Archie stood at the edge, as if trying not to get his feet wet, and took a steady drink.

'Would you like a drink?' Harriet said, removing the rucksack and resting it on the ground.

'Sure.'

'I bought a flask of coffee, milk and two sugars, right?'

Grace smiled. 'Yes.'

'Or there's water if you prefer?'

'Coffee will be great, thanks.'

Harriet removed the flask and two cups.

Grace found herself listening to the running water, lost in her appreciation of Harriet. When she came to focus again, Harriet was smiling at her and she felt her heart skip a beat.

'Here,' Harriet said and handed over a cup and biscuit.

'You like baking?' Grace said, trying to stay focused.

'Yes.'

'You're very good,' Grace said, and she was pleased the jealous voice didn't make some harsh comment. That was new!

'I bake for the café. We should go there for coffee,' Harriet said. 'Drew wants to meet you?'

'Drew?' Grace said and felt a spikey feeling niggle her.

'Drew and I have known each other since we were at school. She's lived here all her life too and we've been best friends forever.'

Grace felt the constriction in her throat and the subsequent battle with the biscuit that refused to budge. She sipped at the coffee. It helped. Even having full realisation of the irrational nature of her intense response to a woman she had never met, didn't make the mention of Drew any less palatable. Maybe it was the fact that Drew had known Harriet all their lives, or the best friend label Harriet ascribed to her, or maybe it was the sense that Drew and Harriet shared something special, that was the threat? Whatever it was, it didn't sit comfortably, and while she wanted to know more, she didn't want to hear something that might disturb the sense of wellbeing she felt around Harriet.

'She's lucky to have you cook for her,' was all Grace could come up with. The biscuit stuck in her throat and she downed the coffee to free it.

'You'll like her,' Harriet said.

I won't! 'Sure,' Grace responded, shaking the dregs from the cup and passing it back to Harriet. 'Want me to carry the rucksack?'

Harriet grinned. 'If you like.'

Grace shrugged. She reached for the bag and lifted it onto her shoulder. 'Bloody hell, did you bring the kitchen sink?' she said, straining under the weight of it.

Harriet laughed. 'I like to come fully prepared,' she said. 'The weather can turn quickly.'

Grace stared into the deep blue sky. Out towards Ferndale, clear blue. 'Right.' She huffed as she positioned the rucksack and secured it around her waist. 'Onwards and upwards,' she said.

Harriet pointed the camera and clicked.

'I bet that was a good look,' Grace said.

Harriet laughed. 'It was,' she said, and started climbing, leaving Grace standing, mouth open, blinking rapidly, heart racing.

9.

Harriet stood what appeared to be a million miles from the house. It had taken another two hours to get to this point and it looked to Grace as though she could literally touch the sky. Harriet clicked the camera and then disappeared out of view.

Grace's heart stopped, irrationally concerned that she had fallen off a cliff. As she approached the same spot, puffing from the climb, a lake the size of an ocean came into view and took her breath away. 'Wow! That's spectacular,' she said. Flo was already swimming, Archie stood on the bank barking at her.

Harriet had the camera pointed at Grace and clicked.

'Another good look!' Grace said.

Harriet smiled and turned towards the lake. 'It's incredible, isn't it?' she said.

Grace scanned the expansive body of water, surrounded by more hills to the left and straight ahead. Looking to the right, down into the valley, Ferndale felt a little closer than it had before. She turned around and located Duckton House, Harriet's cottage and the surrounding fields, and the forestation they had walked through, to get to this point. Only a fraction of the lake had been visible from the house, she realised. She turned to Harriet, who clicked the camera at her again, and chuckled. Harriet wound the film, pointed and clicked again. And, as she lowered the camera, Grace became acutely aware of the intensity in her dark gaze. Harriet seemed to hesitate to speak, looked ever so slightly flustered and then broke eye contact, and turned towards the lake.

'That's Carisfell over there, Cariscarn's further round. You can't see it as well from here,' Harriet said, pointing to the large peak in the distance. 'Carisfell's the highest land in England, apparently.'

Grace hadn't heard of it. Its magnificence was lost on her, her thoughts preoccupied with the person doing the pointing. She said 'Wow!' anyway. She glanced out across the landscape the other side of the lake where one hill rolled into another, small patches of green dotted in crevasses that would transform into villages and towns as one got closer to them.

'Broadermere is in that direction,' she said, pointing again.

Grace had heard of the town, a major tourist destination, but was too distracted to give due attention to Harriet's words. 'Right,' she said.

'Come on,' Harriet said and walked towards the lake.

Grace allowed the rucksack to drop to the ground and breathed a sigh of relief. She rubbed at her shoulders and stood an inch taller and feeling a whole lot lighter.

Harriet pulled out a rug and set it on the ground. The suntrap was perfect, sheltered from the light breeze that blew a little cooler at this height.

Harriet lay back on the rug and groaned with pleasure. 'This is my favourite spot,' she said, and then two dogs descended on her, licking at her neck, causing her to giggle.

Grace watched the dogs, feeling the levity of the moment in a surge of energy that passed through her. She couldn't help but chuckle and lay down on the blanket next to Harriet. There was something intimate in the shared experience, Harriet's presence, and that thought brought a second surge of warmth that felt hotter than the sun on her face. She hadn't been aware of her eyes closing, but when they flicked open Harriet was sat up and gazing across the lake, and Grace gulped. Harriet turned to her as she stirred and sat up.

'I love the way the lake ripples like that,' Harriet said. 'It looks like a ribbed mirror, that creates an abstract of the shadows that fall on it.'

Grace squinted at the water. She couldn't quite see what Harriet was getting at, but the way Harriet talked about what she could see was enough for her to be convinced. And then, a ripple effect made the shadows dance, mesmerised her, and she got it. 'It's spectacular,' she said.

Harriet pointed and clicked the camera. 'Yes, it is.' She looked towards Grace. 'Would you like some lunch?'

'Sure, I'll unpack,' Grace said.

'I'm just going to wander,' Harriet said and jumped to her feet.

'Sure.' Grace watched Harriet stopping to take pictures out towards Ferndale, and then moving further around and pointing back towards the house and finally towards Grace. The light breeze that flapped Harriet's shirt and tousled her hair and the ease with which she skipped from one rocky surface to the next distracted Grace and the lunch was slow to make it from the rucksack to the rug. As Harriet headed towards her, she jumped into action removing container after container. How hungry did Harriet think they would get?

'I didn't know what you might like to eat,' Harriet said.

Grace flushed and smiled. 'I eat pretty much anything,' she said, and felt Harriet's gaze caress her for what felt like an eternity.

Flo bounded up to them, followed by Archie, and both dogs stopped short of the rug. Grace broke eye contact with Harriet seconds before Flo decided to shake off the excess water from her coat. The spray seemed to move in slow motion, covering Grace as she dived to cover the food on the rug.

'Flo, away,' Harriet said, and the dog backed away and shook again.

Archie watched, head on a tilt, and Grace could have sworn the dog had a grin on its face.

'Ugh,' Grace muttered. She reached for the antibacterial spray only to realise she had left it in the house. 'Damn,' she cursed, trying to cuff the water from her face.

'Sorry,' Harriet said. She rummaged in the rucksack and pulled out a pack of wet wipes and handed them to Grace.

Grace pulled out a stream of tissue and wiped her face and hands, all the while, Harriet staring at her. 'I'm not particularly germ-phobic,' she said. 'I'm just cautious when visiting new places. It's a habit that comes from travelling a lot. And, I'm just not used to wet, slobbering dogs,' she added with a half-smile.

'I can see that,' Harriet said and matched Grace's smile.

Grace proceeded to wipe the tops of the containers, gathering a pile of used wipes by her side, Harriet still watching her. Grace couldn't decide whether it was a look of concerned empathy or abject horror.

'I was wondering,' Harriet started, drawing Grace's attention. 'Would you like to go to the quiz night at the pub on Wednesday evening? It's such good fun and you'll get to meet the villagers.'

Grace relaxed. More empathy than horror! Though the idea of going to a quiz night and meeting the villagers did, in fact, fill Grace with dread. 'I...' she started to decline the offer, but Harriet looked dejected at what she had already read to be an impending refusal, and before Grace managed to speak, she found herself nodding. 'Yes, of course, I'd love to,' she said.

Harriet's dark eyes sparkled and she continued to regard Grace for a moment. 'Great,' she said. She turned her attention to the food. She opened one pot, revealing what looked like scotch eggs, and another that had a kind of pickle inside it. She took an egg, dipped it into the relish and bit into it.

Grace couldn't find her appetite, which had nothing to do with the dog spray and everything to do with the attractive woman delving enthusiastically into the pots of food. She sipped at a bottle of water.

'There's pineapple-cheese in that one,' Harriet said, pointing to another container. She opened what looked like a tomato salad, picked up a fork and prodded a slice of tomato. She studied Grace. 'Is it the dogs?'

Grace smiled. 'No. I just drifted; the buffet smells great,' she said turning her attention to the food. She picked out a scotch egg and dipped it into the pickle. As the spicy sweet flavour exploded on her tongue, any residual recollection of having been splashed by Flo disappeared and visceral desire caused her to release a guttural groan. It wasn't a scotch egg at all it was a meatball, seasoned to perfection. 'Wow, these are delicious,' she said.

Harriet nodded and finished the last of hers. 'They're one of my favourites.'

'What herbs did you use?' Grace said knowing that even if Harriet named the herbs, she probably wouldn't be any the wiser. She was familiar with oregano and basil, but the taste that accompanied the minced beef didn't resemble either.

'It's a special blend Delia puts together.'

Harriet wasn't going to go into detail regarding the scope to which Delia's herbal blend was used around the village, but with a tweak here and there the concoction would be used as anything from a food supplement to an ointment. She had used it on her chestnut horse when he had injured his shin, and it had quickly reduced the swelling.

'Another culinary genius in the village, eh?' Grace laughed.

Harriet chuckled.

'Do you come here often?' Grace said, and then realised how inane the phrase sounded. 'I mean, to take photographs,' she added.

'Yes. The weather makes it a unique view every time. Anywhere around here,' she said, pointing out over the surrounding fells.

Yes, Grace supposed it did. The weather didn't change much in London, although sunny, blue-sky days were her favourite, sitting in the park and watching the world go by. Always on the outside, watching others from outside the group, and it dawned on her that she had never really shared this kind of space with anyone. She might sit on a park bench with the sun on her face, but her mind would still be working through the details of the next strategic move for the business, how better to maximise profits, or reduce headcount. She had never taken the time to *be* with nature, let alone to *be* with someone. Had she become so identified with being the unreachable that she enjoyed the distance she maintained?

'I like it here,' Harriet said.

'It's picturesque,' Grace said.

Harriet was studying her quizzically.

'Shall we head back?' Harriet said.

'Sure.' Grace started to pack the rucksack. As she reached for the tomato salad pot, so did Harriet, and then Harriet's hand was on top of hers, and Harriet was looking straight at her – into her – and she couldn't breathe.

'Are you happy, Grace?'

Grace's throat constricted to the point of nearly choking her. She hadn't anticipated that question. Not now and not ever. No one had asked her that. Perhaps no one dared, or perhaps it was assumed she was ecstatically happy given the wealth she had accumulated and the prestigious position she held within the company she owned. She tried to fight the burning in her eyes and wondered if they looked as glassy as they felt hot. Harriet was rubbing her hand with tenderness, and yet it hurt. It wasn't the touch, but the impact of the question that cut deeply and she was finding it impossible to speak. She couldn't answer, because she couldn't face the truth. She broke eye contact and gazed towards Ferndale, wishing she was somewhere over there, anywhere but sitting here with Harriet's hand resting on hers.

Harriet lowered her gaze to the rug, let go of Grace's hand, and finished packing the rucksack. Flo ran up to her followed by Archie and she gave them a chunk of meatball each. The dogs devoured the snack in seconds then sat as if waiting for the next treat.

'No,' Grace said in a quiet voice, avoiding eye contact. She stood from the rug, picked it up and folded it. She added it to the rucksack and then lifted it. It wasn't much lighter than on the journey out. Throwing it onto her back, she clipped the waist buckle and only then looked up.

Harriet looked sad.

Grace smiled. 'It's okay, Harriet,' she said. But it wasn't. 'Come on, let's get back.' She didn't need to ask Harriet the question. She radiated happiness. Maybe that was what made her so attractive, so comfortable to be around, so easy to enjoy spending time with, and so interesting to get to know.

'I need to replant the seedlings tomorrow, if you'd like to help. Perhaps we can go to the café for breakfast first?' Harriet said as they walked.

Grace smiled. 'Sounds great,' she said and she realised she was looking forward to spending more time with Harriet.

10.

Grace had thought twice about opening her laptop and checking her emails, and now she wished she hadn't bothered. The email from the Chair had been short and to the point.

Hi Grace, Apologies for not being in touch sooner, but there still isn't anything to update you on. The Board is unable to come to a decision at this time. I realise this is difficult, but I'm sure you want us to do the right thing for the business. Rest assured we have your best interests at heart. Regards, Stephanie.

Grace stepped into the hot bath, lowered herself slowly, and leaned back against the headrest at the end of the tub.

This should be done and dusted by now. Stephanie hadn't foreseen a problem when they had spoken at the outset. It was just that the Board needed to apply due diligence to do justice to the process. Any complaint against a senior executive must be given time and appropriate attention to ensure the perceptions of the *business* are managed. It's not just about the shareholders, she had said. We need to be sure our people get the right message. Allegations of this nature must be taken very seriously.

Grace sighed, the warm water comforting her tender muscles, and closed her eyes. Thoughts of Sandra fucking Floss tried to irritate and she felt a flash of fire behind her eyes. And then, inexplicably, tears pressed through the gaps and trickled onto her cheeks. She couldn't remember the last time she had cried, not with this kind of heartfelt emotion. The essence of it seemed to start so deep inside and it flowed so freely, it felt both liberating and alarming in equal measure. And then a strong feeling of helplessness gripped her and caused her to sit up sharply. She wanted to run and the only person she wanted to run to was Harriet. Harriet, Harriet, Harriet! She splashed her face with warm water, eased back against the tub and let the tears flow.

Harriet had made her feel something she hadn't realised she was capable of. It was as if Harriet saw her for who she was, rather than what she perceived herself to be. The CEO of a multi-million-pound events company held no sway in Harriet's world. Instead, there was innocence and purity, and a genuine sense of kindness that emanated from Harriet, and it wouldn't matter who you were or what you did, Harriet would care about you.

And then there was London, and Sandra fucking Floss!

She slid her head under the water and stayed there for as long as she could hold her breath, giving her mind a new challenge to focus on. Sliding back out of the water, she released the breath and sat up holding her head in hands and staring vacantly at the water. Thought-after-thought streamed relentlessly, her mind refusing to settle. She hadn't realised her heart was racing and her jaw had clamped tightly, and then her breathing became shallow and her head was spinning.

Standing up, her focus narrowed and she felt as if the world was closing in around her, her heart pounding, her body heavy; she was fighting for air. Voices rattled in her ear; and then there was confusion. She scrambled to the floor, knelt, and started blowing into cupped hands. Slowly at first, short breaths becoming longer, and then the voices faded into a ringing sound. Collapsing to her side, in the foetal position, she sobbed until shivering brought her to her senses and she moved herself to sit leaning against the bath. Studying the room as if seeing it for the first time she pulled her knees to her chest and remained still, shivering uncontrollably.

Unsure of the time that had passed, Grace slowly stood. Her body had dried itself, but her hair still trickled a single trail of water down her back. She picked up a towel, wrapped it around her head in a turban and pinched the bridge of her nose. She had never had a panic attack before and she never wanted to have another one.

Exhausted, she collapsed onto her bed and sobbed herself to sleep.

*

A banging noise attracted Grace's attention and then dogs barking, and she opened her eyes to bright sunlight. The banging came again and she blinked at her phone. Seven-thirty. Bloody hell, the dogs! Throwing on a pair of jeans and a t-shirt, she ran downstairs and pulled open the door. With a sleepy voice, 'Harriet,' she said.

Harriet seemed to swallow, her eyes settling momentarily on Grace's bra-less state before returning to hold her gaze. She cleared her throat. 'Hi. Sorry, I thought you'd be up already.'

Grace sensed heat flushing her cheeks, acutely aware she was sporting a badly ruffled I-went-to-bed-with-wet-hair look that could compete with the best, and her nipples had reacted to the cool air pressing them into the light material for the whole world to see. 'Sorry, I slept in,' she said. 'Come in. I just need to feed the dogs and get dressed,' she said. She went through the kitchen to the hunting room and opened the door into the side garden. Flo sped out the door and bounded across the lawn to pee at the hedge in the far corner. Winnie pottered to the first patch of green and squatted. Grace filled the dog's bowls with food and placed them on the floor. 'Can I get you a drink?'

Harriet shook her head. 'I'm okay, thanks.'

There was something different about Harriet. 'Where's Archie?'

'He can stay at home while we go for breakfast,' Harriet said.

'Oh. I'll leave the girls here too, then.' Harriet had her hands in her jeans-pockets, a gentle smile, and looked hellishly cute. 'I'll go and get ready,' she said and headed for the stairs.

Fully dressed, she returned with her hair still looking a little the worse for wear. As they left the house, Grace felt a sudden surge of guilt. 'Will the dogs be okay?' she said.

'They'll be fine. We won't be long and they can play in the garden while we're working later.'

'Right.'

They walked in silence along the narrow footpath leading into the village. They passed the thirteenth-century stone church, perched up on the hill, and then the cricket field and pavilion. 'This is where we hold the summer fete,' Harriet said.

Grace glanced across, the small hut, cricket pitch, and children's playground area with two swings a slide and roundabout. It wasn't much and it didn't compare to the outdoor event-venues she had visited over the years, but she could imagine the locals gathering here. It was a quintessentially British village fete location, absent of adequate facilities and yet enchanting.

They entered the café to the smell of coffee and approached the counter.

'Hey!' the woman working the coffee machine greeted them.

'Morning. Grace, this is Drew. Drew, Grace,' Harriet said.

Drew left the machine to percolate the coffee, stepped up to the counter wiping her hand on the cloth attached to her hip and then held it out to Grace. 'Hello Grace, I've heard a lot about you,' she said.

Grace took the firm grip and smiled. 'Drew, it's good to meet you.'

'What can I get you to drink,' Drew said, addressing Grace.

'White Americano, please.'

'What would you like to eat?' Harriet asked Grace. 'The full English is worth a shot if you're really hungry,' she suggested.

Grace smiled. 'Full English it is then.'

'Same for me, thanks,' Harriet said to Drew.

'Two full English coming up. Take a seat and I'll bring your coffee over.' Drew ushered them away, but not before Grace had noticed the way Drew smiled at Harriet.

Grace headed to a window seat, as she often did when drinking coffee in London. Somewhere she could sit and watch the world go by. 'It's quaint,' she said.

The door opened and Sheila entered. She walked to the counter and ordered a Mocha coffee, with extra chocolate. While she waited, she glanced around the room, spotted the girls, and turned as white as a sheet. 'I'm going to the pub,' she announced, and without waiting for her drink marched straight out of the café and across the road to the shop.

Drew shook her head and shrugged. 'What was that about?'

Grace's expression shifted from wide-eyed to a frown.

Harriet chuckled. 'That's Sheila Goldsworth. She was the school secretary for years. I think she's losing her marbles,' Harriet said, in a tone that conveyed compassion. She watched Sheila approach Esther just short of the shop and then both women looked towards the café. They were gossiping.

'There you go.' Drew placed their drinks on the table. She looked at Harriet with a broad grin and winked.

Harriet felt the groan rumble inside her, thankful she didn't let it out. Could Drew be any more obvious? Grace was looking from her to Drew and back again. 'I need to pick up some copper tape before we head back,' she said to get Grace's attention.

Grace frowned.

'Keeps the slugs and snails off the plants,' Harriet said,

Grace shuddered and put two spoons of sugar into her coffee and stirred. 'Right,' she said.

They sipped coffee in silence.

'Drew seems nice,' Grace said.

Harriet flushed.

'Did you make all the cakes?'

Harriet shook her head. 'No, Drew bakes too,'

Of course, she does. Damn, there was that voice again. 'Nice,' she said.

'You seem a bit out of sorts,' Harriet said.

Grace sighed. 'I'm sorry. It's just work.'

'I thought you were on a break,' Harriet said.

Grace sipped the coffee. 'I am, but it still occupies my mind,' she said. That wasn't a lie.

'Do you miss it?'

Grace nodded.

'I would miss my work,' Harriet said.

It was of little comfort.

'I find it so refreshing. Totally engrossing,' Harriet continued.

Grace wouldn't describe her work as refreshing. Engrossing, maybe? Draining, definitely! And yet, the absence of it left a gaping hole and sense of purposelessness. It was like a constant itch that could never be satiated, and yet there was a quality to that itch that was also deeply disturbing. Unhealthy. An addictive kind of quality. 'You're lucky,' she said.

'There you go,' Drew announced, and breakfast landed in front of each of them.

'Bloody hell, you meant hungry!' Grace blurted.

Harriet chuckled.

Two eggs, two sausages, two rashers of bacon, two hash browns, two large flat mushrooms, a buffalo tomato cut in half and two large servings of baked beans stared up at Grace. And then, Drew returned with two side plates, each with two slices of buttered toast.

'I won't need to eat again today,' Grace said.

'You wait 'til the country air gets to you. We've got a lot of planting to do when we get back.' Harriet cut into a sausage, smothered a piece with baked beans and ate it.

Grace mirrored her and moaned as the food melted on her tongue. 'That's really good sausage,' she said.

Harriet smiled. 'What do you like about your work?'

Grace chewed while she pondered. 'It's challenging. There's a huge buzz that comes from running a successful event, I think because it's so time pressured. You can't afford to miss a deadline, or the event won't happen, so when it all comes together it's a huge thrill.'

'Like our summer fete?' Harriet said.

Grace considered. 'Yes, exactly! Imagine your summer fete for twenty thousand people.'

'That's a lot of cream-teas.'

Grace chuckled. 'It's a lot of everything. A logistical nightmare in the making if it's not planned properly. Getting it wrong can literally fold your business.'

'I guess that's a bit like bad weather for us.'

Grace pondered. 'It's harder for you. You don't have control over the weather whereas we should have control over our planning, and we have contingency plans for everything.'

'Sounds stressful! Do you do all that organising yourself?'

Grace shook her head. 'No. I have teams that do the hard work.'

'What do you do then?'

'I make decisions I guess.'

'What, on your own?'

'Not anymore, we make decisions as a team now.'

'Oh, right. So, if you don't make decisions, what do you do? What is it you enjoy about what you do?'

Grace was stumped. 'I take responsibility for the decisions we take as a business.'

'Oh! A bit like deciding whether to grow carrots or cucumbers and how many of each?'

'Something like that, yes.'

'I prefer getting my hands dirty,' Harriet said. 'The tending and nurturing bit is more fun than deciding what to grow. I find it really rewarding to watch the plants mature and produce something that other people can enjoy.'

'Yes, I get that too. We aim to put on events so that people have a great experience.'

'That's lovely. What sort of events do you run?'

'Music events, skiing and snowboarding – indoor slopes, of course, other sports and health-based events.'

'Equestrian?'

'No, we haven't done one of those.'

'You'll be great at organising our summer fete then,' Harriet said, and she didn't look as though she was joking.

Grace was shaking her head. 'That's your baby,' she said and chuckled.

'I'm sure everyone would welcome your input this year. We could do with a makeover,' Harriet said.

Grace pondered the idea. She had thought Harriet was joking the first time she mentioned attending one of their meetings. She clearly wasn't!

'Seems the bit you like most, you don't really get to do in your job,' Harriet said.

Grace gazed at Harriet and smiled. 'Yes, I guess you're right.' It had been a long time since Grace had got her hands dirty, having removed herself from the day-to-day management of the events and even the interaction with audiences at the events her company managed. Did her job make her happy? Being the figurehead?

'So, you'll help us with the summer fete?'

'When is it?'

'The fete isn't until late July, but the first planning meeting is on Friday evening. Will you come?'

Grace knew she wouldn't be around for the fete, she'd be back in London by then, but there would be no harm in helping with the planning. 'Sure.'

Harriet smiled and her cheeks turned a healthy shade of pink. She looked adorable.

11.

'What do you want me to do?' Grace said, rolling up the sleeves of her jumper.

'Here, take this tray and start setting these out in the small pots over there,' Harriet instructed, handing Grace the seedlings and pointing to the bag of compost and pile of small plastic pots in the corner. 'One seedling in each pot and then put the pots on this tray.' She lifted the large plastic tray onto the bench in the greenhouse. 'I'll show you,' she said. She took a small pot, half filled it with soil, seemed to squeeze out a tiny seedling from the batch and set it in the middle of the pot, and then filled the space around it with more soil, pressing gently around the edges of the plant with her thumbs. Within a few seconds, the single shoot stood proudly in its own space, and the first pot sat in the plastic tray.

That looked easy enough.

Harriet smiled and her dark eyes held Grace until the point Grace became restless. 'Got it?' Harriet said.

'Sure.' Grace shrugged.

'I'll be working outside,' Harriet said and stepped out of the greenhouse. Grace watched her until she disappeared into the shed.

Grace turned to the plants and considered them intently. Right, here goes. She reached for one of the seedlings, twisted and tugged. She could feel tiny string-like roots snapping and pulled back from the plant. Am I doing this right? She poked her fingers into the soil again and closed her eyes, concerned that she was damaging the baby plant. Eventually easing it from the pack she went to place it in the pot. Fuck! She'd forgotten the soil. She placed the plant carefully on the bench, grabbed a handful of soil and half-filled the pot. Reaching for the plant, she knocked it through the gap between the slats of the bench and it tumbled to the floor. Fuck it! Plucking it from the floor, she eased it into the pot and filled the surrounding area with soil as she had seen Harriet demonstrate. She placed the pot next to the one Harriet had done and studied them side-by-side. Hers looked as though it had been on a journey through hell and back, the tiny battered shoot was struggling to stand. Fuck!

She filled a second pot, determined to model Harriet's confidence, pull the seedling from the batch, pop it into the pot, fill around the edges and bam, pot on the tray. Nice idea. She eyed the next victim, reached into the soil surrounding the roots and tugged. Snap! Fuck it! The top of the plant rested in her hand with the roots still embedded in the soil. 'Shit.'

'Everything okay?' Harriet's voice caused a chill to slide up her spine and her heart to race in a state of panic. Harriet was walking towards the greenhouse.

Fuck, fuck! 'Oh, hi,' Grace said, looking flustered.

Harriet assessed the two plants that had been potted and bit down on her lip, in a vain attempt to hold back the laughter. She chuckled. 'Here, let me show you again. You need to be quite firm with them,' she said.

Harriet moved closer and Grace froze. She couldn't tell whether Harriet intended to pin her between the bench and her own body, but the squeeze had been inevitable if she was going to see exactly how Harriet uplifted the seedling without killing it. Harriet's arm rested against hers and as Harriet moved, Grace inhaled the scent of her perfume. If that hadn't been confusing enough, Harriet's next move really caught Grace by surprise. Harriet half-filled the pot then took Grace's hand and plunged it into the batch of seedlings, her fingers intertwined between Grace's and guiding her to feel the roots. Oh, she was feeling them all right! Pushing down and then rotating, together they lifted the small plant and placed it into the pot. With a handful of soil to fill the pot, Harriet put the rehoused plant onto the tray.

'How was that?' Harriet said.

Grace couldn't breathe. Her hand tingled and her stomach was stuck in somersault mode. Harriet's smile added insult to the injury and Grace was surprised she didn't groan out loud. 'Huh hmm, fine. Thanks,' she croaked. She thought she'd heard Harriet chuckling as she wandered back to the shed, or maybe she was just shaking her head in despair.

Grace approached the seedlings again then remembered she needed a half-filled pot from the start. Pot in hand she dived into the plants, closed her eyes, pressed, twisted and pulled. When she opened her eyes, a tiny seedling sat in the palm of her hand. Chuckling, she placed the delicate plant into the pot and filled around its edges. It too sat proudly in its pot on the tray.

Sweat beaded her forehead and she started the process again. Pot after pot, she was on a roll now. Even the first plant had perked up a bit by the time she finished.

Harriet returned to the greenhouse with a can of water. 'They need a sprinkle of water, now,' she said and handed the container to Grace.

Grace followed Harriet's instructions to the letter then wandered into the garden. She stretched her back and stood watching Flo and Archie chase around the field. Winnie lay on the grass at the side of the veggie-plot chewing on something.

'Would you like a drink?' Harriet said.

Grace nodded.

'We need to dig this up next, so we can plant the tubers,' Harriet said, indicating to the muddy patch of ground. 'I'll go and get some water. If you want to make a start, just lay out a row of tubers from the bag over there and then pile the soil on top. It should look like that,' she said, pointing to the row she had already done. 'Tubers first, remember?'

'Tubers?'

'Potatoes,' Harriet confirmed.

Grace gave the thumbs up and turned to pick up the shovel.

'Tubers first, Grace. They need to be about three inches deep and twelve inches apart,' Harriet shouted.

Fuck! Grace went to the bag of tubers, grabbed a handful and started to lay them out. Three inches apart, twelve inches deep. Twelve inches deep, that doesn't sound right. Harriet returned with two glasses of water, Grace studying the soil, tubers in hand.

'Here,' Harriet said, handing over the drink. 'I'll place the tubers, you cover them.' She smiled warmly, downed the water and took the tubers from Grace.

Grace finished her water, enjoying the view of Harriet as she worked, and then picked up the shovel and turned the soil onto the tubers. By the end of the row, the two rows looked identical. Grace stood and rubbed her back. This was fun, kind of.

After the seventh row, Grace stood up and rubbed her back for the umpteenth time. This was bloody hard work. She wandered to the gate enclosing the horses and enjoyed the light breeze on her face.

'Do you ride?' Harriet asked as she approached.

Grace chuckled. 'No, never.'

'Would you like to have a go?'

Grace turned to face Harriet with a look of abject horror, but Harriet's dark eyes regarded her with unwavering confidence and she melted.

And then Grace realised she was nodding and the word, 'Sure,' slipped from her lips.

Harriet whistled and the chestnut approached. 'This is Buzz,' she said. 'That one's, Fizz,' she added. 'My brother named them.'

Grace smiled.

'I'll just saddle him,' Harriet said, and wandered off, returning a moment later. She entered the field, talked to the horse and slipped the saddle over his back. She disappeared again, returned with a hat and plonked it onto Grace's head. 'You'd better be safe,' she said. Shifting the box next to the horse she waved to Grace.

Grace moved tentatively towards the horse.

'Don't be scared, he won't bite you. He's a gentle giant, and frankly, you're more of a liability than he is.'

'Thanks!'

Harriet chuckled.

Grace would have laughed had terror not taken control of her senses. She took a deep breath and approached with as much confidence as she could muster. She stood on the box and put a foot through the stirrup, following Harriet's instructions. She swung her leg over the saddle and sat.

'Fuck, that's a long way up,' she blurted.

Harriet chuckled. 'You'll get used to it. Hold onto the saddle, and I'll guide him around.'

Grace wanted to scream. 'We're going to move?' she said.

'Yes, that's why it's called horse riding, not horse sitting.'

The horse started to turn from the fence and Grace had the feeling of being launched sideways. She squeezed her thighs into the saddle and tightened her grip. Harriet was looking at her with a curious gaze.

'Try to relax and rock with the movement of the saddle,' she said.

Easier said than done. Grace tried to relax the pressure in her thighs and the horse took a step forward. She wobbled and squeezed hard again and then her heel inadvertently jabbed the horse causing him to think he needed to walk faster. The sudden increase in pace elicited a muffled shriek from Grace and a 'whoa boy' from Harriet, who stroked the horse's cheek, keeping him under control. Grace's shriek faded into a yelping sound, and then into a moan and eventually a normal breathing pattern. Buzz had taken a few more paces and she was beginning to adjust to the rhythmical movement of the saddle.

'Try and sit upright,' Harriet said, and Grace became aware that she was close to hugging the saddle.

Grace lifted herself up, feeling even further from the ground and fear came over her again. She resisted the urge to crouch down to hug the horse.

'Look to the horizon,' Harriet said, and she did.

The feeling slowly subsided and she found the tightness in her shoulders easing too. She started to smile.

'There you go,' Harriet said. 'You're doing great.'

Grace had never been one for needing encouragement but coming from Harriet it felt positive and supportive. She found herself watching Harriet as she guided the horse around the field, the way her hair lightened under the sun and lifted on the breeze.

Strong, competent, hands controlled the horse's movements with sensitivity and words of reassurance spoken to Buzz, and again to Grace.

Grace climbed off the horse in a state of euphoria, and relief. Feet back on solid ground, she found she wanted to do it again. Harriet was smiling at her and her own face ached with the broad grin that spanned from ear to ear. 'That was quite something,' she said.

'It's an exhilarating feeling, riding,' Harriet said. She removed the saddle and Grace followed her back to the shed.

Grace handed over the hat. 'Thanks, that's a first for me,'

'Yes, and for me! I don't normally teach screaming adults,' Harriet said and started to chuckle.

'I didn't scream,' Grace said.

'Oh yes, you did.'

'I won't next time,' Grace said.

Harriet's intense gaze held Grace. 'Good,' she said.

Grace felt vibrations ripple through her then heat. 'I'd better go and get cleaned up,' she said.

Harriet nodded. 'Will you come over for a drink and some supper?'

Grace grinned. 'Sure, I'd love to.'

'Do you fancy a barbeque?'

Grace nodded. 'You want me to bring anything?'

Harriet shook her head.

'Right, I'll see you in an hour or so then.'

'Great. The dogs can stay with me if you like?'

'Okay.' Grace walked to the house wondering if Harriet had felt as awkward as she had, or whether it was her imagination. She went upstairs and turned the tap for the bath. Nothing. She kept turning. Still nothing. 'Fuck!'

She grabbed a change of clothes, the bottle of gin, and wandered back to the garden.

'That was quick,' Harriet said, noting the clothes and gin. 'What's up?'

'There's no water?'

Harriet frowned. 'That's unusual. I'll check mine and call dad.'

'Is he a plumber?'

'He does a lot of odd jobs around the village,' Harriet said walking into the cottage. 'He might know if there's a local problem. Let me just check,' she said and turned the kitchen tap. It was running perfectly. 'Strange. I thought both houses ran from the same source. Are you okay running a bath while I try and get hold of him?' she said.

'Sure.' Grace made her way upstairs to the bathroom.

Harriet picked up the phone.

'Darling, I can't get over there tonight. I can come first thing tomorrow. There's nothing locally that I'm aware of, and if your place is fine then it must be to do with Vera's. Very odd,' Bryan said.

'Dad,' Harriet said, in a tone that implied she had a question.

'Yes, petal.'

'Are mum and Delia up to something?'

Bryan went silent. 'What makes you say that?'

'Grace saw Hilda Spencer in the house, things keep moving, and every time I see Sheila, she tells me she's going to the pub. And now the water.'

Bryan guffawed. 'I think Sheila's losing it. Can't say for your mother, though she probably is too.' He lied convincingly.

'Well, if she's up to something, you can tell her from me to stop meddling.'

Bryan went silent again. 'Well, I think she's a bit concerned you're going to run off to New Zealand, petal,' he said.

'What?' Harriet started laughing then stopped suddenly. 'Where on earth did she get that idea from?'

Bryan went silent and then there was a muffling sound that didn't quite make sense.

'Where?' Harriet insisted.

'I think Doug overheard you talking at the Duckton Arms,' he said.

'Oh, for heaven's sake. If Doug Pettigrew heard anything then it was me telling Grace that was where Annabel ended up, with her boyfriend.'

'Oh! The woman who left you for a man?' Bryan said.

'Yes, dad. That one. The one and only woman in my life.' Harriet was shouting.

'Ah, right, that explains it then. I'll let your mother know,' Bryan said, oblivious to the fact that his ambivalence had caused offence.

Harriet put the phone down and turned, straight into Grace.

'Sorry, I.' Grace started to say. But it still looked as though she had been snooping.

'Hey. It's okay. It's nothing, just dad being dad – clueless and tactless,' Harriet said. 'How about a G&T? Seems there's nothing wrong with the water in the village so it looks like it's specifically to do with the house. Dad will pop round in the morning and see what he can work out.'

'Gin sounds great. I feel I've deserved it after all that digging,' Grace said, pondering Harriet's conversation with her father.

'Yes, we have.' Harriet led the way and poured two large drinks. She handed one to Grace, turned on the oven, and wandered into the garden. 'I'll get the barbeque fired up,' she said.

'Can I help?' Grace said.

'Can you grab the gas bottle from the shed?'

'Sure.' Grace took a long sip from the drink and placed the glass on the window ledge. She admired their work as she wandered round to the shed and back. 'How long will it take for the potatoes to be ready?' she asked.

'About ten weeks,' Harriet said. 'There's more over there that'll be ready in a month or so,' she added. 'The seedlings you potted earlier are runner beans. When they grow big enough, they'll need to go into the soil around that frame,' she said, pointing to the bamboo trellis.

'It's quite some plot you've got here,' Grace said.

'Yes, it's taken a while to get it to this point, and the crop is always dependent on weather, but I'm happy with it.'

Harriet lit the gas and stood and sipped her drink.

'Are you okay?' Grace said.

Harriet's smile lacked the intensity Grace had become familiar with for a moment, and then it seemed to return to normal. 'Yes, sorry. I was distracted. Are burgers okay with you?'

'Of course. I eat anything. I'll feed the dogs,' Grace said, surprising herself.

Harriet whistled loudly and three wagging tails ran at varying speeds towards the house. 'Everything is in that cupboard,' she said. She went to the fridge and pulled out two burgers wrapped in paper. She tipped some frozen chips – with skins on – onto a tray and put them into the oven and carried the burgers on a plate into the garden. Grace followed her, leaving the dogs to eat. Flo shot past Grace before she reached the barbeque and chased around the garden after what turned out to be a moth, which she caught and ate.

They stood in silence, the fat from the burgers starting to crackle and spit, sipping their drinks.

'Sorry, I'm being a bore,' Harriet said.

Grace shrugged.

'Village gossip gets to me sometimes.'

Grace could imagine. Gossip wasn't her favourite topic, either. Gossip could be divisive and damn right destructive.

'You'd think I'd be used to it by now?' Harriet said.

Grace shrugged again. 'Gossip isn't always easy to handle,' she said.

'It's just people caring. They don't think of it as intrusive; they just worry. Mum worries.'

Grace nodded. 'Mums do worry. Apparently, it's in their genes,' she said and chuckled.

Harriet smiled and when Grace held her gaze, she flushed.

'It's certainly in my mother's genes,' Harriet said.

'Mine too,' Grace admitted. 'It was a deciding factor for me setting up in London,' she said and smiled.

'Really?'

'One of them.'

Harriet inspected the burgers. 'They're ready,' she said.

'Can we eat inside?' Grace said.

'Germs?' Harriet said.

'No, I'm not that bad. It's getting bloody cold.'

'Wimp,' Harriet said and nudged Grace in the arm as she passed.

They sat at the kitchen table and ate in relative silence, Grace commenting on the quality of the food and discovering that the frozen chips had been hand made.

Grace studied Harriet as she tucked into her supper. The woman seemed so self-assured, so comfortable in who she was and the life she led, and Grace found herself drifting in admiration. Not only was Harriet exceptionally smart, interesting, confident and personable, the intensity of her gaze whenever she spoke said that she was interested to know about you – that she cared about you. She had Grace enthralled in a world Grace hadn't realised existed.

London seemed so shallow, so false, the people so arrogant and self-obsessed. God knows she had been one of them. She hadn't seen it clearly until now, though. Self-importance dressed up as entrepreneurship, used to further oneself ahead of others. Harriet was right; it was vulgar. And Harriet was beautiful. Everything about Harriet was beautiful. Even the way she ripped the bloody seedling from its bed and set it in its own pot. Everything she touched, she touched with purposeful passion, kindness, tenderness, and yet, in the vulnerability and openness that she displayed, there was also great strength. Grace felt weak by comparison.

Harriet watched Grace in deep reflection. She didn't want to pry but she did want to be there for Grace. She wanted to know what it was that seemed to distract her with what appeared to be concerned thoughts. She smiled, drawing Grace's attention to her.

Grace focused. 'Sorry.'

'You were frowning.'

'Was I?' Grace finished the last of her burger and tried to smile as she chewed, Harriet gazing at her causing a battle to ensue between her throat and the meat she needed to swallow. 'You're so beautiful,' she said and felt heat flush her cheeks.

Harriet blushed too. 'Would you like a mint tea?'

Grace chuckled. Harriet looked cute when she blushed. 'Please,' she said.

Harriet made the tea and wandered through to the living room. She slumped into the two-seater sofa and Grace flopped down next to her.

Grace caught Harriet gazing at her again and a surge of lightning zipped down her back. She hesitated to speak and then, the questions that she had wanted to ask since hearing about Harriet's girlfriend started to flow, 'How long were you with your ex?' she said.

Harriet looked away, sighed, and then held Grace's gaze. 'Six years,' she said. 'We had been together since our early twenties.'

Wow! Grace couldn't imagine being in a relationship with anyone for that length of time. She'd barely managed a long weekend in any one stint of co-habiting. 'When did you split up?'

'Five years ago.'

'And you're still not over her?' she asked then wished she hadn't. Harriet seemed to take the question well though; the grimace hadn't lasted long.

Harriet took in a deep breath and released it slowly. She was looking at Grace but locked in distant thought.

'Sorry, I didn't mean,' Grace started.

'No, it's okay. I'd like to talk to you about Annabel. You'll relate to her, I'm sure.'

Oh, that's not good! Grace swallowed.

'She was ambitious and creative and wanted to explore life. In the end, I got the impression she was just seeking a high all the time. She would climb without a safety harness and take the kind of risks that others wouldn't dare to take. She was fun to be around. Exciting, I guess. But, when it came down to it, we had different values. She had itchy feet and always needed the next fix.'

'Was she?' Grace hesitated, suddenly worried whether she could be as direct with Harriet as her thoughts had been with her. She was familiar with some of the behaviours as Harriet had described in Annabel at the pub, she recognised them in herself, and had been relieved that Harriet hadn't. That drive for the heady, rush of achievement and a feeling of failure when it didn't come, the constant striving for bigger, better and more. It could be relentless. She had seen the same qualities escalate within her Board in recent years too and that had given her cause to reflect on her own behaviour. She had known *that* person wasn't who she was, but it was who she had become. Maybe, in some unexpected way, the Sandra Floss situation had done her a favour? 'Was Annabel, obsessed, addicted?' Grace said.

'Yes, I think so. Not like an alcoholic but addicted to the adrenaline rush for sure. And if there wasn't something going on, she could get quite down too.'

'Hmm. That must be hard to live with.' Grace said. She sipped at the tea.

'I hadn't realised she had been seeing other women behind my back until after she left. And men, as it happened.'

Grace lowered her gaze to the cup in her hands. 'Ouch!' She might be lousy at relationships, but she'd never two-timed anyone.

Harriet smiled, tight lips holding resignation and acceptance in equal measure, and huffed. 'Yes, it's amazing how many women you can find around here, even when you don't want them,' she said.

Grace looked up. 'So, there hasn't been anyone since?'

Harriet sighed again and sipped. 'No. I've had offers, but I've never been ready to go there again. I was deeply in love and got badly burned. I'm not a slow learner, but I guess I don't carry a broken heart too well.'

Grace couldn't relate to either having a broken heart or not having had sex for five years or more.

'Don't you miss the physical contact?'

Harriet shook her head. 'It's not worth paying the price. Having someone get inside your soul, only to have them rip it open and stamp all over it.'

Fuck! Harriet had been truly burned.

Harriet held Grace with enquiring eyes. 'Have you ever been betrayed, Grace?'

Grace shook her head.

'You're very lucky.'

Right now, Grace didn't feel like the lucky one.

'It is the worst feeling in the world. The one person you trust with everything you have, everything you are, everything you want to be, destroys it piece by piece.' Harriet smiled.

Grace flushed, speechless. Fuck! The urge to pull Harriet close, to hold her tightly and protect her from the world overcame her and then rage filled her. How could anyone do that to Harriet?

'Tricked into a world that is driven by pain and avoidance, you eventually find your confidence eroded. That's what I came to realise that kind of addiction is all about – avoiding pain, bad feelings, things you can't handle. My failing was that I thought I could help. I thought we could be happy together. But I know now that never works. People have to be happy in and of themselves before they can be truly happy with another.'

Grace swallowed, minded of the question Harriet had asked her. Are you happy Grace? No, she had said. Fuck it! She thought she had started to understand Harriet, and she was really attracted to her, yet it seemed she didn't know her at all. Harriet didn't need anyone in her life; Harriet was happy. Grace suddenly felt very small and insignificant. She needed Harriet. She wanted to spend time with Harriet. Christ, she had even had thoughts of kissing Harriet, and if she were honest, she thought Harriet was similarly attracted to her and had had thoughts of kissing her too. Harriet's tender touch after she had seen the ghost, the body contact when they had been bird watching, and then again in the greenhouse. And Harriet had certainly flushed, several times, and looked at Grace with such intensity. Those looks didn't come without some intimate thoughts, at least not in her world.

Harriet seemed to focus back on Grace. 'I'm sorry, I'm ranting at you,' she said and smiled with those dark penetrating eyes.

Grace was shaking her head and struggling for words. 'Are you happy?' she said, feeling naked and exposed with the frankness of their conversation.

'Yes,' Harriet said, emphatically.

Fuck! Grace was right; Harriet didn't need anyone. 'That's good,' she said, her voice broken.

'That doesn't mean I wouldn't like to share my life with someone, Grace,' Harriet said.

'Oh! Of course.' There was hope after all.

'I'm just not in a rush and I'm not one for putting myself out there to get trampled all over. Intimacy is important to me, and I feel it in lots of ways. It would be nice to share my life with someone who feels as I do,' Harriet said, and Grace smiled.

'That's good,' Grace said, and then wondered whether Harriet had noticed that her tone sounded more upbeat?

Harriet chuckled. 'Thanks for your company today. I really enjoyed it. Would you like to do more tomorrow?' Harriet stood and Grace followed. 'You can stay here overnight if you like, but I need to get to bed now.'

'It's okay. I can do without water overnight.' She studied Harriet. 'I've enjoyed the day too,' she said and a wave of sadness flowed through her.

Harriet walked to the door and Flo leapt to her feet, Winnie staggering behind her. 'Thanks again,' Harriet said and held her arms open.

Grace felt the warmth of Harriet against her chest, and Harriet's cheek felt hot against her own. And then a sense of loss came to Grace and tears started to well in her eyes and trickle onto her cheeks. Harriet was squeezing her and she had to work hard not to sniffle into her exposed ear, the scent of Harriet tormenting every cell in her body. Harriet shifted slightly and Grace became acutely aware of the lips pressed to her cheek.

'Good night Grace.' Harriet said, easing out of the embrace. Then her eyes widened at the tear-stained cheeks and she lifted her hand to Grace's face and brushed away the wetness with such tenderness it caused the tears to flow even faster. 'Hey,' she said, and there was that look again.

Grace felt consumed. The softness of Harriet's fingers against her skin, the gentleness of the palm resting on her cheek, the eyes that seemed to delve inside her and undo her from the inside out. 'I'm sorry,' she said.

Harriet brushed the tears away again, and pulled Grace into another hug, kissing the top of her head, and cradling her to her chest. 'It's okay,' she said.

The scent of Harriet, the warmth, so close, Grace lifted her head and turned, immediately finding Harriet's lips. Grace's lips parted and she was aware of the groaning sound that

119

spurred her to discover Harriet with more depth. Then a cold blast of air and a hand pressing against the middle of her chest caused her eyes to snap open.

'No, Grace!' Harriet was frowning, shaking her head back and forth.

Grace lurched backwards and stood, mouth agape, head in hands. 'Oh, fuck. I am so sorry, Harriet.' Heat flared and churned her stomach, ripped through her chest, and then flamed in her cheeks. Oh, fuck! 'Shit!' she said in anger, rubbing her hand frantically through her hair. 'I am so sorry.'

Harriet still had her hand up in a defensive posture that caused a wave of nausea to pass through Grace.

Grace put both hands in the air, shaking her head. 'I'm so sorry, I wasn't thinking. I need to leave. Harriet, I am so sorry.'

Grace stepped past Harriet, whose hand had made it to her mouth, and walked out the door. Flo leapt past her as she strode and Winnie waddled to keep up. Grace started to run across to the house and slammed the door behind her. She leaned against the solid wood, tears flowing down her cheeks. 'Bed,' she said, with as much confidence as she could muster. Whether by fluke or respect, both dogs headed towards the hunting room and she shut the door behind them.

12.

'Good morning Mrs Haversham.' Drew said. She always greeted Harriet's mum with the more formal title; it was a habit.

'Good morning Drew, I'll have a Latte please.'

'Coming right up.' Drew turned to the machine and started preparing the coffee. 'How's the plan going?' she said.

Jenny looked at her as if assessing whether she could be trusted. Yet, it was clear she had found out from one of her parents, Doug or Esther. 'I think it's going very well, now we're over the first hurdle.'

'What was that?'

'Well, there was a rumour of Harriet moving to New Zealand, but I've been reliably informed that was just an unfortunate misunderstanding,' Jenny said.

'No chance. That's where her ex ended up,' Drew said.

'Oh, right!' Jenny said and fiddled with her cardigan. 'Anyway, it seems they're both getting on very well. They went for a picnic together the other day and then spent all day yesterday in the garden working together. That's good, isn't it?'

Drew was nodding, working the creamy milk into the coffee. 'Sounds good to me,' she said. 'They had breakfast here yesterday too. Seemed to get on really well, chatting, eating, chatting.'

'Oh, right. That's very good. Bryan's gone over there this morning though. Something to do with the water not working.'

'Strange.' Drew placed the coffee on the counter. 'Can I interest you in a piece of carrot cake? Harriet made it.' Drew was smiling encouragingly. 'You know we have a special deal for old-age pensioners on Wednesday mornings – coffee and cake for a fiver,' she said.

Jenny huffed. 'I'm not an old-age pensioner yet, I'll have you know.'

'Offer still stands,' Drew said, already putting a piece of cake onto a plate.

'Oh, go on then,' Jenny conceded and took the treat to the nearest table.

'Grace has seen Hilda Spencer, you know!' Jenny said. 'Twice.'

'Blimey.' Drew pondered. 'Has a stranger ever seen her before?'

'Nope. Not that anyone can recollect. Do you think it's an omen?'

'Must mean she's destined to stay here if you ask me.'

'Ooh, do you think so?'

'What else can it mean? A stranger seeing a ghost that us locals have only ever seen. Even then not everyone here has seen Hilda. It must mean Hilda sees her as one of us.' Drew shrugged, leaned on the counter, and sipped at her drink.

'Ooh, I never thought of that. Do you know, I think you could be right! That sounds very positive, doesn't it?'

Drew shrugged and smiled. She didn't really give a shit, but if it kept the rumour mill running, the coffee flowing, and for entertainment value alone, it was worth the input. Delia Harrison would be in next.

The door opened.

'Morning Delia, your usual?' Drew said, with a beaming smile. 'Mrs Haversham here was just telling me that Grace has seen Hilda Spencer walking these parts. Twice, apparently.'

'Really,' Delia said, racing to join Jenny at the table.

'Once in the house,' Jenny said, in a tone that carried high suspense.

'Ooh, now that's interesting,' Delia remarked.

*

122

'Ah-right, petal?' Bryan said, climbing out of his car and walking to the boot. He lifted out a toolbox and walked to Harriet's side. She looked uncharacteristically out of sorts. 'You're not still mad at me, are you?' he said, trying to be chirpy.

'I'm fine,' Harriet said, though she didn't feel it. She had had the worst night's sleep in a long time, worrying about Grace, and, more specifically, how she had responded to Grace kissing her.

Clearly, the things she had talked about had upset Grace, and she felt bad enough for that, but then when Grace kissed her at the door and she pushed her away, Grace had become angry and stormed off without a second word. Harriet had stood for a good length of time, trying to reconcile her feelings. On the one hand, the touch of Grace's lips, so soft and tender, so eager, had drawn her in, stirred something inside, and on the other, she had been gripped with anxiety. She couldn't deny it, she had become fascinated with Grace in the few days they had spent together, and under normal circumstances, she might have considered something developing between them. But Grace would be leaving, and she wouldn't – couldn't – expose herself to being hurt again.

'Is Grace in?' Bryan said. 'I need to check the stopcock. There aren't any issues locally, according to the waterboard.'

'I haven't seen her this morning,' Harriet said.

She looked distracted.

'Dogs not out?'

'No.'

Bryan approached the front door and knocked. Nothing. He knocked again. He lifted the flowerpot. No key.

'No dogs,' he said. 'They must be out.'

'She knew you were coming to sort the water.' Harriet said, overwhelmed with conflicting feelings.

'I'll try the back door,' he said and wandered along the front of the house to the corner then disappeared out of view.

Seconds later, he reappeared. 'It's open,' he said and disappeared again.

Grace must have gone out with the dogs. That would explain why she hadn't seen her. She was expecting Grace to show up, to carry on gardening. Grace had seemed keen enough, though that had been before the incident. Harriet felt tension rise within her. What if Grace fell and injured herself? What if the weather changed as predicted today? You could never tell, and what if Grace got lost? Flo wasn't trained well enough to show her the way home, and Winnie wouldn't even realise they were supposed to be heading home! Oh my God, this was all her fault. Grace had been so upset, and all she had done was reject her.

Bryan appeared from the side of the house, toolbox in hand. 'Not sure what all the fuss was about. Water's working fine,' he said.

Harriet frowned. 'I'm confused,' she said.

'Anyway, I told your mother to stop her meddling,' he added.

'Right.' Harriet was preoccupied.

'She only has your best interests at heart, petal. We both know you got badly hurt with Annabel. It's only natural to worry, but it's been a long time, and Vera said Grace is a good woman. She wouldn't harm anyone.'

It was Jenny talking, Harriet knew that, but at least he was trying. 'Thanks dad,' she said and rubbed his arm.

'Anyway, there's no one in the house,' he said and put the toolbox into the boot.

'Okay,' Harriet said and started towards the veggie-plot.

'You coming to the quiz night later?' Bryan said, one foot inside the car.

Harriet turned and smiled. 'Sure. We'll both be there,' she said, though she wasn't entirely sure Grace would want to go.

'Good, good.' He climbed in, turned the engine and drove off.

Harriet petted Buzz as she walked past the gate, but it was a quick pat and lacking her normal considered attention. He snorted as if to tell her so, but she walked on and into the shed. Fork in hand, she went to a new plot and started to turn the soil. Archie lay in the grass between two plots, eyes closed. It felt as if something was missing.

She tried to find the mental space she always adopted when working the land, but it wouldn't come, and her thoughts juggled images of Grace in trouble and then memories of Grace with her engaging smile, thoughtful gaze and considered perspective.

She had tried not to let her fascination with Grace show, but she had caught Grace looking at her at times, when they were at the lake and eating together, and she had felt it as an intense wave that seemed to penetrate all her defences. She had been sure Grace had noticed, and deep down she had wanted her to.

She hadn't intended to upset Grace. When she had said you couldn't be happy with another without first being happy within yourself, she had been referring specifically to Annabel because Annabel could never be happy within herself. She had seen glimpses of Grace looking happy in a way that hadn't been possible for Annabel. They had laughed together, enjoyed spending time in each other's company, and Grace had shown genuine interest in Harriet's life and work, and at no point had Harriet felt inadequate in Grace's presence. Being with Grace felt good and she had found herself looking forward to spending time with her. She was attracted to Grace; and more.

And then, Grace had to open a can of worms and kiss her. She hadn't meant to push Grace away; it had simply happened, but she had known at that moment that she cared deeply for the stranger from London and she sensed that Grace had similar feelings towards her.

She had wanted to kiss Grace. To press her lips with tenderness to the damp eyes that had melted her heart. To kiss the wetness from her soft warm skin and take in the texture, the essence of her. The urge had been there, more strongly than she had experienced since Annabel, and then it happened. The memory of Annabel leaving her, and the lie that had devastated her world had flooded her and the visceral response had been out of her control. It wasn't Grace she pushed away at that moment. It was Annabel. She needed Grace to know that. She wasn't sure if she was ready for a relationship. And there was still the issue of Grace leaving. But, she needed Grace to know the truth.

She slammed the fork into the ground and turned the soil at an increased pace, stopping briefly to sip water, until the whole patch had turned a reddish-brown-black shade. She stabbed the fork into the ground and walked to the gate, leant over the top of it, and gazed out to the horizon and then up to the edge of the lake. Maybe Grace had walked the dogs to the lake? She would be back soon enough. Winnie can't walk that far.

Harriet went inside, washed her hands, made a cheese sandwich, removed the film canister from her camera and headed to the cellar. The darkroom would be a great place to occupy the time. Grace would be back soon and she could talk to her properly. She sat on a stool and ate then put the plate on a low shelf. She sat at the workstation, switched off the lights, removed the film from its canister and threaded it through the spiral then set it inside the developing tank. Sealing the tank, she turned on the lights and prepared the chemicals.

Working diligently through the process she stood over the tray watching the black and white image slowly appear. Grace's dark eyes held such intensity as she gazed in wonderment for the first time across the lake and the surrounding hills, her lips rested slightly apart, the shading in her cheeks highlighting her cheekbones and strong features, her hair ruffled by the breeze. There was something pure and unpretentious about Grace at that moment, and deeply, disconcertingly sensual, and as the image developed further, bringing greater contrast and sharper focus, looking at it took Harriet's breath away and caused her heart to race. She lifted it carefully to the next tray with trembling hands, and then the next. She ran it under a cold-water tap, then placed it in a fourth tray her hands still struggling to steady the image. She stood, gazing at the image of Grace finding it difficult to breathe. God, she was striking.

She started the process again with a new image. She had caught Grace gazing at her and snapped just before Grace shifted attention out towards Ferndale. She smiled, watching closely, as the shading on Grace's cheeks appeared on the paper, the passion coming through in a quizzical gaze, long dark lashes, and the soft smile that lightly wrinkled the corner of her eyes and made them sparkle. Harriet had felt the unfiltered emotion directed at her as she had clicked the camera and here it was, evidenced in print and forever etched in her soul. She groaned involuntarily, feeling Grace as if she were in the room touching her.

With four images hung up to dry, she turned away from the bench, picked up her empty plate, and exited the room. They wouldn't be her best pictures, her concentration wasn't right for that, but the two of Grace that had caught her attention, still caused the hairs on her neck to rise and her heart to pound as she walked back to the kitchen.

Archie jumped up from his bed and skipped to greet her as she approached. 'Hello boy,' she said and ruffled his curly coat. 'Have you seen Grace?' she said. His bark had all four feet leaving the ground and Harriet looked out the kitchen window, across to the gate and Buzz eating grass in the field beyond.

'Come on, let's go and see if we can find Flo, shall we?'

She looked to the sky, puffy clouds had formed, and it was half-past three. It wouldn't be dark for a few hours yet, but the weather could deteriorate and it was still a fair hike to the lake and back.

She crossed the driveway to the house, Archie trotting at her heel and banged on the door. Nothing. No dogs. Not a sound. Her heart sat in her throat with the lingering thought that Grace lay in a ditch, dead. It was totally irrational, but the feeling wouldn't leave and she had a dreadful sense of having lost something precious.

'Right, come on Archie, we need to take a walk.' She marched back to the house, put on her hiking boots and stuffed a few provisions into the rucksack. Grabbing Archie's lead on the way out, she shut the door and headed around the back of the house, retracing the route Grace knew – to the lake. 'Come on, Archie,' she said, encouraging the dog to run freely. 'Go find Flo,' she said.

Archie wandered off into the forestation running alongside the track, and then moments later appeared at her feet and trotted along merrily.

'Go, on Archie, where's Flo.'

Archie barked and dived into the ferns and foliage, sniffing and exploring, and then cocked his leg and peed.

Harriet, head down, lengthened her stride. She needed to cover the ground quickly. She stopped after a short distance, puffing, and looked around. 'Grace?' she called out. 'Grace, Flo?' She waited, birdsong interfering with her sense of hearing. Sshh, she wanted to say. She called out again and continued to hike. Specs of rain blew on the breeze, darker clouds approaching giving cause for concern.

By the time she reached the stream beads of sweat trickled down her temples and her thighs burned. She threw off the rucksack, pulled out a bottle of water and swigged. Archie lapped from the stream, dipped his nose under the water and snuffled, shaking his head before trotting on up the slope. Harriet swigged again, did up the cap, put the bottle back in the rucksack and slung it on her back. Come on, Grace, where are you? 'Grace!' she yelled, feeling as frantic as the word sounded. Drops of heavier rain had started to fall, and she wondered if her impulse to set off and find Grace hadn't been the wisest of decisions.

As she approached the lip of the path leading down to the lake, she hoped her heart would stop with joy. Instead, it sunk with alarming speed into a pit of despair. Rain-wet hair hung loosely around her face and she rubbed the tears of despair from her cheeks. There was no sign of Grace and no sign of the dogs. There was no sign of anyone and little point in trekking any further. If Grace had gone beyond the lake, then God knows where she might have ended up. Harriet shuddered at the thought. 'Fuck,' she screamed, and Archie looked at her with his head at an angle. He jumped up; his front paws clawing the length of her calf. 'Come on, boy,' she said and turned back down the slope. Shit, shit, shit. Archie leapt off, taking full advantage of the adventure.

The route back seemed to happen at breakneck speed, Harriet's heart pounding, her legs pumping. As they reached the house, the rain having passed, the movement through the kitchen caught her eye and she cried out with relief. Overcome by light-headedness and a sense that her legs were about to give way beneath her, she stopped and leant into a tree, puffing for air. Archie bolted towards the side garden, where Flo and Winnie were playing.

Grace strolled into the garden, gazed up at the overcast sky, and Harriet felt another tear slip onto her cheek.

'Hello Archie,' Grace said.

Archie bared his teeth and barked at her from the other side of the gate.

Did he just growl at me?

Harriet approached Grace with a look resembling a drowned rat and then Grace noticed the damp, bloodshot eyes and fiery glare that shaped Harriet's jawline. She winced, bracing herself for the onslaught.

Harriet opened the gate and Archie raced over to Flo who ran off. She stood in front of Grace, hands on hips. 'Where have you been? I was worried sick,' she blurted.

Grace looked down then lifted her head slowly, unable to avoid staring at the straggly wet hair that dangled seductively and turned her insides into a quivering mess. 'Shit!' she said.

'Where were you?' Harriet said. 'We've been searching all over for you.'

Grace turned her head, unable to observe Harriet's distress, the pain of which had reached into her chest and was squeezing tightly. 'I went for a long walk and ended up at the Duckton Arms. I needed some space to think,' she said. She turned back to look at Harriet and the pressure in her chest increased. Harriet looked wounded, her cheeks pale, her eyes glassy; her sadness, raw. Grace stood, waiting for the next blast of frustration. It didn't come. Instead, Harriet fell towards her and threw her arms around her, pulling her into the heat of her body.

'I'm sorry I ran off without saying anything,' Grace whispered.

'I'm sorry I reacted as I did. It wasn't about you,' Harriet said. She pulled Grace closer, cradled her head, breathing close to her ear. 'It wasn't about you,' she repeated and released Grace.

Grace nodded, swallowed, and tried to form a smile. It was a lame attempt, a reflection of the turmoil that had sent her running to the hills before the break of day.

Thoughts of Sandra Floss had haunted her. And then other women had come to mind and caused her to question. How many hearts had she broken over the years? The women she had crushed with her arrogant and flippant approach to relationships. Good women. Kind women. Some had held deep feelings for her, and maybe even loved her. Had she stomped all over their emotions, as Annabel had Harriet's? Seeing Harriet in pain, hearing the words she used to describe her experience with Annabel, and then being on the receiving end of the residual effect of that impact had stirred her. Harriet was right. You cannot love another unless you first love yourself, and right now she hated herself. Perhaps she always had. Had every interaction with women just been a business deal to her? A fix? A transaction? Did she know what love was? Had she, too, spent her life seeking a high? Harriet was staring at her oddly.

'I didn't mean to push you away,' Harriet said.

'I deserved it,' Grace said.

'No, you didn't.' Harriet paused. 'I like you,' she said.

Grace tried to smile but with tight lips, she huffed through her nose instead.

Harriet reached out and took Grace's hand. 'I think you're interesting, fun, and.' She stopped speaking, drawing Grace's eyes to her. 'And, I'd like to get to know you better.'

Grace squeezed the hand in hers and released a long breath that seemed to come out in a shudder.

'I am so scared of getting hurt, Grace. I don't think my heart could take it,' Harriet said.

Grace held the dark gaze, feeling the ache beneath her ribs, challenged by her own fears. 'I would never do that to you, Harriet.'

Harriet nodded, averting Grace's gaze and letting go of her hand. 'Will you still come to the pub?' she said. 'It will be fun, and everyone's dying to meet you.'

'Sure. I was just about to feed the dogs.'

Harriet sighed and looked down at her wet clothes. 'I'll need to get changed. We just hiked to the lake and back in the rain, in record time,' she said.

Grace flushed. 'I'm so sorry,' she said.

'Me too,' Harriet said. She turned away, took a couple of paces to the gate, and then turned back again. 'By the way, dad came to fix the water, but said it was working fine,' she said.

'Ah, yes, I found a stopcock in the hunting room and fiddled with it. Seemed to do the trick,' she said.

'Right,' Harriet said and walked through the gate frowning. 'Come on Archie.'

Grace watched Harriet move out of sight and walked back through to the hunting room and continued filling the dog's bowls. She didn't have words to describe the warm feeling that accompanied her and she didn't need them. Dealing with her past could wait for now. She vowed to give Harriet her undivided attention and engage with the locals at the quiz night. What she wouldn't do was make a pass at Harriet. Not tonight and not any other night. She couldn't afford to get it wrong again and she had made a promise to herself she intended to keep. She would never hurt Harriet's feelings, ever.

13.

Grace entered the Crooked Billet with Harriet at her side and gazed around the room. Three large round tables occupied what might also double-up as a dance floor in their absence. Wood-carved, team name-cards sat in the middle of each table, and two of the tables were already filling with people. 'Where's the Parson's Nose?' she asked Harriet.

'At the arse end of the chicken,' Doug yelled from the table labelled The Duckton Arms. Laughter filled the small space, and groans hummed from the Parson's Nose table.

'Any new jokes, Doug?' a man retorted from the competitor's table.

'It's a paradoxical delicacy,' the woman sat next to him added.

'Old ones are always the best,' Doug said and held his drink up in a toast.

Harriet stopped chuckling. 'It's the Lower Duckton village pub,' she said.

Grace smiled.

'Hi Dad, Elvis.'

'Hello, my petal.'

'Good evening Harriet; your usual?' Elvis said.

'Hello Grace,' Bryan said. 'How's your waterworks?'

Grace felt the heat hit her cheeks. 'Fine thanks, Bryan. I'm sorry, I should have let Harriet know I'd fixed it. I was a little distracted this morning,' she said.

'God bless you, Grace,' Elvis said. 'G&T?'

Grace pondered the Vicar pulling a pint and handing it across the bar to another customer. 'Yes, thank you.' She paused. 'Umm, Vicar,' she said.

'It's usually Elvis in here,' he said, with a welcoming smile.

'He blesses everyone on their first visit,' Bryan said, with a wink.

'And every time they buy a drink,' Harriet whispered to Grace as Elvis poured their drinks.

Grace chuckled.

Two long drinks were placed on the bar, a slice of lemon wedged on top of the glass and a cherry on a stick resting on the ice.

'He always puts a cherry in long drinks,' Harriet said. She picked up the stick, pulled the cherry into her mouth and chewed.

Grace winced. 'Do you want my cherry?' she asked, holding up the fruit. Harriet looked at her with raised eyebrows, tilted her head and smiled. Grace felt the heat in her cheeks flame and send fire to her toes.

'Thanks,' Harriet said and took the stick and ate the fruit.

They turned towards the banter flying across the three large tables, the Crooked Billet table starting to fill.

Bryan passed in front of them and headed to the door, accosting Sheila Goldsworth on his route and whispered something in her ear. Moments later they both returned to the bar and Shelia approached Harriet and Grace.

'Hello, you must be Grace; how lovely to meet you,' Sheila said. 'How was the cruise?'

Bryan closed his eyes for a long time and pursed his lips then opened them. 'What would you like to drink, Sheila?' he said, drawing Sheila's attention.

Grace frowned. 'I think you're referring to Vera, my aunt, Vera,' she said.

'Oh,' Sheila said, looking most confused. 'I thought she was with her sister in Devon,' she added.

'Sheila, what can I get you?' Bryan said, his voice louder and more insistent.

Grace was shaking her head, Harriet was frowning. Both women sipped from their gin in unison, leaving Sheila mumbling to Bryan something about Jenny, Delia, and the café culture.

'Hello, you must be Grace,' another older woman said. She held her handbag firmly hooked in the crook of her arm, hands across her middle and strained over the top of her glasses.

'Hello Mrs Akeman,' Harriet interjected. 'I've been telling Grace all about our summer fete and what an amazing organiser you are.'

Doris Akeman seemed to straighten at the news. Grace nodded along corroborating Harriet's account.

'Right, well. It's lovely to meet you, Grace. I assume you will be attending the meeting on Friday evening?' she said.

'Umm, yes, of course, if you'll have me?'

Doris muttered, smiled, and took the orange juice that Elvis had placed on the bar for her. 'I'm sorry, I must dash, I have my quizmaster hat on tonight,' she said, and tottered towards the small podium in the corner of the dance floor overlooking the team-tables.

Grace smiled at Harriet.

Harriet sipped her drink. 'She has a big heart,' she said.

'Harriet, Harriet, I've been so worried.'

'Hi Mum,' Harriet said, ignoring the dramatic tone and rolling her eyes to Grace. 'Mum, this is Grace,' Harriet added before her mother could dive into any further elaboration of her traumatic concerns.

Jenny eyed Grace up and down. 'Hello, Grace, aren't you a cracker,' she said.

'Mum!'

'She is,' Jenny defended. 'Look at her, she's positively gorgeous. Vera said she was a good-looking woman, and smart with it. Damn right she is.'

Grace choked on the bubbles that had tried to make their way down her throat and, flushing crimson, started to laugh. 'That's very kind of you, Jenny. You're a cracker too,' she said and winked at the older lady.

'See, she's got a good taste too,' Jenny said to Harriet, tapping her on the arm.

Harriet cupped a hand to her shaking forehead.

'Harriet tells me you've seen Hilda Spencer?' Jenny continued.

The hum in the room quieted.

'Mum!' Harriet interjected. 'We're out for a fun evening. Will you please keep your tittle-tattle to yourself?'

Mumbling noises increased in volume and soon the chatter was back to its previous level.

'What do you want to drink?' Harriet asked her mother.

'Just a glass please, darling,' she said and opened her handbag to reveal an unlabelled green bottle.

'You can't drink that in here,' Harriet objected.

'Of course, I can. Elvis doesn't mind and I'm trying out a new formula,' she said.

Harriet turned to the bar. Elvis was nodding and smiling and handed over an empty tumbler.

Oh my God. 'Let's take a seat,' Harriet said to Grace.

Grace was chuckling. 'Sure.'

Jenny put her hand on Grace's arm as she turned to follow Harriet. 'Tell me about Hilda later,' she said and winked.

Grace nodded and patted the hand on her arm.

'Right, if I could have your attention please.' Doris's voice squeaked through the loudspeaker as Harriet and Grace took their seats.

Doug leapt from the Duckton Arms table and joined them.

'If everyone is settled, it's quiz time,' Doris announced. She almost sounded excited.

The mumbling died down and all eyes were on Doris. Doug had the pencil poised, as the designated scribe for the Crooked Billet's table.

'We're starting with a general knowledge question this evening.' Doris looked up, scanned the three tables, and then lifted her glasses as she looked down at the paper.

'Bloody hell, woman, get on with it,' Doug muttered, delaying the process even further as Doris eyed him over the top of her glasses.

'According to the Beatles, who 'Picks up the rice in the church where a wedding has been'?'

'Elvis, this one's for you,' someone shouted, fully aware that Elvis was neither a Beatles fan, nor did he allow rice in the church at weddings. It was a health and safety issue, apparently.

'Eleanor Rigby,' Doug said, and his team nodded. He scribbled.

Grace looked at Harriet as she listened attentively to the questions. The delicate lines that appeared in concentration, the intensity of that concentration reflected in her posturing as she colluded excitedly with her team to come up with an answer and the thrill she displayed, bouncing up and down in the seat, when they came to an agreement. Enamoured, she sipped at her drink, smiled at Harriet when she looked towards her and flushed when Jenny spied her watching Harriet closely. She wished she hadn't kissed Harriet, the timing couldn't have been worse, but she couldn't deny the impulse to kiss the beautiful woman sat at her side. It was still there and stronger than ever.

Bryan arrived with a tray of drinks and Grace enjoyed watching Harriet as she leaned over the table and moved around the group handing them out. And then Harriet caught Grace staring at her and she felt caressed by Harriet's smile and when Harriet returned to sit next to her, warmth flooded her and Jenny was still smiling at her, which made matters worse. She pulled her attention back to the quiz.

'What is the full name of the first man to climb the Matterhorn?'

'What kind of question is that?' Doug complained. Groans echoed from all three tables.

'Edward Whymper,' Grace whispered to Harriet.

Harriet studied Grace and nodded towards Doug.

'Who's he?' Doug said.

'The first man to climb the Matterhorn,' Grace said and shrugged, and Harriet chuckled.

Doug scribbled their answer on the paper.

Harriet smiled at Grace. 'How did you know that?' she whispered and Grace noticed a sexy slur in her voice.

'You would be surprised at the useless facts I have accumulated over the years while killing time in airports and the like,' she said.

Harriet gazed longingly at Grace.

The door opened and Jarid entered the bar drawing Harriet's attention. She grinned at him and he waved. Drew was close behind him and Harriet grinned at her too.

'What is the procedure called where an anaesthetic is injected close to the spinal cord?'

'Epidural,' Jarid announced to the whole pub as he waited for a drink.

'Jarid!' Doug complained.

'Everyone knows that, Doug.' He was grinning as he took a seat at the table. 'Hey Grace,' he said.

'Hey you two,' Drew said.

'Hi,' they said in unison.

'Could we all settle down, please?' Doris announced.

'Thank you, Doris,' Doug said.

'The next round is TV and films,' Doris said.

'Ooh lovely,' Delia said. She took a seat next to Jenny and presented an empty glass. Jenny pulled out the green bottle and poured. 'Gnat's piss, the wine in here. Thanks, Jen,' she said.

'Bloody hell, here we go,' Doug complained.

'The Slaughtered Lamb features in which movie?'

'*Silence of the Lambs*,' Delia announced to her team and sipped her drink.

'There wasn't a bloody lamb in *Silence of the Lambs*,' Doug said.

'*Shaun the Sheep*,' Jarid said and started laughing.

Doug was incensed. 'You're not taking this seriously, are you?'

Harriet, Grace and Drew burst into hysterics and Doug, without consulting anyone further wrote '*An American Werewolf in London*,' on the paper.

The group was still giggling when the next question came.

'Where could you find Isaac, the bartender, serving drinks and relationship advice on the Lido deck?' Doris said, her voice rising above the laughter.

'*The Love Boat*,' Delia whispered excitedly across the table.

Doug hesitated; pen poised.

'It's, *The Love Boat*,' Delia insisted. 'Write it down Doug.'

Doug's hand couldn't form the letters. 'Are you sure?' he said, stumped for an alternative answer.

Grace nodded. 'She's right,' she said.

Harriet gazed at Grace, then whispered in her ear. 'You didn't strike me as a Love Boat kind of girl!'

She was sounding even more pissed, but the lower pitch adding to the soft lazy words reached even lower down in Grace's anatomy and seduced her with effortless ease.

Grace struggled to find the words. 'It was a long time ago. I saw it once on TV,' she said then stopped. Harriet's dark eyes sparkled and she realised she was being teased.

Doug scribbled.

'Right, last question of this round.' Doris announced.

'Which chief medical officer and coroner could be found drinking in 'Danny's Bar'?'

All eyes around the table shifted to Jarid.

'How the hell am I supposed to know that?' he said and sipped from his pint.

'You're the doctor?' Delia said.

'Anyone?' Doug asked, scanning each of the shaking heads around the table and noting the smug looks directed at him from the Parson's Nose table.

'No idea,' Delia said. 'Wasn't that an American programme? Come on Doug, you should know.'

'What's the question?' Bryan asked, approaching with more drinks.

'Chief medical officer drinking in Danny's Bar?' Doug repeated.

'E.R.,' Bryan said, and Doug wrote it down.

'Time,' Doris called, the scribes for each team put down their pens.

Harriet hiccupped and Grace chuckled.

Doug walked up to the podium among the chatter and handed over their answer sheet. They had better not be eliminated in the first round or there would be hell to pay.

'How was that?' Harriet said, grinning at Grace. Her cheeks had a healthy glow and her eyes a glazed soft look to them.

She looked so fucking cute. 'I don't think we got that last question right,' Grace said.

Harriet shrugged. 'It's just a bit of fun,' she said.

'Don't you want to win?'

Harriet chuckled and hiccupped again. 'I don't mind either way.'

Grace frowned. 'I can get very competitive,' Grace said.

'About everything?' Harriet said, with raised eyebrows.

Grace paused. 'About most things, yes. I like to win, I guess.'

'You and Doug will get on like a house on fire. Would you like another drink?'

'Don't you like winning?'

'Not at the expense of others, no. If something's important to me I'll fight for it. But that's not about winning, so much as protecting the things you care about, I suppose. Drink?'

Grace had had plenty already and Harriet seemed as though she had had more than enough, but she was enjoying her company, which was a relief after their earlier upset. What the hell! 'Sure,' she said, 'Let's celebrate.'

'What are we celebrating?' Harriet said.

'That we like each other,' Grace whispered. She had intended the comment as a light-hearted truth, but Harriet's perfume sent a spark to her core and it dawned on her that she liked Harriet a lot more than she had allowed herself to admit.

'To us,' Harriet slurred, lifting her glass in a toast.

Grace laughed and clinked her glass to Harriet's.

Jenny elbowed Delia sharply in the ribs. 'Did you hear that?' she said, excitedly. 'They're getting married,' she said, in an excited, whisper.

Delia pulled out the pack of cards, shuffled them and turned over the top card. 'The Wheel of Fortune.' Delia said. 'It's fate' She smiled, smugly. 'Fill my glass, Jen' she added, popping the cards back in her handbag. 'That does sound positive.'

*

'That was fun,' Grace said as they walked down the road. Harriet linked arms with her and leaned into her shoulder.

'I'm glad you enjoyed yourself. Doug wasn't best pleased that we came last,' Harriet slurred.

Grace tensed, 'Neither was I,' she said and started to chuckle.

'They're good people,' Harriet said, still snuggling into Grace.

Grace reflected with a smile. 'Yes, they are.'

'I apologise for my mother's directness,' Harriet said.

'She's funny. I thought she was never going to let me go from that bear hug.'

'Yes, she does drama really well.'

'Hey, I'm not that bad,' Grace said.

Harriet staggered. 'Oh, no! I didn't mean it like that.'

'I was teasing,' Grace said.

'If you really want to know, I was a little bit jealous,' Harriet said.

Grace stopped walking and turned to face Harriet, assessed the glazed look in her eyes and smiled. 'You're teasing me,' she said softly. Harriet was more than a little tipsy and the way she looked at Grace touched her deeply.

'No, I wasn't.' Harriet said. 'I was really worried about you earlier. I need you to know, it wasn't about you, my reaction last night. I like you, Grace.'

Grace reached up, tucked Harriet's hair behind her ear and smiled. 'I like being liked by you,' she said. She pulled Harriet into a hug, inhaled the scent of her, savoured the warmth of her, and then let her go. 'Come on, it's cold,' she said.

Harriet linked arms again and they walked in silence to Harriet's front door. They stood, hands in pockets, looking at each other and then into the darkness. Buzz snorted and the sound of insects brought the silence to life.

'I'd better get to bed,' Harriet said.

She was swaying.

'Sure.' Grace started to walk, then stopped and turned.

Before she could speak again, Harriet had moved towards her and now seemed to be hurtling directly at her.

142

Grace tried to brace herself but was taken out more effectively than a prop-forward rugby tackle and found herself flat on her back, Harriet on top of her.

Grace groaned at the impact of being sandwiched between the hard ground and Harriet.

'Shit!' Harriet slurred. 'I'm so sorry, I think I tripped,' she said.

'Ouch!' Grace moaned then started to chuckle. 'Harriet Haversham, you certainly know how to make an entrance,' she said. She tucked the hair around Harriet's ear, but it fell away instantly, and then without warning, Grace couldn't breathe. Harriet's lips, warm and moist, were pressing against hers and the sensation was electric. Every cell in her body ignited in an explosive response so strong that it would provide power to service the village in electricity for a week. She groaned and Harriet responded by biting down on her lip, tenderly, teasingly. Grace was paralysed; she hadn't expected this. She hadn't expected Harriet to kiss her, and she certainly hadn't expected Harriet's kiss to turn her insides out and render her motionless.

Harriet eased out of the kiss and stared into Grace's eyes. 'I just wanted you to know that I like you,' she said, and then slumped on top of Grace's chest.

Oh my God. Harriet weighed a tonne! 'Harriet,' she said, hoping to rouse her. She shook her shoulders gently, and a muffled sound came back at her. She rolled Harriet off her chest and studied her for a moment. She was strikingly beautiful. 'Right, come on, we need to get you to bed,' she said. She fumbled in Harriet's pocket and pulled out the front door key, eased herself from the ground and hobbled to the front door.

Archie met her with a wagging tail then seemed to realise it wasn't who he was expecting and barked; then his lips curled and he bared his teeth. 'It's okay, boy, it's only me,' Grace said. The words seem to settle him and she returned to Harriet and stared at her. How the hell would she get her into the house?

Grace bent down and tried to turn Harriet onto her side but she wouldn't stay. 'Fuck!' She put a hand under each armpit and managed to get Harriet into a sitting position. 'Come on Harriet, help me out here,' she said.

Harriet moaned.

Grace heaved, and it seemed Harriet had heard as she took a little of her own weight on her feet and slumped into Grace's chest. 'Ugghhh, she groaned with the effort. 'We've got you,' she said, reassuringly. She pulled Harriet up and wrapped Harriet's arm around her neck, her own arm around Harriet's waist. She bundled her clumsily through the front door. Keeping the momentum going, she staggered slowly up the narrow stairs. 'Come on Harriet, work with me here,' she said, talking Harriet through every step, and then she helped Harriet into the bedroom and flopped her onto the bed.

Grace groaned with the release, lifted Harriet's legs onto the bed and removed her shoes. There was no way she was going any further down the undressing route. She took the stairs, filled a glass of water and returned to the bedroom, placing it on the bedside cabinet. She studied Harriet for a moment, turned and went back down the stairs.

She was just about to shut the door when a meowing sound alerted her. The ginger tom! 'Terence,' she said. The cat meowed again, nuzzled up to her ankles and started purring. 'Fuck, where's the cat food?' She searched the cupboard, spotted a tin of tuna and opened it. Terence sprang effortlessly onto the work surface and pranced up and down, purring loudly. Before she could tip the contents onto a plate, the cat had its nose firmly entrenched in the food, purring noisily as it ate. She stroked its back and it looked up at her for a split second before continuing. Grace smiled.

Terence finished the tuna and ran up the stairs, and Grace closed the front door behind her, hoping Harriet wouldn't have too bad a hangover in the morning.

14.

'You look rough,' Drew said, gazing at Harriet with enquiring eyes and a wry smile.

'Can I get a double Espresso and pancakes with maple syrup?' Harriet said.

'That rough! Can't remember the last time you ordered that combo.'

'It always works. Oh, and vanilla ice-cream on the side.'

'Anyone would think you were pregnant,' Drew said and laughed.

'Good God, no! It was a fun night, though.'

'You two look to be getting on well,' Drew remarked. She hadn't seen that look in Harriet's eyes since the early days with Annabel and even then, there was a subtle difference. Tenderness conveyed through quiet confidence. It was as if Harriet and Grace fitted together – hand in glove – and as if they had always known each other. With Annabel, Harriet had been more volatile, needy and dependent. When Drew had walked home from the pub, she was certain that Harriet and Grace were in love with each other. Maybe, they had yet to realise that fact for themselves. But it was unmistakable to the onlooker. She had caught them in silhouette walking down the road, Harriet leaning into Grace and then Grace touching Harriet's face.

Harriet accepted the coffee, loaded it with sugar and drank it in three gulps. She held Drew's attention with the shine in her eyes giving away the excitement that had managed to mediate the worst of her hangover. 'I think I kissed Grace,' she said.

Drew laughed. 'You think you did?'

'I did, I kissed her,' Harriet said.

'And then what?'

'I passed out.'

'What!'

'I know.' Harriet broke eye contact and looked towards the window.

Drew was laughing.

'You passed out?'

'Yes. I woke up in bed with Terence,' Harriet said.

'The wrong pussy,' Drew quipped. 'Were you naked?'

'No, fully dressed.'

'Honourable, eh? That's a good sign.'

Harriet gazed dreamily. 'Yes, she is.'

'Here, take this and I'll go get your pancakes.' Drew handed over a large glass of fruit smoothie.

'Thanks.' She sipped, recognised the taste of Delia's special ingredient and smiled. That would do the trick. She took a seat and pondered the exquisite pleasure that had been the kiss before she had passed out the previous evening. She had woken with the taste of Grace on her lips or at least a hazy memory of the taste of her. Grace had felt so soft and supple, though more tentative than she might have expected. The last thing she had remembered was the tingling that radiated throughout her. And then, Terence purring loudly in her ear and rousing her to the early dawn.

'Here you go.' Drew plonked a stack of pancakes in front of Harriet, dripping with syrup, ice cream starting to melt on the side.

'Perfect.'

'So, are you two an item then?' Drew said.

Harriet choked on the first mouthful. 'I wouldn't go that far.' A wave of discomfort prodded her as the memory of pushing Grace away just hours before the kiss, and the distress she had caused, came to the fore.

'Your mum and Delia were checking Elvis's availability when I left the bar.'

147

Harriet struggled to retain the juice she had sipped to help the pancake down and sprayed the table. 'What!'

'Heard you guys toasting each other, apparently, and there you go – married overnight.' Drew started laughing.

'Jesus Christ!' Harriet spluttered.

'Yep, seems you have his official approval too,' Drew said.

Harriet was shaking her head.

'Ah, they mean well,' Drew said.

'Mum had hit on Grace within thirty seconds of setting eyes on her,' Harriet said.

'That's good – she likes her.'

'Embarrassing.'

'Nah… It's just your mum. Anyway, Grace is good looking. Who can blame her. If you weren't into her, I'd think about it myself,' Drew said.

Harriet studied her friend. She was serious.

'Don't worry. I won't get in your way. But if it doesn't work out between you guys.' Drew turned her head towards the opening door. 'Morning Doug, what can I get you?'

'Ah, Harriet, there you are. I was wondering if you would ask Grace if she would like to join the team for next month's quiz? She kept us in the competition with that Whymper bloke last night. She's a smart cookie that one,' he said.

Harriet felt the dull ache fill her chest. 'I don't think she's planning to be here that long, Doug,' she said.

'Oh! I heard you two were planning to get married. Delia's cards confirmed it apparently, so must be true. Right? Damn shame. Latte extra strong please Drew. Damn shame. I reckon we could take the trophy if Grace was on our side for the rest of the season,' he muttered.

For fuck sake! Harriet swayed between near boiling at her mother's rumour and dejection at the thought that Grace would be leaving. She knew it was something she needed to face. Denying how she felt wasn't going to make the process of acceptance any easier. Yes, it was a damn shame. No, it was a fucking nightmare. She rammed pancake into her mouth and chewed, the sweetness going some way to tempering the anger and comforting the disappointment.

'See you at the meeting tomorrow then,' Doug said picking up his coffee and heading for the door.

'You okay?' Drew said.

'Yeah, I'll live,' Harriet said.

'You like her a lot, don't you?'

Harriet nodded. 'I think I do,' she admitted.

'Just go with the flow, honey. Don't let this lot get to you. Maybe you can find a way to make it work?'

'Maybe,' Harriet said. She would like to think so. She looked at Drew. 'I pushed her away,' she said.

Drew frowned. 'I thought you said you kissed her?'

'I did, last night after the pub. But the night before, she kissed me and I pushed her away.'

'Oh! That's...' she paused.

'Confusing,' Harriet said.

Drew tilted her head back and forth. 'A little.'

'It wasn't Grace's fault,' Harriet said. 'It was a reaction to Annabel.'

'Ah, yes.' Drew stared at her friend.

Harriet sighed, forcing another piece of pancake into her mouth.

'Does Grace know?' Drew said.

'Yes, about Annabel, and that it wasn't her fault.'

'It'll be okay then,' Drew said. She reached across and took Harriet's hand. 'You deserve to be happy with someone Harriet. If you like Grace, then at least give it a shot,' she said.

Harriet seemed to relax, and smiled. 'What if she doesn't feel the same way?'

'She kissed you first, right?'

149

'Oh, yes, I suppose she did.'

Drew released Harriet's hand. 'She seems like a good person to me, Harriet.'

'Yes, she is.' Harriet smiled.

Grace would be up and about when she got back and they could spend the day working together. There would be time for an honest conversation then. She needed to let Grace know how she felt. She didn't know what a long-distance relationship was like. How it could possibly work?

*

Grace gazed out over the fields from the bedroom window, Ferndale disappearing into a bank of greyness. Grey and white, white and grey – wall-to-wall cloud had decapitated the hills and rain looked imminent. She shivered and rubbed her arms. Fucking freezing! Buzz stood perfectly still in the field, Fizz at his side. There was no sign of Archie and no sign of Harriet. The pain in her right shoulder from hitting the ground with the full force of Harriet paled by comparison with the burning sensation that had kept her mind – and body – agitated for the best part of the night. The memory of Harriet's tender lips, the soft moan that had ignited every cell in her body as the deadweight of Harriet slumped across her chest, had thrown Grace into turmoil. Harriet liked her. That was a good thing. But did Harriet know the effect she had on Grace? Did she realise how completely undone she had felt as a result of that kiss? If Harriet had been sober, she would not have been able to hold back. She might have lost control, and what if Harriet had then said no? Fuck! Is that how it was with Sandra Floss?

She had thought about the times she had noticed Sandra Floss over the previous weeks before that fateful night, their eyes locking across the boardroom table when Sandra had presented an event plan, and the casual conversations they had shared when making coffee. There had been a few notable moments, laughs, looks. Had she just been keen to please the boss, hungry for promotion? Not that Grace had ever made any promises. She wouldn't do that. When Sandra Floss had put her hand in the small of her back to gain her attention at the post-event party, Grace had felt it as an electric wave tingling up her spine and the hairs on her neck had paid attention. Sandra had teased with her fingers, ever so subtly, only pulling back from the contact when Stephanie had approached. Sandra hadn't even had anything specific to say, other than congratulating Grace on a brilliant event, but she had maintained eye contact with her as if searching, asking, seeking. Later, Grace had become aware of Sandra Floss watching her, and the woman had smiled at her suggestively. When their paths had crossed again towards the end of the evening, Grace was intoxicated to the point of not processing the consequences of anything. High on success, seduced by the attractive event manager, she had taken her a drink. Perhaps that had been her first mistake but she wasn't thinking; she had acted on instinct and the drive for sexual gratification that she was sure was mutual.

It had been Sandra Floss who made the first physical contact, brushing up close, pressing her ample breasts against Grace when she tried to whisper into Grace's ear. It had been Sandra Floss who had suggested they go to Grace's room. She couldn't be clear about whether Sandra Floss had moved to kiss her first or not, but she certainly hadn't backed off – at least not in the beginning. Even as Grace had slowly started to undress her, Sandra Floss had flung her head back and moaned in pleasure, her eyes closed, biting down on her lip. Their mouths had been hungry together, urgent, penetrating, and Grace had taken Sandra's cries of 'Oh no,' as an erotic response, that had simply urged her on. 'Please,' Sandra had cried out, but she hadn't tried to move away from their contact. On the contrary, she had closed her eyes and moaned. And then, it was as if the world had been turned on its axis and Sandra Floss had flown at her, thumping her and screaming. Grace had backed off instantly in a haze of confusion. Sandra Floss had laid into her further, pulled her shirt on frantically and escaped the room.

In the silence Grace had slumped to the floor, head in hands, trying to make sense of the scene. She hadn't slept, and she hadn't made eye contact with Sandra Floss again. And now, the letter of complaint, the allegation of sexual harassment sat with her Board of Directors. Not only her career at stake but also her part in the company she had built from scratch. It all now rested on their decision. Harriet had talked about fighting for what was important to you. Well, if she had to, she would fight Sandra fucking Floss all the way. She just hoped it wouldn't come to that.

Grace studied the sky; a few drops of rain had started to pattern the window and she felt cold again. She picked up a jumper, threw it on, and went down the stairs. As she entered the kitchen, Flo greeted her with a whimpering sound and then ran back into the hunting room. Grace followed the dog and then her heart skipped a beat. Winnie lay in her bed, seemingly unable to move. She knelt and stroked down the dog's back. Winnie blinked, but she lay still. 'What's up Winnie?' she said, in a calm voice, her heart racing. 'Stay here girl, I'm going to get Harriet,' she said, hoping the dog would understand.

Grace sprinted through the house and out the front door, followed by Flo. Harriet was walking towards the house, shopping bag in hand. 'There's something wrong with Winnie?' Grace said, panting for breath.

Harriet followed Grace into the house.

'What's happened, Winnie,' Harriet said. She touched the dog's nose and gently stroked over her head and down her back. 'It's okay, old girl.' She stood and held Grace's gaze. 'We need to get her to Kelly,' she said. 'I'll call dad. He'll drive us to the vets. We need to put her in the carry case.' She pointed to the container on the shelf with a slatted top half and Grace pulled it down. Flo had returned and was sitting staring at the two women.

'Flo can come to mine,' Harriet said. Slowly, she lifted Winnie into the box. The dog didn't object and just lay out on the fitted blanket. 'Come on. Flo,' she said, picking up the container and heading for the door. Flo bounded out the door.

Grace followed, shutting the door behind them.

Archie greeted them with enthusiasm, sniffed at the box then chased Flo into the living room. 'They'll be fine. I'll just call dad and let Kelly know we're on the way,' Harriet said.

'Will she be okay?' Grace said. She felt sick.

Harriet reached out and rubbed the top of her arm. 'She'll be fine. I suspect she's got an infection. Dogs bounce back very quickly.'

Grace nodded. She still felt sick.

*

Harriet approached the receptionist, just as the door to the surgery opened. 'Hi, Kelly.'

'Harriet, hi.' She held out a hand to Grace. 'Hi, you must be Grace?'

'Hi.' Grace tried to smile and failed.

'I've heard a lot about you, it's lovely to meet you.'

'You too.'

'What have we here then,' she said. 'Come through.'

Harriet lifted the container onto one end of the large table and removed the lid. Winnie lay still with her eyes open.

'Hello Winnie,' Kelly said.

Grace thought the vet had a comforting voice and felt reassured. She watched Kelly as she gently lifted Winnie and laid her on the table. She assessed the dog, touching along the length of her body.

'Right, let's take your temperature,' she said. She reached for the thermometer, lifted the dog's tail, held it in position for a time, and then studied the result.

Grace looked from Kelly to Harriet, to Winnie and back to Kelly until she couldn't stand the tension anymore. 'Will she be okay?' she said.

Kelly smiled. 'She's got a temperature, so she'll need antibiotics. I'd like to keep her in for a while if that's okay?'

Grace nodded.

'Has she been off her food at all?'

Grace shook her head. 'I don't think so. Then she thought about it, remembering that she had caught Flo finishing Winnie's meal on a couple of occasions in the last two days. 'Maybe,' she added. 'It's hard to know. I don't know what she's normally like,' Grace admitted, and then felt bad for not knowing.

'It's okay. Dogs can be particularly challenging to monitor,' Kelly said. 'Has she been sick, diarrhoea, at all?'

Grace had seen what looked like small mounds of regurgitated food in the garden but hadn't thought anything of it. She'd never seen Winnie being sick. 'A bit sick, I think.' Grace was feeling really shit.

'Lethargic? Not wanting to go out?'

'Not until now, no. She seemed fine yesterday,' Grace said, mildly relieved with the fact that at least one response didn't feel devastatingly awful.

'Anything else unusual?'

Grace shook her head. She hadn't noticed.

Kelly checked inside the dog's mouth, down her body and her stomach. Winnie's gut gurgled loudly. 'Let me get some antibiotics into her.'

Kelly left the room and Grace looked at Harriet. 'Is she going to be okay?'

'I'm sure she'll be fine,' Harriet said.

154

Harriet wasn't smiling though and Grace studied the concerned expression for some time. 'I'm worried,' Grace admitted.

Harriet put an arm around Grace and pulled her into her shoulder. 'Kelly will work her magic,' she said softly.

Grace felt Harriet's comforting warm breath with the kiss to her forehead, just as Kelly returned through the door.

Kelly smiled at the two women. 'Right, little lady, let's get this into you and you'll be right as rain in no time,' she said. She stuck the needle into the bottle of liquid, sucked up the fluid and then injected it into the scruff of the dog's neck. Winnie snuffled and blinked. 'Come on, let's get you settled,' she said to the dog. 'I'll just get the nurse to take care of her,' she said to Grace. She left the room again and returned with a young woman in tow who picked Winnie up and carried her through the door to the rear of the clinic. 'She should be fine. We'll get some checks done while she's here. She should respond to the antibiotics quickly, but if you're concerned please do call me. If there's anything comes up, I'll let you know,' she said.

Grace nodded. 'Thank you,' she said.

'Thanks, Kelly,' Harriet said. 'Are you going to the meeting on Friday?'

'Wouldn't miss it for the world,' she said, rolling her eyes. 'It's a three-line whip isn't it?' She chuckled. 'I'm sure I'm already down for the dog show. Goes with the territory,' she added for Grace's benefit.

'We'll be there,' Harriet said.

'Well, it's lovely to meet you, Grace. Sorry, it wasn't under more sociable circumstances, but please don't worry. There's nothing you could have done differently,' she said.

Grace smiled. 'Thank you.' She wasn't convinced. 'Do I need to pay anything?'

'Don't worry about that now. Vera has the dogs insured, so we can deal with it later.' Kelly smiled and led them through to the reception.

'How is she?' Bryan asked.

'Kelly thinks she'll be fine, but they will keep her in for a while until the drugs start working,' Harriet said.

'Right, right, that's good,' Bryan said. 'Do you want a lift back?'

Harriet looked to Grace. 'Would you like to walk?' she asked.

Grace nodded. 'I think I need the fresh air,' she said.

Harriet nodded and Bryan wandered back to his car.

'How old is Winnie?' Grace said as they walked. She shuddered at the chill and wondered if walking hadn't been the best idea to walk. It must only be about eleven degrees, but at least it wasn't raining anymore.

'Thirteen, I think,' Harriet said.

'That's old, isn't it? Do you think it could be something serious?'

'I don't know,' Harriet said. 'It's possible,' she admitted. She reached across and took Grace by the hand.

Grace enjoyed the tenderness against her skin. 'Thank you,' she said.

'I'm glad I was there for you both.'

Grace was too.

15.

Harriet stopped at the front door and turned to Grace. 'Don't worry, Winnie will be fine,' she said, gazing into glassy eyes.

Grace nodded, avoiding eye contact. Harriet reached up, cupped Grace's cheek and drew her to look at her. She moved closer, leaned forwards and met Grace's lips with softness. The kiss was brief, but the depth of it filled Grace and the absence of it reduced her to tears.

'Just in case you were wondering,' Harriet said. 'I remember kissing you last night and didn't want you to think it was because I was drunk,' she added. 'Though I clearly was, drunk,' she added. 'But that wasn't why I kissed you.' She was wittering.

Grace wiped the tear from her cheek and started to smile.

'Would you like to help with the gardening? I need to get stuff ready for the market tomorrow and it will be a good distraction.'

Staring at Harriet was already proving to be the best distraction. Grace looked to the darkening sky over the hills. 'It's going to rain,' she said.

Harriet laughed. 'Rain doesn't stop play here,' she said. 'We'll be working in the greenhouses. Would you like a coffee before we get started?'

Grace nodded.

Harriet opened the door and they entered the kitchen. Archie bounced towards Harriet, followed by Flo, and then Terence appeared and circled Grace's ankles purring loudly.

'Someone else's taken a fancy to you,' Harriet said and flushed. She turned sharply and started preparing the coffee.

Grace reached down and stroked the cat who nuzzled her hand. When Grace stood up, Terence continued to circle leaning into her leg as if she was a scratching post, purring loudly. She chuckled and felt the tension ease.

'Dad will get a message to mum and she will let Vera know,' Harriet said, handing over a mug of coffee. 'Come on, we've got work to do.'

Flo, Archie, and Terence bundled out the door, the dogs heading to the field and the cat perching himself on top of the fence post and pawed it as if plotting his next move. Harriet led Grace into one of the large tented greenhouses, filled with long rows of various types of vegetation, and Harriet handed her a pair of gloves. It was much larger than the small greenhouse in which Grace had potted the seedlings. 'We need to unearth the potatoes from the sacks over there and put them in the buckets with holes in the bottom. The buckets are over there. Once we've washed them, we can then bag them in batches of twenty,' she said and pointed.

Grace noted the row of thirty or more cloth-like sacks on the far side of the tent and the bench at the end of the row. 'Right,' she said. Didn't sound too complicated.

'Empty the bag into the wheelbarrow, dig out the potatoes and then dump the soil in that pile.' She pointed again, and Grace nodded.

'I'll be working in the tent next door,' she said.

Grace felt abandoned and Harriet hadn't even moved. 'Oh, okay,' she said and the phrase had disappointment written all over it.

'Actually,' I'll do the onions first, they're down this row,' she said, pointing to the green shoots.

Grace smiled and noticed Harriet's eyes firmly fixed on her.

Harriet stepped closer, her gaze never lifting from Grace. 'Thank you for being here with me,' she said and placed a soft kiss to Grace's lips.

Grace could feel the tingling sensation move from her lips to her core and then spread through her body, covering her with warmth. She put her cup on the bench, walked to the sacks and studied the yellow-brownish looking leaves hanging limply over the side of the sack. Buckets, wheelbarrow! She collected both, returned to the sack and started tipping the soil into the barrow and hunting down the small white potatoes.

Harriet gazed across at Grace and smiled. Grace was working tirelessly and it looked as though she was enjoying herself. It would appeal to her competitive nature. There was something oddly thrilling, rewarding, about hunting down new potatoes; even better if you planted the tubers in the first place. Next time? Grace looked at ease and hadn't reacted badly to being kissed again either. That was good. She turned to the onions and started pulling them from the soil, placing them carefully into a second barrow.

Buckets of potatoes and a barrow of onions soon sat at the bench awaiting the next stage in their processing. 'We need to wash them down,' Harriet said, picking up the hose and switching on the water. Spray flew out the end of the hose and Grace ducked.

'Hey,' she shouted, and Harriet looked at her menacingly, with a broad grin.

'Get your hands in here and turn the onions as I spray,' Harriet said.

'You sure know how to spoil a girl,' Grace remarked.

'Try me,' Harriet quipped.

'Hmm!' Grace damn near groaned at the surge of energy that challenged her concentration and guided her thoughts to Harriet, naked. Fuck! Exactly. Onions! She brought her attention back to the vegetables removed her gloves and followed the instructions.

'If they look clean, can you pop them on the bench?'

Grace obeyed.

'Now the potatoes,' Harriet said, and they worked systematically through the buckets until a clean pile of potatoes sat on the bench next to the onions. 'Do you want to bag the potatoes in twenties or band the onions into fours?'

'I can count to four and twenty,' Grace said and smiled.

Harriet chuckled. 'You can do the potatoes then. The onions can be fiddly.'

'I don't mind a bit of fiddling?' Grace said and raised her eyebrows.

'Hmm!' Harriet mumbled. 'We can swap if counting to twenty becomes too taxing,' she said and grinned.

As Harriet moved around the bench, Grace stopped her. She reached up and swept the hair softly from her face. 'I really like you Harriet Haversham,' she said. She leant forward and met Harriet's lips, lingering a moment before easing away. 'Thank you for this,' she said.

Harriet flushed. 'You're slowing down progress,' she said and grinned. 'We need to get the beets and carrots next.'

'You say the nicest things to a girl, Ms Haversham,' Grace said and kissed her again. Harriet didn't object.

*

Lunch came and went and they moved into the next greenhouse. The aroma struck Grace instantly. Rows of tomatoes, cucumbers, lettuce, and herbs of various varieties filled the space.

'Wow, it's quite the enterprise you've got going,' Grace said. She hadn't realised the scale of the business Harriet was running. She gazed at Harriet awe-struck. 'Wow,' she said again, only this time the object of the expression was the woman staring back at her.

'It's expanded over the years,' Harriet said.

'How many of these do you have?' Grace asked. She had noticed several from her aunt's house and a good number of vegetable plots, but the greenhouses extended way beyond her view from the landing window.

'Eight,' Harriet said. 'It's mostly the same produce at different stages of growth, and bedding plants. There's a small orchard beyond the greenhouses – just apples and pears,' she said, with a shrug.

'Impressive.' Grace would never have guessed, and she hadn't even thought to question. 'How do you get it all to market?' Grace said.

'Dad will bring the van over later.' Harriet smiled. 'I don't drive,' she said.

Grace's eyebrows shot up. She couldn't imagine someone of Harriet's age not driving. 'Oh!' she said, stumped for a response.

'It's never really been of interest to me, though really I should, especially with this getting bigger,' she said, indicating with her eyes to the surroundings.

'Dad enjoys being involved too, though, and I think he'd be put out if I didn't need him for something.'

Grace smiled. 'He could still help,' she said, her tone soft.

'Yes, I guess so. Maybe I'll learn someday,' she said.

'I could teach you, if you like? It's really easy.'

Harriet chuckled.

'What's so funny?' Grace said.

'I've seen you on a horse,' Harriet said.

'That's not the same thing at all.'

'It would be for me. It would be as scary to me as riding a horse is to you.'

161

'Yes, I guess so. Well, how about I get back on the horse and you get into the driving seat, how about that?'

Harriet was grinning at her and Grace held her with affection, sensing the apprehension, and then the trust that came. She felt the essence of it, spill through her, unlocking something. A wave of anxiety rose up and she continued to maintain eye contact. 'I'm scared too,' she said.

Harriet nodded. 'Yes,' she said, her voice struggling to be heard.

Grace continued to stare, feeling the heat between them intensify.

'Cucumbers.' Harriet announced.

'If you say so,' Grace quipped.

'I'll do the tomatoes.'

'Let me guess, they're really fiddly,' Grace said.

'Don't worry you get to do the gooseberries while I do the strawberries. Prickly little fuckers!'

Grace burst out laughing. She'd never heard that language from Harriet, and it seemed all shades of odd and hot at the same time. Harriet had already started walking towards the tomato plants and Grace stood, watching, admiring her. She became lost in the idea of cupping the perfectly sized buttocks that teased in front of her eyes, delving into the curve of her hips and kissing the line that tracked up to Harriet's tempting neck; the scent of Harriet infusing her thoughts. Fuck! Harriet turned and Grace felt fire course through to her core and then flame in her cheeks.

'Are you working or watching?'

Grace tried to swallow. She tried to say working, gave up, cleared her throat and headed towards the cucumbers. So not helpful!

'Bloody hell, are they always this difficult to pull off?' Grace said, exhausted from having removed three fruit.

Harriet looked across to her and started to chuckle. 'Sorry, I should have said, use the cutters, they're on the bench.'

Grace groaned. 'That's an act of sabotage,' she said, rubbing sore hands.

Harriet put her hands in the air in submission and that image brought a whole new train of thought to Grace. Stop it! Grace picked up the cutters and returned to the act of systematically removing the fruit and placing them into the boxes, as instructed, trying her best to curb her imagination.

And then she saw it and all her efforts failed!

'Oh my God. It looks like a rabbit,' she blurted, cutting the oddly shaped cucumber from the stem.

'What?' Harriet said, looking across to Grace, shaking her head.

Grace held up the offending plant, which resembled the vibrating sex toy as if it had just been plucked from the shelf of an Ann Summers' shop, two prongs, appropriately distanced of course, and when she started waving it vigorously and making a buzzing noise, Harriet couldn't help but laugh out loud.

Grace looked up from the waving fruit and eyed Harriet curiously. Her imagination driving her feet, she set off on a chase, buzzing and waving, Harriet screaming as they circled the rows and benches.

Bryan entered the greenhouse at a pace and caught sight of the scene. 'Ah-right,' he said, puffing.

Grace tucked the cucumber behind her back and a fit of giggles came over her.

Harriet stood sniggering hands behind her back, like a child about to be disciplined. 'Hi dad,' she said.

'I thought for a minute old Hilda Spencer had come to life and was causing merry hell,' he said. 'You two look to be having fun,' he added, eyeing one woman and then the other. 'That's good.'

'You alright, dad?'

'Yep. I just popped in to see if you needed a hand,' he said. 'Oh, and to say, Kelly phoned to say Winnie seems a bit brighter. She's still going to keep her in overnight and do some tests, but at least the antibiotics are helping. She did leave a message on your answerphone. Oh, and Vera sends her love and says please not to worry, oh and mum says not to forget the meeting tomorrow night and that she still needs to catch up with Grace. I think that's everything,' he said, scratching his head.

Harriet looked to Grace. 'What does mum want with you?' she said.

'She just collared me in the pub, to catch up about Hilda.' Grace smiled.

Harriet rolled her eyes.

'Anyway, what do you want me to do?' Bryan said.

'Gooseberries,' Grace said.

'No chance, they're all yours, lady,' Harriet insisted.

'Can you start with the lettuce, dad? About forty should do it.'

'Right-oh,' Bryan said and set to work.

Grace held Harriet's gaze. 'That's good news about Winnie,' she said.

'Yes, it is.'

Grace waved the cucumber at Harriet with a wicked grin and Harriet snatched it from her.

'Back to work, slave, or I'll have to beat you into submission with my vegetable of much pleasure,' Harriet teased, threatening her with the cucumber.

Grace's eyes widened at the image her mind presented. 'Yep, that would certainly do it,' she said. And grinned as Harriet flushed.

Harriet slapped her on the arm with the fruit and headed back to the tomatoes.

*

All three workers stood, hands rubbing their backs, admiring the boxes of fruit and vegetables stacked and ready to go.

'Great job,' Harriet declared.

'Time for a gin,' Grace announced.

'I thought you'd never ask,' Bryan said.

We didn't, was the first thought that went through Grace's mind. 'You've earned it,' she said and smiled at Harriet. Much as she would rather be alone with Harriet, they had worked as a team and Bryan's help had quite literally saved Grace from total physical destruction. It had been hard work, but a lot of fun.

Grace staggered into the cottage and made the drinks. Harriet fed the dogs.

'Will you stay and eat, dad?' Harriet said as Bryan supped the last of his drink and placed his glass on the drainer.

Grace froze. Right, that's one step too far.

'No petal, I've got to get back,' he said.

Grace breathed in and released the air slowly. There is a God after all.

'I'll come back first thing and load the van.'

Harriet kissed him on the cheek. 'Thanks for the help,' she said.

'Pleasure. Keeps the old body ticking over,' he said, his cheeks rosy. 'Right, you ladies have a lovely evening, and don't do anything your mother wouldn't do?'

Well, that left a whole load of options up for grabs!

Harriet chuckled. 'See you at five?' she said.

FIVE! Grace couldn't imagine that. 'See you later Bryan,' she said meaning a lot later than five am.

'See you at five too,' he said and smiled.

It didn't sound like an option.

165

Grace groaned.

Harriet started laughing.

'Five?' Grace said.

'Yep.' Harriet stopped chuckling and gazed at the muddy patches that marked Grace's face. 'You want a bath?' Harriet said.

Grace's eyebrows raised and the mischievous grin that appeared made her eyes shine. 'I thought you'd never ask,' she said.

Harriet swallowed, colour sweeping up her neck and into her cheeks. She seemed entranced, lost in thought.

Grace became acutely aware that Harriet might be considering the proposition seriously and was suddenly overcome with the nervous tension of a teenager about to engage in their first romantic encounter. It was an alien feeling. She hadn't even felt this way with her first sexual experience, and yet the idea of making love with Harriet seemed altogether more frightening even than riding a horse. Way more terrifying.

Harriet seemed to regain focus and grinned. 'Now there's a thought,' she said, and Grace felt Harriet slowly, and excruciatingly painfully undress her with her eyes.

And then Harriet took a pace towards Grace, and Grace froze. This is ridiculous! She had never been immobilised by the idea of intimate physical contact. Fuck! The penny dropped with a resounding thud. She'd never experienced intimate physical contact. Not of this kind, not of the rip your heart out and steal your soul, meaningful kind of intimacy. Fuck, fuck, fuck. She was falling in love with Harriet. And now Harriet was moving closer, licking her lips, and she knew that if Harriet's lips came that close again, she wouldn't be able to stop herself from going all the way. Shit, she was even starting to think like a love-struck teenager. Harriet had stopped and was assessing her intently, reaching the tips of her fingers into her mouth and licking seductively. Why are you so fucking tempting to me? Then,

Harriet was reaching out and wiping something from under Grace's eye. Grace was struggling to breathe and her heart was racing.

'You had a lump of dirt close to your eye,' Harriet said. She moved away, picked up her glass and went to pour another gin.

Fuckety fuck! Grace felt as though she was gulping for air and hoped it wasn't obvious to Harriet.

'Another one?' Harriet said, holding out her hand for Grace's glass.

Grace responded with a nod because the words wouldn't come.

'Can you go run a bath?' Harriet said, making up the drinks.

Grace nodded, and it took a few seconds longer before her feet complied with Harriet's instructions. Harriet wasn't serious about them bathing together, was she? Grace wouldn't be able to take that. It would tip her over the edge.

Grace turned the taps and sat on the ledge of the bath, working her breathing to slow her heart rate. Flo bounded in, all tongue licking and tail wagging and she smiled. She petted the dog, suddenly aware that the dog had eyes of two different colours. She stared in fascination, the dog nuzzling her hand playfully. She ruffled the dog's head, the silky soft ears; Flo enjoying the attention and making sure Grace didn't stop. Grace hadn't expected Flo to lift her front paws up and onto her lap, let alone the weight of the dog as she edged forward. She hadn't braced herself for it, and when it happened, she had zero resistance to the movement. Upended by the Great Dane, she landed with a splash, water waving over the top of the bath, Flo barking excitedly and wagging her tail and dipping her nose into the soapy bubbles and snorting. Great game, eh?

'We usually undress in this part of the world before jumping into the bath,' Harriet said, two gins in her hand, and a broad grin that spanned from ear to ear.

'Seriously!' Grace wiped the water from her face but couldn't stop the chuckle from developing into hysterical laughter, Flo taking the hilarity as a command to continue and water soaking the floor at her paws as she splashed.

Harriet, still chuckling, put the glasses down, grabbed Flo by the collar and moved her away from the bath. She looked at the dog and in as serious a tone as she could muster said, 'Bed.'

Flo looked at her with a tilt of her head, barked and ran down the stairs.

Harriet looked at Grace quizzically, the wet t-shirt clinging, revealing, and drawing Harriet's eyes to linger longingly and her teeth to pull on her lip. She reached out a hand and Grace took it.

Grace stood, dripping from head to toe, Harriet still observing her.

'I'll leave your gin there,' she said, picking up the second glass and heading out the bathroom. 'I'll put some dry clothes outside the door for you,' she added and shut the door behind her.

Grace took a deep breath and released it slowly, her heart pounding.

16.

Grace's phone alarm screamed at her, forcing her eyes to blink and open. She reached out and slapped at the snooze button then lay still; dazed by the rude awakening and drifting back into a deep sleep. She rolled onto her side. The covers felt so warm, her head so heavy on the downy pillow, and then the alarm intruded again and she slapped it, harder. She moaned, squinted her eyes to open and sat upright. The first signs of daylight teased through the gap between the curtains and it irrationally occurred to her that she might be late. Four-thirty, her phone said, and her body responded with a yawn. Staggering, she jumped into the shower and allowed the hot water to entice her into wakefulness. Dressing quickly, she went to the kitchen then stopped when she remembered that Flo had stayed over with Archie. Crossing the driveway to the cottage, the front door was already open and she walked in to be handed a mug of steaming coffee.

'Morning,' Harriet said.

She looked as if she had been awake for hours and seeing the packed rucksack simply confirmed that fact to Grace. 'Morning,' she said and sipped the coffee.

Bryan parked the white transit van on the driveway and walked towards the cottage. Harriet handed him a coffee, finished her own and headed out the door round to the stacked boxes and trays.

Grace downed her drink and followed Harriet feeling marginally uplifted, and between them, and then Bryan, they loaded the van, locked up the dogs and headed into town.

Harriet guided the setting up exercise and before they had the stand fully stocked, Grace had sold a bag of potatoes, two strings of onions, carrots, and three beetroots to an early customer.

'Ah-right, Harriet, Bryan,' the man said, catching sight of the two of them as they returned from the van with trays of strawberries and gooseberries.

'Ah-right, Fred,' Bryan responded.

'See you got yourself a new un then?' the man said, tilting his head towards Grace.

'How are you, Fred?' Harriet said, ignoring the comment.

'Mustn't grumble. That brother of yours tells me, me bowels are just fine and that I need to eat more green veg. What does he know, bloody dietician now, eh?' he grumbled and pottered off.

'Have a good day, Fred,' Harriet said and smiled. Fred waving his hand in the air shuffled away, dragging the tartan shopping bag on small, white wheels behind him.

Grace watched Harriet as she worked and smiled.

'If you've got nothing to do, go get some coffees and breakfast from the café,' Harriet said, throwing a soggy lettuce leaf at her. 'Dad 'll have a sausage sarnie and I'll have bacon, with ketchup, please. Drew will put it on our tab and I'll settle it at the end of the day,' she added.

Grace continued eyeing Harriet up and down for a bit longer, sighed, and then headed to the café.

'Good to see you two getting on well,' Bryan said to Harriet.

Harriet flushed; her eyes firmly fixed on the back of Grace as she meandered down the street. 'Yes,' she said then turned her attention to the trays of fruit.

'Morning Grace,' Drew said as Grace entered the café. 'What can I get you?'

'Two coffees for Harriet and Bryan, please.'

'That'll be a Cappuccino for Harriet and Latte for Bryan.' Harriet only ever took an Espresso with a hangover and those days Drew could count on one hand. There had been a few immediately after Annabel had left, but none until yesterday morning. 'Their usual, one sausage, and one bacon sarnie with ketchup?' she said.

'Yep.'

'What about for you?'

'I'll have an Americano and a bacon sandwich please, with ketchup.'

Drew smiled. 'Right you are,' she said and started preparing the drinks. 'You helping today, then?' Drew said.

'Yes.'

'How are you finding village life?' Drew said.

Grace didn't know if she was being interrogated, or she was just imagining it. 'It has its moments,' Grace said.

'You enjoying the scenery?' Drew said.

'Very much,' Grace responded and had to work hard not to blush. She looked away from Drew. 'It's a pretty place,' she added.

'With pretty people,' Drew added.

Grace smiled. 'That too,' she agreed and Drew was staring at her oddly.

'Do you like her?' Drew said, and Grace couldn't stop the fierce heat that had her flushing. 'Thought so,' Drew said, shaking her head in affirmation of her hypothesis. 'She's really into you, I know that much,' Drew continued, and placed three take away cups with the initials A, C, and L, written in black ink, respectively on each lid.

Drew was looking at Grace and Grace got the distinct impression that Drew had more to say on the matter, but instead, she turned and went to the kitchen.

'I'll just get the sarnies made up,' Drew said, leaving Grace wondering how she was going to manage to carry three cups and three sandwiches with two hands.

Drew returned with the sandwiches in a carrier bag, pulled a cup holder from under the counter and slotted the cups in it, answering her concerns. 'There you go,' she said. 'I'll put it on the account.'

Grace nodded. 'Thanks,' she said. She turned away from Drew, feeling the woman's eyes on her as she went to the door.

'You will look after her,' Drew said, causing Grace to turn.

Grace paused. She held Drew's concerned gaze. 'I will try,' she said, and then wondered if *try* sounded lame. She stepped out onto the bustling street, buzzing with life. Chatter and laughter filtered across the square and the flow of traffic was more constant than it had been before.

'Morning, Grace,' a passer-by said and Grace looked towards the stranger.

'Morning,' she said. She had no idea who the person was but they were now busy talking to the owner of the scented candles and perfumes stall. The owner of the stall waved to her as she passed and she smiled in response.

'Morning, Grace,' the butcher said and waved to her as she passed the meat waggon.

'Morning,' Grace said and smiled back at him. His ruddy cheeks shone and he had a welcoming smile. She had seen him in the pub on quiz night but hadn't been introduced. The wagon said Bill's Butcher, so assumed he was the Bill McKenzie, she'd heard Bryan talking about. He supplied the pub, she recalled.

'Morning Grace.'

The voice came from behind her and she turned to see Doug running to catch up with her. 'Morning Doug.'

'They got you up bright and early this morning then?' he said and chuckled.

'That they did,' Grace said.

'Is there any way I can persuade you to hang around for next month's quiz night?' he said. 'We could really do with your brain on our team.'

Grace laughed. 'I'm not sure I'll be here,' she said.

'Damn shame,' he said, nodding his head. 'Thought I'd ask in person,' he said and shrugged and continued to mumble. 'Will you think about it?' he said.

Grace nodded.

'Great,' he said and beamed a smile before stopping at the bread stall.

'Morning Grace,' the woman at the bread stall said and waved.

'Morning,' Grace said and smiled.

She had been watching Harriet for a while as she approached the vegetable stall, before Harriet spotted her. And when Harriet smiled, Grace melted inside. She needed to do more than try and look after Harriet.

They ate as they worked, the flow of customers relentless. 'Where do they all come from?' Grace said, just short of lunchtime.

'Surrounding villages.' Harriet smiled. She brushed past Grace, making sure that their bodies touched and whispered in her ear. 'We have a reputation, you know.'

Grace chuckled. 'Is there anything else you might like to share, about the nature of that reputation,' she whispered back, emphasising the word reputation.

'I need four onions and two bags of potatoes,' Harriet said, indicating with her eyes.

Grace laughed. 'You can boss me around anytime, Ms Haversham,' she whispered to Harriet, as she reached across her to get to the onions.

'I'll remember that,' Harriet said, slipping away and grabbing two punnets of strawberries and a punnet of gooseberries.

Grace was flagging by 2.30 and grateful the flow had started to ease. The stand had the appearance of a food hall that had been raided by a troop of starving monkeys. Bits lay strewn around the floor, empty trays stacked to the rear of the stand.

Bryan was shouting encouragement for the few remaining bags of potatoes, beetroot, cucumbers, and tomatoes.

'We can start packing up,' Harriet said and lifted an empty crate into the van with as much enthusiasm as she had shown at the beginning of the day.

Grace's body felt wrecked. Not only had the physical exercise taken its toll in the last few days, the unwitting and repeated incidents that had resulted in her being upended either by the dog or Harriet had left their mark at various points on her body. A Thai massage would go down a treat right now.

'Are you helping or watching?' Harriet quipped.

Grace moved slowly; the stiffness having taken on a new level of rigidity following a short period of standing still. She picked up a crate and groaned. She stepped up into the back of the van and stacked it onto the pile. As she turned, she met Harriet's dark gaze; Harriet's hands were empty. Harriet stepped closer, reached out and traced a line from her cheek, down her neck, and rested in the apex of her cleavage. Grace smiled. 'Are you helping or watching?' she said.

Harriet chucked.

Grace so loved that sound.

Harriet leaned closer. 'I guess that depends who's asking,' she said, and she brought her lips to rest briefly against Grace's before easing back. 'Thanks for helping today,' she said. 'I've enjoyed it.'

Grace cleared her throat. 'Me too,' she said, struggling to control the vibration that rippled through her in waves.

Harriet turned and stepped out of the van, and Grace followed her.

'Thank you, Mrs Goldsworth,' Bryan said, handing over a sack of potatoes and the last punnet of tomatoes. 'You have a great day now,' he added.

'Thank you, Bryan,' Sheila said, and then she spotted Harriet and Grace. 'I'm going to the pub,' she blurted and scampered off.

'Great idea, I'll be there in a jiffy,' Bryan said and chuckled. 'Last two of potatoes,' he shouted, leaving Harriet and Grace to continue packing up.

*

'Oh my God, I'm exhausted,' Grace said and slumped into the kitchen seat.

Flo and Archie had spent the time that they unpacked running around the field and then continued to chase up and down while Harriet fed the horses. The fact that Harriet had the energy to give them such loving attention had had Grace looking on in awe.

Now, the dogs were munching merrily from their bowls and Grace was nursing her aching body. Kelly had left another message saying she was going to hold onto Winnie until the test results were back, which would now be Monday and for a split-second Grace became aware of the fact that there was nothing in that moment they needed to do. She groaned as she rubbed tired legs.

'Want a beer?' Harriet said.

Grace nodded. 'Do you do that every week?' she said.

'Every Friday.'

'It's knackering, I don't know how you do it,' She yawned. 'I ache from head to foot,' she complained.

'Not aided by diving into the bath,' Harriet said.

'Or being flattened by a dead-weight trying to take advantage of me the other night,' Grace added.

Harriet sniggered and handed over a bottle. 'Have I apologised for that?' she said. She hadn't remembered how she had come to be laying on top of Grace. Just the kissing bit had etched in her memory, and that suited her fine.

Grace leaned back in the chair and gazed at Harriet. 'You know, I don't believe you have,' she said, and sipped the chilled beer.

Harriet plonked her bottle on the table, stepped up to Grace and then straddled her and wrapped her arms around her neck. Grace slid her bottle onto the table then moved her arms around Harriet's lower back and pulled her closer.

'I've been wanting to do this all day,' Harriet said.

'What, sit on my lap?' Grace said.

'No, this,' Harriet said. She tilted Grace's chin upwards eased her hips into Grace and looked at her with pure desire.

When Harriet's lips closed around Grace's, Grace felt it in every cell in her body. Harriet tasted so sweet, and the slight chill on her lips was quickly replaced by wet heat and then the throbbing at her centre became a distraction. Grace fell into the kiss and groaned in pleasure when Harriet's cold fingertips grazed the flesh on her abdomen and traced a line round to her back and upwards. As Harriet touched the back of Grace's neck and toyed with her hair, their tongues dancing, exploring, teasing, Grace shuddered beneath the erotic sensations.

Harriet softened her lips, licking, nipping and then eased back and gazed at Grace with dark eyes that glistened like coal. 'That,' she said.

Grace studied the dark, intensity. 'I might not be able to stop,' she said.

'I might not want you to,' Harriet said.

Harriet hadn't meant to sound indecisive, but that's what registered with Grace. She reached up and brushed a thumb across Harriet's swollen lips. So, tempting. So delicious. 'I need you to be sure,' she said, her voice broken.

Harriet wetted Grace's thumb, cupped Grace's hand and kissed her palm. 'I am sure,' she said. 'I know I was drunk the other night when I kissed you, but I'm not drunk now, and I want to do more than kiss you.'

Grace tried to swallow and struggled. 'What about me leaving here?'

Harriet looked away and then focused on Grace again. 'I've thought about that a lot, she said, and I don't have any answers. But I do know.' She hesitated. 'I know I feel strongly enough that I want you,' she said.

There it was. The energy behind Harriet's gaze would have floored Grace had she not been sat down. Why was she hesitating?

Harriet eased off Grace's lap and held out her hand. 'Come to bed with me,' she said and Grace stood.

'Can I get a shower?' Grace said, gazing down at her dusty state.

'Come shower with me, and then come to bed with me,' Harriet said.

The hesitation was like a pressure imploding in her chest. Why was this suddenly so difficult? She looked away, closed her eyes and tried to make sense of the turmoil that now consumed her. It was the Sandra fucking Floss allegation, and the undisclosed truth, hanging over her head. She pinched the bridge of her nose, praying that turning down Harriet's offer wouldn't create a rift between them. The gentle touch on her cheek roused her and she turned to face Harriet.

'It's okay,' Harriet said. 'If the timing isn't right for you, I get it.' She was smiling, and the intensity in her gaze was lighter than a moment earlier. Grace didn't sense any friction in Harriet and released a long slow breath. On the contrary, Harriet seemed to exude nothing other than love and compassion.

'I want to,' Grace said.

'It's fine, Grace. Just being close is good. If that's okay with you?'

Grace nodded, and when Harriet leaned in and kissed her, she felt as if a weight had been lifted. The time would be right at some point, she knew that. Harriet eased out of the kiss and Grace cupped her cheek. 'You're beautiful,' she said. She paused and then it dawned on her. 'And, isn't there a meeting tonight we need to go to?' Grace said.

Harriet froze. 'Oh, shit! I'd forgotten. Damn it! Yes.' She chuckled. 'We'd better get changed. We can eat in the pub afterwards,' she said.

Grace nodded. 'I'll go and get washed,' she said, pointing over her shoulder to the door.

'Hmm!' Harriet mumbled and smiled. 'I'll hold that thought,' she said.

Grace smiled, thankful for the banter and feeling even closer to Harriet.

17.

'Good evening, everyone,' Doris announced, her voice projecting over the busy voices and coaxing them into a low hum and, in the absence of any further sound from Doris, near silence. 'Welcome to our first meeting for the organising committee of this year's summer fete.'

Doug glanced around the room noting that, apart from their special guest, it was the same bloody group of people who had attended the previous parish meetings, the annual general meeting and last year's fete committee meetings. He huffed, checked his watch and laid a private bet. Two hours and thirty-five minutes. That would take them to eight thirty-five and beat last year's record of two hours and forty-five minutes. It was optimistic for sure, but the bar was open because Bryan, the lucky bastard, had agreed to open it for Elvis, who was already fidgeting with his dog collar, and efficiency was therefore critical. 'Evening Doris,' he said, aiming to keep on the right side of the chairwoman.

'Firstly, I would like for us to welcome our guest, Vera's niece, Grace, whom I'm sure most of you have already had the good fortune of meeting. Welcome Grace,' she said.

Bloody hell, she's making it sound like presidential speech. 'Grace,' he said, nodding in welcome.

Mumbles of welcome circled the table.

Harriet grinned with something akin to pride and squeezed Grace's leg when she wasn't expecting it.

Grace shot up from her seat and let out what might have been interpreted as a squeal that she managed to disguise as a welcome returned to the group and pulled in her chair. She glared at Harriet who was holding back a chuckle.

'We're very excited to have Grace with us, and for those of you who don't know, Grace is in the events organising industry. She is an expert and I'm sure will make a massive contribution to the organising of our event this year, won't you Grace?'

Grace hadn't been expecting the question, that sounded more like a statement, and stuttered out, 'Yes of course,' and then wondered whether she had committed to something she might later regret. She had intended to just turn up to the meeting, observe and then support Harriet. Instead, Grace now found herself sitting to attention and making sure she was listening to Doris's every word. She was also aware of the eager eyes around the room that had zeroed in on her and especially the disconcerting, dark gaze of the woman sat next to her. Having been drawn into Harriet's world, she was having a hard job trying to maintain the distance needed to protect them both from the inevitable – her leaving – and added to that, she had come to realise she didn't feel inclined to leave. She had never felt more exposed, vulnerable, fragile, and yet, she'd never felt more certain of anything either. She was falling in love with Harriet and powerless to stop her heart in motion.

'Right,' Doris said. 'Are we all in agreement that the fete will be held on the local cricket pitch on the 25th of July, between ten-thirty and half-past-four?'

'Shall I minute that, Mrs Akeman?' Shelia said.

'Wait, we need a proposer and seconder,' Doris said.

'Bloody hell,' Doug said. 'It's been in everyone's diary since last year.' He rolled his eyes. 'I'll propose.'

'I'll second,' Esther said.

'That's agreed, Sheila,' Doris said.

Sheila made a note.

'Now, let's move on to the activities for the event.'

Well, that opened a can of worms.

Grace watched agog as individual conversations broke out around the room. She heard someone ask whether the Morris Dancers were booked and no one answered and then the school Maypole dancing was mentioned and she couldn't quite work out whether that was instead of or as well as the Morris Dancers. Someone else had shifted to the races, someone mentioned a sheep race, God forbid, and Grace drifted, suddenly challenged by a vision of Hilda Spencer and the sheep-looking poodle legging it across the cricket square. And then, Delia piped up about doing her Tarot readings again this year and Doug seemed insistent that the cards had been the final downfall of the Mayor's visit the previous year when Delia had insisted that there was going to be a birth in his family that same year. The fact that he had shouted, 'that's not possible, I've had the snip,' at the precise moment the jukebox stopped playing *Always the Last to Know* by Del Amitri, didn't go unnoticed by a good number of visiting guests. Though, it had all started going wrong long before that, when he had sampled the adult punch without realising it had been doctored with the special brew from Jenny's kitchen and then opened the *Fuckton Date*, much to the amusement of those whose hearing was still intact. Delia was rebuffing smugly, reminding Doug that her predictions had come true – his wife had indeed given birth during the year, and if the Mayor had continued with the reading instead of running off, he would have been forewarned about her infidelity.

Grace's eyes widened, the voices merging into a blend of battle and banter, and then Grace felt the warmth of Harriet's hand on her thigh, immediately followed by the banging of a gavel on the table. She jumped from her chair, her ears slowly recovering from the sustained assault.

'Thank you, Elvis,' Doris said and proceeded to address the group. 'Ladies and gentlemen, might I please remind you that we need to conduct this meeting with an element of decorum. So, if you would please kindly wait until asked before speaking.'

Doug raised his hand.

'Yes, Doug?'

'Should we raise our hand to speak?' he said and started to chuckle.

'That's a very good idea, Doug. A very good idea indeed.'

'Bloody hell,' he mumbled.

'So, let's start with the games. Are we going ahead with the wellie tossing this year?'

Jenny put up her hand and started to speak before permission had been granted. 'Remember, our Jarid had to tend to old Mrs Laverty last year when little Jonny, thinks of himself as 'Jonny Wilkinson' Jones's wellie damn near took her head off. Swept her cream tea clean off the table. The shock of it nearly killed her,' Jenny said.

Doris was shaking her head. 'Yes, terrible affair,' she said.

Grace was biting down on her lip and Harriet was also struggling not to chuckle.

'Why don't we move it to the bottom of the field, Doris?' Elvis suggested. 'You know Neville would be most disappointed not to be running the activity this year. He prides himself in measuring the throws with pinpoint accuracy,' he added.

Harriet leaned towards Grace and whispered, 'Neville is Doris's husband. He's the local undertaker, he's good at measuring,' she said.

Grace sniggered, receiving a stern look from Doris.

'It can't go too far down, or it'll clash with the coconut shy and plate smashing,' Delia said. 'Jarid says the plate smashing is important for the community because it provides a therapeutic outlet for those in need of venting their spleen,' she added.

'Bloody hell,' Doug remarked. Was that why he had spent his time oscillating between the beer tent and throwing balls at the crockery last year? He hadn't decided which of the two was his preferred choice of medication. 'Can't we just fence it off better, with the cricket nets or something?' he said.

'Good idea,' Doris said.

'We need the cricket net for the coconut shy,' Delia said.

Grace's lips had parted and she couldn't help the words flying out. 'Do you have a health and safety policy for the event? A risk assessment for the activities?' she asked.

Silence.

Grace gazed around the room.

Still silence.

Doris cleared her throat. 'We endeavour to make sure all our activities are appropriately supported, and Jarid is in attendance for any medical emergencies,' she said.

Grace nodded. 'Would you like me to write one for this year?' she asked.

Harriet felt warm and tingled with the gentle kindness in Grace's tone, and the offer of support rather than any accusation.

Everyone in the room seemed to breathe at the same time.

Doris cleared her throat again and studied Grace over the rim of her glasses. Harriet recognised the look in Doris's eyes. She had seen the same supportive gaze all those years ago.

'That would be very kind, Grace, thank you,' Doris said.

'So, the wellie tossing is a yes?' Sheila said.

Doris nodded. 'I think we're also in agreement to the coconut shy and plate smashing, and Grace's offer to write an assessment,' she said.

Sheila made a note.

'Let's move on to the races,' Doris said.

'Kev and Bryan have agreed to coordinate the sheep races,' Doug announced.

Oh my God, they were serious. Grace looked to Harriet with raised eyebrows and Harriet smiled.

'It's an annual event, draws people from all over these parts. There'll be twelve teams,' Harriet whispered.

Fuck! Grace couldn't imagine that.

'They'll run along the bottom behind the coconut shy, same as last year,' Doug said.

'Fine. Agreed.' Doris said, and Sheila made a note.

Grace felt the warm hand on her thigh again and turned to Harriet.

Harriet winked.

Grace smiled. She was thinking about the risk assessment.

'Children's and adult races,' Doris stated. 'Three-legged race, no carrying allowed. There was a lot of cheating last year from competitive dads. And we need to make sure the children don't have any sticky tack if they're taking part in the egg and spoon race. Jonny 'Wilkinson' Jones was instrumental in last year's debacle. Fortunately, he went to uni but his two younger brothers know all the tricks,' she said.

Everyone nodded.

'Sheila, will you manage the races again, dear,' Doris said.

Sheila straightened her back and smiled. 'Of course, I'd be delighted. Thank you, Mrs Akeman,' she said and made a note.

'Bloody hell,' Doug mumbled. 'Therein lies the first problem,' and Esther dug him in the ribs with her elbow.

'I'll speak to the school about the children doing the Maypole dancing, and Eric regarding the Morris Dancing,' Doris said.

'Oh aye!' Doug mumbled, referring to Doris's not-so-well-hidden attraction to the handsome head of the Morris men of Upper Duckton. He received another elbow to the ribs.

Doris ignored his facetious comment and studied the list in front of her.

Doug checked his watch. An hour in – not too shabby!

'The Brownies will pick up face painting, of course,' Doris continued.

She seemed to have good control of things.

'Dog show?' Doris said.

Good God, no! Grace sat up in the chair. Seriously? With sheep races?

The door to the hut opened and Jarid and Kelly walked in, drawing the attention of the room.

'Sorry we're late, Jarid said.

'Shall I minute that, Mrs Akeman,' Sheila said.

Doris nodded. 'Come in, come in. Take a seat. We were just discussing whether to have a dog show this year or not?'

'We'll have the sheep races, I assume?' Jarid said.

'Yes,' Doris confirmed.

'It was touch and go at-one-point last year,' Jarid said, Kelly, nodding furiously in agreement. 'If we're going to do it, we should separate the two activities, maybe one in the morning and one in the afternoon?' Jarid suggested.

That they were even considering it was a mystery to Grace and she thought about voicing her opinion then thought again. It wasn't her event. Sheep and dogs just didn't mix; it had disaster written all over it, and she now realised why they'd never written a risk assessment before. 'I assume the two activities will be well fenced off?' she said, for the purpose of the assessment.

No one was nodding.

'It's a bit tricky to fence the area completely, and we do rely on people applying common sense,' Doris said.

'Bloody mistake that is,' Doug quipped.

Grace agreed with him.

'Running them at different times would work. We can't cancel the sheep racing, it draws too many people, and so does the dog show. Vera's Flo won puppy of the year last year,' Doris said, heads nodding around the room.

'There were only two entries,' Harriet whispered to Grace who chuckled and then received another look from Doris. Or was that look directed at Harriet?

Harriet's hand squeezed and Grace felt the warmth of it move through her. Very disconcerting.

'So, sheep or dogs in the morning?' Doug said, wanting to move things along.

'Can we do the dogs before lunch is served?' Kelly suggested. 'It helps them stay focused,' she added.

'Good point,' Kelly, 'Everyone agreed?' Doris said. 'I assume I can put your name down to coordinate the dog show, Kelly?'

Kelly nodded. 'I'll get Vera to help,' she said.

'We'll have the beer tent, of course, wine and soft drinks,' Elvis said. 'I'll get that sorted, with Bryan and Doug.'

Grace couldn't help herself. 'Have you thought of something like Gin tasting?' she asked.

'Ooh, what a good idea,' Delia piped up.

'Gin tasting, what all five types,' Doug said and chuckled to himself.

'You're right Doug, there are five types but there are around fifty different flavours and then there are the liqueur gins too,' Grace said. 'I can organise it if you'd like?'

Delia's hand shot up, immediately followed by Jenny, Esther Kelly and Sheila. Everyone looked at Sheila, who didn't drink, with a united frown. The door opened and Drew walked in, carrying a cake box.

'Hands up for a gin tent,' Delia said to her, and Drew plonked the box on the table and raised her hand as she sat.

'I'm in,' Drew said and smiled at Harriet and Grace. 'There's cake if anyone wants it?' she said. 'Sorry, I'm late.'

Sheila scribbled a note.

'Gin tent, eh,' Harriet whispered to Grace and squeezed her leg.

Grace could feel the colour in her cheeks shift and Drew's eyes on her with a crafty looking grin on her face.

Doug opened the box. 'Well, I'll have cake,' he said, removed a slice, and passed the box to Esther.

The box moved around the table, murmurs of 'ooh' and 'ah' and other mumblings of pleasure halting the meeting.

'Did you bake this?' Grace said to Harriet.

Harriet nodded.

Grace fell apart inside, just as the cake melted in her mouth.

'I suppose it would be a good time to agree on the cake stall this year,' Doris announced.

'Great timing, Doris,' Doug said, licking his lips.

'Yes, I'll do the cakes and café, Harriet can help bake and set up,' Drew announced, nodding to Harriet, who nodded back.

Grace felt a prickly sensation alert her, and then her chest tightened enough for it to affect her jaw. That's ridiculous! They do the cakes together every year.

'I'll organise the horticultural show, and judges,' Harriet offered.

Grace looked at Harriet in wonder. This event was already more complex than one of her own, which were both, professionally organised and by large teams of experts. This small band of enthusiastic people seemed to be redefining the term productivity.

'Can we make sure Colin's cucumbers end up in the right judging category this year, please Harriet?' Doris said.

'Yes, we'll have someone watching the tent all day,' Harriet said.

Grace frowned.

'Jonny 'Wilkinson' Jones,' Doug started. 'Moved Colin's prize cucumber into the marrow section for judging last year.

Needless-to-say he didn't win and the cucumber that won was half the size of his. Never heard the end of it since,' Doug said.

Grace tried not to smile. 'Is there a novelty vegetable section?' she said, thinking of the cucumber that she had chased Harriet around with, and then flushed. Harriet squeezed her thigh, tightly and she winced.

'There's a thought,' Doug said.

'Right, thank you, Doug. Sheila, can you minute that please?'

Sheila scribbled.

Elvis, looking over her shoulder smiling said, 'I don't think Doris was referring to Colin's cucumber specifically, Sheila.'

Sheila gazed up at him. 'Oh, thank you, Vicar,' she said. She picked up the ruler at the side of her pad and drew a straight line through the note.

'Do you have a band or any musical entertainment?' Grace asked.

'We have the Morris Dancers and Maypole,' Doris said. 'And Elvis brings the jukebox over from the pub.'

'What about background music and intervals between the main activities?' Grace asked. Harriet squeezed her leg, and she cleared her throat. 'I might be able to source something if a band would be of interest?'

Elvis was nodding. 'I think that would be a wonderful idea. I'm happy to give the jukebox a rest this year,' he said, approvingly.

'How exciting,' Delia said. 'Will it be a famous band?'

Grace grinned. 'I can't promise that, but I'll see who I can reach out to.'

Jenny smiled smugly, confident that the two of cups and wheel of fortune were showing their hand. Unity and fate!

'Is it time for the pub?' Doug announced, looking at his watch.

'One last thing,' Doris said. 'Harriet, do you think we could do the pony rides again this year? I don't like to ask, but I think the children really missed it last year.'

Harriet nodded. 'I know. It was tricky last year. Obviously, there'll only be one, but I'm sure Fizz will be up for it,' she said.

Doris was studying Harriet over the top of her glasses, and Grace noticed compassion and gratitude passing from the elderly eyes. 'Thank you, Harriet, we are most appreciative,' she said.

Sheila made a note.

'Right ladies and gentlemen, have we missed anything?'

Shaking heads and low mumbling came back in response and then the scraping of chairs across the floor as people started to free themselves from the shackles of the meeting.

'Excellent, then I declare this meeting closed. Thank you, everyone.'

Elvis banged the gavel again and Sheila made a note.

Grace took in a deep breath and released it slowly. That wasn't too bad. She smiled at Harriet.

Doug announced, 'two-hours-and-forty-three-minutes,' and turned up his nose. He was sure they could have done better.

'Food?' Harriet said.

'Starving,' Grace responded.

18.

'Hey, Kelly, how's Winnie?' Grace said, catching the vet's attention as they set off for the pub.

Kelly put a gentle hand on Grace's arm. 'She's doing well. She perked up in the last few hours so if she's still good in the morning you could probably come and collect her,' she said.

Grace felt her shoulders relax. 'Thank heavens,' she said and noticed Harriet grinning.

'That's great news,' Harriet added.

'Do you guys have plans over the weekend?' Kelly said.

'Just Luce coming over for riding on Sunday,' Harriet said. 'And I'll need to give this one another lesson,' she teased Grace.

Grace flushed, her mind toying with any number of lessons she would like to work through with Harriet, none of them involving a horse.

'Hmm!' Kelly murmured and studied Grace with a knowing look.

Grace blushed and Kelly spared her any further embarrassment by giving her attention back to Harriet.

'We're having an open barbeque tomorrow, running from midday, if you fancy it?' she said.

Harriet nodded. 'Thanks.'

Kelly dropped back to join Jarid who had been drawn into deep conversation with Doug.

'How did you find the meeting?' Harriet said.

Grace smiled. 'Touch and go at times,' she said. 'The sheep racing and dog show running alongside each other had me a bit on edge, I have to confess. And at one point a vision of Hilda Spencer came to me, undecided as to which activity she should be lined up for,' Grace said. 'It was a scary moment.' She grinned at Harriet.

'You saw Hilda again?' Harriet said.

Grace looked at her oddly. 'Not that kind of vision,' she said and Harriet nudged her in the arm.

'Look how well they're getting on,' Jenny whispered to Delia, observing the two women from a few paces behind Jarid, Doug and Kelly.

'It's in the cards,' Delia said as if to say, what did you expect? One thing irked her though! The upside-down justice card – dishonesty, and the eight-of-cups – walking away, still hadn't appeared, and she knew they would. It was only a matter of time, though she wouldn't mind being proven wrong in this instance. Harriet and Grace looked good together, and it was a blessing to see Harriet back to her old self.

'Thank you for offering to help,' Harriet said to Grace. 'We've looked at having music before, but it's always proven too expensive,' she said.

'I'll sponsor the event,' Grace said.

'Really?'

'Sure.'

Harriet gazed at Grace in profile as they walked. 'Hmm,' she murmured and there was no doubting the inference in Grace's mind.

Grace smiled. 'You're staring at me,' she said.

'Yes,' Harriet said.

The depth in Harriet's tone sent goose bumps up Grace's back and the hairs on her neck tingled.

'You're going to trip if you keep staring in this direction,' Grace said as they walked.

Harriet wrapped her arm through Grace's and leant towards her ear. 'I won't now,' she whispered.

Grace felt her insides flip with the warmth of Harriet and the soft, indisputably seductive, tone in her voice. Thought evaded her.

'You are very kind, Grace,' Harriet said.

Grace looked at Harriet. She'd never thought of herself as kind per se. She'd always done what she felt was right, usually backed by a great deal of logic and most often, evidenced using statistical data. 'Thank you,' she said, unable to define how she felt about the feedback.

They entered the pub and approached the bar. Elvis was already serving.

'Hey, dad?' Harriet said.

'Hello, petal,' Bryan responded. 'G & T?'

Both women nodded.

'Thanks Bryan,' Grace said.

'Here.' Harriet handed Grace a menu from the bar. 'Fish and chips is the Friday special,' she said.

'That'll do for me,' Grace said and put the menu on the bar.

'Two fish and chips?' Bryan said, placing their drinks on the bar.

'Thanks,' Harriet said. She moved away from the bar and headed for a small table, set away from the main hub of the pub and in the opposite corner from the dance-floor area. It was a little quieter and more private.

They sat and Grace leaned her head back in the large soft seat. 'I'm knackered,' she said.

Harriet laughed.

Grace sat up, sipped at her drink and held Harriet's gaze, hesitating to speak. 'Did you have another pony?' she said, softly.

Harriet's gaze drifted and she clamped her lips with her teeth for a moment before speaking. Looking back to Grace, 'Yes,' she said. 'She died suddenly the year before last, a few months after the fete,' Harriet said.

Grace frowned. 'I'm sorry,' she said.

Harriet sighed. 'I'm fine now. It was a heart problem. She was five, Fizz's twin sister. I stopped the riding lessons after she died. Only Luce comes now. It used to be really busy at the weekends,' Harriet said, lost in reflection. She smiled.

'Must have been difficult?' Grace said.

'Yes, it was. We cancelled the rides at last year's fete, but I think it would be good to get them back. The children really do love it,' Harriet said.

Grace observed Harriet, falling more in love with her in every revealing moment. She sipped at the gin for want of some small distraction, the pain of losing something precious registering in the emptiness that settled in her chest. 'You're so beautiful,' she said.

Harriet assessed Grace and smiled. 'I happen to think you are too,' she said. 'It's going to be a bit awkward with one pony, there's usually a queue with two,' she said.

'Have you ever thought of getting another one?'

'The timing hasn't been right,' Harriet said.

Grace nodded.

'Anyway, what did you think of the meeting. How did it compare with organising a real event?'

God, she was so fucking adorable. 'Yours is a real event. I'm, honestly, really impressed. I've no idea how the hell you're all going to pull it off, given the number and scope of the activities proposed,' Grace said. 'I would have had a team of thirty doing this kind of thing.'

Harriet flushed and hesitated before speaking. 'So, might you come back and help us on the day?' she said.

Grace smiled and heat flushed her cheeks. She had already considered the idea. She'd had thoughts about sourcing and running the gin tent on the day. Shooting up to Duckton-by-Dale for a weekend – she could manage that. 'Maybe,' she said and flushed further as Harriet's face lit up.

'Two fish and chips,' Bryan said, presenting the food to the table.

Jarid stepped in front of his mother as she made her way past the bar, heading in Harriet and Grace's direction. 'Leave them be, mum,' he said.

Jenny gazed up at him. 'What do you think?' she said, trying to peak around him on the basis that she had no chance of seeing over his towering shoulder.

'I think they're doing just fine, so how about you and Delia have a nice relaxing evening. Did you hear? Hilda was seen again today,' he said, escorting her back to the table Delia sat at. Delia was shuffling the cards.

'Really,' Jenny said. 'Where?'

'Ferndale.'

'Really!' Jenny said, an octave higher. 'Delia, did you hear that?' she said as she sat. Delia looked up. 'Hilda spotted in Ferndale,' she said. 'She's never been seen that far out before.'

Delia's eyes widened. 'Ooh, Ferndale,' she said. She started to shuffle with greater urgency, Jenny pouring their wine and Jarid returning to Kelly.

'Has there really been a sighting in Ferndale?' Kelly said to Jarid.

'Nah,' he said. He picked up his beer and took a long slug.

Kelly chuckled. 'Jarid Haversham, you're a bad man,' she said and laughed.

Jarid wiped the beer-foam off his top lip. 'It'll keep them entertained for days,' he said. 'And takes the heat off Harriet and Grace,' he added.

'They seem to be getting on well,' Kelly said.

'They do,' he said and smiled.

*

Harriet and Grace hadn't reached the doorstep of the cottage before Harriet stopped and turned sharply towards

Grace. She didn't even study Grace for any length of time either, before seeking out Grace's lips with focused determination. She moved her hand to cup Grace's cheek, another toying with the back of her hair and pulling her deeper into the kiss, moaning in pleasure.

Grace groaned, her earlier reticence dissolving in the liquid heat that seemed to impede her ability to rationalise the situation. Urgency building, she wrapped her arms around Harriet's waist and tugged her closer. She slid a hand under Harriet's jumper, finding soft warm skin at her fingertips.

Harriet let out a guttural groan and pulled out of the kiss. 'Please come in with me,' she said.

Grace held the caressing eyes, the intensity and depth pleading to her, the goose bumps on the skin under her palm a reflection of Harriet's desires. She nodded, and her heart raced. She let her hand drop from the contact and followed Harriet into the cottage.

Flo and Archie greeted them enthusiastically and at that point Grace resented their presence.

'Go pee,' Harriet said, and the dogs ran into the garden, returning a moment later. 'Bed,' and they went.

Impressive. Maybe they weren't so bad after all.

Harriet tilted her head indicating towards the stairs and started walking.

Grace followed her, her heart pounding, louder with every step closer to the bedroom. She stood, just inside the room, her back to the door, her insides in a spin.

Harriet closed the door.

Grace could feel Harriet behind her, assessing her, but something in the unspoken told her not to turn around. She moaned at the tingling sensation that ran from her spine to her fingertips, as Harriet kissed the nape of her neck and trailed a finger down her back. Harriet lifted the jumper over Grace's head and dropped it to the floor, removing her own and

195

dropping it on the same spot. Harriet found the nape of her neck again and kissed around and up to her ear, nipping the lobe and breathing into her ear. Harriet's hands reached around Grace and slowly, one by one started to unbutton her shirt.

Grace moaned, feeling disempowered by the fact that Harriet remained behind her and in control, every cell in her body screaming to her to turn around and kiss Harriet, to touch her, to discover every inch of her sexy body. She went to move and Harriet tugged her closer, and Grace moaned again at the sensation of Harriet's breasts pressing into her back, the hands firmly against her abdomen. And then Harriet moved a hand down and undid her jeans and teased along the line of Grace's underwear and Grace groaned loudly.

'Harriet,' Grace moaned and Harriet teased lower, the lips at her neck becoming more urgent, biting and searching.

'God, you feel good,' Harriet moaned.

'Touch me,' Grace said, and Harriet's hand slipped down further and Grace's desire exploded at the sensation of Harriet's fingers at her wet centre.

Urgency overtook Grace and she turned swiftly and found Harriet's mouth with hers, her hand around Harriet's head and pulling her closer. Clashing teeth, tongues desperately licking, biting, tasting, the intensity soared. Grace pulled out of the frantic kiss, struggling for breath, and held Harriet's dark gaze with her own. 'Fuck me,' she said, her voice broken.

Harriet kicked off her shoes, and Grace did the same. They ripped off their clothes, dropping them where they stood and faced each other, naked, unashamedly admiring each other.

'You're so fucking adorable,' Grace said, her tone subtly deeper. She reached out and ran her fingers over the soft, fleshy part of Harriet's breast and then lingered at the swollen bud at the centre, watching it transform and heave with Harriet's breath. She studied the delicate quivering of Harriet's lips, the desire in her eyes; her own response evident in the throbbing and wetness at her centre.

Harriet placed her index finger at Grace's lips, and Grace could smell her own scent there.

She kissed the finger taking it into her mouth, stealing the essence of herself, then moved to Harriet and gave herself back to her in a lingering kiss.

Harriet's arousal propelling her, she backed Grace to the bed, stopped kissing her and held her attention with a piercing gaze. She reached up, teased Grace's nipple, and rested her palm in the centre of Grace's chest. Then, unceremoniously, and without warning, she pushed Grace backwards onto the bed.

Grace's feet remained firmly fixed to the floor and she landed on her bottom before falling onto her back, Harriet stood over her, admiring her form with enquiring eyes.

Harriet lowered to her knees and ran her palms from Grace's knees up to her centre, and when Harriet's thumbs continued the journey, the first exposing her and the second taking advantage of the swollen bud, Grace's head flew off the bed, her body jerking violently.

'Fuck, what did you just do to me?' Grace said, and then groaned as the sensation faded and she fell back to the bed.

Harriet grinned and repeated the movement, trailing along the excruciatingly sensitive inside of Grace's thighs and again, her thumbs had Grace jolting from the bed.

'Fuck!' Grace said. She leaned towards Harriet and tried to kiss her, but Harriet pushed her back and she flopped down again, the back of her hand finding her forehead, her teeth finding her lip in anticipation of what was to come. 'Ahh,' she groaned, jerking again and again as the electric flames grew stronger, each time driving her closer to the edge.

Harriet moaned with pleasure and teased with fingers and thumbs exploring Grace with delightful sensitivity and precision.

Grace cried out in the absence of the pressure and the burning fire at her core eased, and then it came again, and she felt the sensation more deeply and it stayed with her for longer.

Harriet was relentless, and her timing and touch in perfect harmony with Grace.

'Oh, fuck,' Grace moaned. 'Harriet, no, wait. Kiss me.'

Harriet grinned, ignoring Grace's pleas, and continued to explore her. She watched the tension build in Grace's expression, fall away, and build again, sensed the shift in Grace as the vibration started to take hold of her.

'Kiss me,' Grace murmured, and then groaned as Harriet's lips took hers. And then she could feel Harriet inside her and it was as if she were floating inside a kaleidoscope, drowning in sensations, vivid colours dancing, forming and then dissipating. With every movement, Grace descended. Lower, deeper, drowning in wave after wave and then rising, rising, rising, and then she couldn't breathe and the explosion that followed stayed with her, holding her in a space and time in which she wanted to remain, forever. Harriet's lips, against hers, came into her awareness. The kisses were tender and she could taste iron. She tugged Harriet down to rest on top of her, inhaled the scent of her; every part of her tingling from the aftershock of orgasm. 'Where did you learn to do that?' she said.

Harriet kissed Grace as if to quiet her, then pulled back and studied her with deep affection.

Overcome by the giggles Grace started chuckling and tried unsuccessfully to move her legs. 'I'm stuck,' Grace said and moaned as she lifted herself onto the bed.

Harriet eased up onto her elbows and grinned at Grace. 'You expected a country bumpkin?' she said, raising her eyebrows.

'If that's country bumpkin, I've been living the wrong side of town,' Grace said and ran her thumb across Harriet's sweet lips. 'Of course, we might need to compare notes,' she said, with a wicked and wild-looking grin.

'Oh yeah?' Harriet teased.

Grace shifted up the bed, pulled Harriet with her. Grace turned onto her side, lifted onto her elbow and rested her head against her hand, observing Harriet, the softness of her skin, the fine bone structure, the perfect breasts and then the curve of her hip.

Harriet watched Grace watching her.

Grace reached out and rested her palm lightly in the centre Harriet's chest and closed her eyes as if sensing her.

Harriet watched the subtle shift in Grace's expression, the change in her breathing, aware of her own racing pulse and the sense of anticipation pulsing between her legs.

Grace's touch lightened, barely making contact.

Harriet felt nothing, and then her breathing hitched as the lightest touch caused her skin to goose bump and a swift surge of energy to head south. She bit down on closed lips to silence the rising groan and closed her eyes. Oh my God, this was excruciating. And then a tingling wave swept through her. Sensing Grace close to her, the goose bumps continuing to spread down her abdomen and up her spine and yet she couldn't locate Grace in her mind's eye. It seemed she was everywhere. 'Oh God,' she moaned as Grace slipped fingers between her legs and teased the slick wet heat. Harriet's back arched as if seeking out everything Grace could give. And Grace entered her and was giving to her, slowly, and deeply and Harriet was demanding more. And then the softest touch sent a flash of fire through Harriet, as Grace tenderly awakened the sensitive bud at her centre with the delicate pressure of her tongue. She could feel Grace inside and out, drawing her in, lifting her up, and taking her to screaming point. 'Oh God, Grace, Grace!' The words came on a wave that swept her into insensibility. The pounding of her heart came into her awareness, and then soft vibrations consumed her. Warmth radiated close to her, and then there was the fire and wetness between her legs. She flicked her eyes open to find Grace's dark gaze on her. The intensity of the look stole her breath, and then the kiss that followed left her heart open and aching.

Grace breathed Harriet in, tasting her, imprinting her, etching the essence of her into every memory of Harriet, and she placed tender kisses to her forehead, her cheeks, her lips, her eyelids. She eased back and regarded Harriet with tenderness. 'I'm in love with you,' she whispered and watched a tear appear at the outer edge of Harriet's eye and slide down her temple. She studied the glassy eyes and pressed a thumb to Harriet's lips.

Harriet reached up and cupped Grace's face. 'Please don't say that,' she said.

Grace took Harriet's palm to her lips and breathed in their scent. 'I am,' she said. 'I'm sorry, I didn't mean to fall in love with you, but I have.'

Tears rolled freely from Harriet's eyes and she rubbed at them with the back of her hand.

'Harriet,' Grace said softly, drawing Harriet to look at her. Grace smiled at her, stroked her damp cheek. 'I have never felt this way, ever. I can't help it and I can't just have it go away. It's the most terrifying and yet the most wonderful feeling I've ever experienced,' she said. 'I'm not going to deny it.'

Harriet pulled Grace into a deep, lingering kiss, knowing full well. She had fallen in love with Grace, too.

19.

Grace blinked her eyes open to find the space next to her in the bed empty. She squinted into the sunlight, arousing images of Harriet coming to her, and groaned. She sat up, rubbed her hands through her hair and smiled at the sensual sensations. Climbing out of bed, she threw on her clothes and went downstairs and into the kitchen, the coffee aroma drawing her eyes to the pot on the hotplate. She poured a cup, spotted Harriet tending to the horses, and felt the truth tug at her heart again. She sighed, sipped the coffee and wandered out to the gate. 'Hey,' she said as she approached.

Harriet stood up from checking Buzz's shoe, patted the horse, and came to the gate. 'Hi,' she said.

Harriet looked radiant and was closing the space between them. She kissed Grace firmly on the lips, creating a chain reaction that had Grace's legs weaken, and when Harriet released her, Grace expressed her appreciation in a guttural moan.

'Later,' Harriet said and smiled. She returned to Buzz and lifted his rear leg, continuing to work.

Grace couldn't stop looking at Harriet, admiring the shape of her as she bent over to lift the horse's hoof from the ground, and she considered what she might like to do with Harriet later and have Harriet do with her. She grinned and then chuckled.

'You going to help or watch?' Harriet said, not looking up.

'Definitely watch,' Grace said, and sipped from her coffee. She wasn't joking.

Harriet glanced in her direction. 'Where's mine?' she said.

'You want, I get?' Grace said.

'Anything?' Harriet said, with more than a hint of suggestion in her tone.

Grace held Harriet's gaze and cleared her throat. 'Yes,' she said.

'Pastries.' Harriet said.

'Pastries.' Grace repeated.

'Can you get some from the café? And we need more sugar,' she said.

What a comedown.

'Sure,' Grace said.

'Thanks,' Harriet said and continued to give her attention to Buzz.

Grace wandered back to the house, put her cup on the counter and made her way into town to pick up the sugar and pastries. Her thoughts drifted to the previous evening, the night, and her admission of love. In the cold light of day, she felt even more certain of her feelings. She felt exposed, yes, the get inside your soul and rip your heart out kind of exposed, but also strangely fulfilled. And the feeling transcended every part of her. No part of her objecting, finding excuses, or challenging her in any way. Absolutely, she was totally in love with Harriet Haversham and that truth wasn't going away any time soon.

Uplifted, she lengthened her stride. It was a fabulous, amazing, magnificent day. She breathed in the familiar aromas; the blossom on the hedgerows and in the trees that had come into their fullest form over the week, aided by the sunny warmer weather, the ferns and wildflowers that dotted the undergrowth with colour, even the heady scent of the earth that formed the hills. It all combined to provide a signature that was, Duckton-by-Dale. And that signature had been imprinted on her. It was a part of who she had become. Maybe it was part of who she had always been? It felt right and it felt so fucking good. She looked up with a broad grin, blue skies as far as the eye could see. It would be another warm day. Fucking amazing! She wanted to laugh hysterically and pondering the idea of doing so decided that no one here would give a monkey's if she did. She chuckled to herself, her inhibitions holding her back as she became aware of people moving around in the village.

'Hello, Mrs Akeman,' Grace said, waving to Doris across the road as she headed in the direction of the shop.

'Good morning, Grace,' Doris said and waved back.

'Morning Doug,' she said as she entered the shop.

'Morning, Grace, you survived last night then?' he said.

'I did indeed Doug. Very informative,' she said and chuckled.

'Got that policy written yet?' he teased. He stepped the two paces from the shop counter and to the post office counter, picked up an envelope and returned to the till. 'This came for you,' he said. 'Needs signing for,' he added. 'Saves Gary a trip over to your place.'

Gary was Doris's son and the local postman. Grace had rarely seen the man reputed to be the most eligible bachelor in the village. Apparently, he took his commitment to support the community seriously; his personal services extending beyond licking stamps to frequent special deliveries to preferential customers, it was rumoured, and Grace didn't doubt his dedication to the task.

Grace smiled. 'Thanks. I need some sugar.'

'Next to the cereal, lower shelf,' Doug said, pointing.

Grace followed his directions picked up a bag and set it on the counter.

'Here you go,' Doug said, presenting a book and pen. He handed over the envelope and she signed for the letter.

'Cheers, Doug. Have a great day,' she said. She paid for the sugar and studied the envelope, curious to know what was inside. It could only be from her work, and that realisation elicited an unpleasant feeling and her stomach churned. She left the shop and walked across the road to get the pastries.

'Hey, Grace, what can I get you?' Drew said.

'Two pastries, please?'

'Which ones?'

Fuck! 'Umm, I'm not sure. What does Harriet prefer?'

'Pecan and maple syrup,' Drew said, and Grace felt a slight twitchiness niggle her.

'If she's got a major hangover, it will most likely be pancakes with maple syrup or a full English, and whichever it is it has to be with a double Espresso,' Drew said, popping the Danish into a bag. 'What about you?' she asked.

'When I have a hangover?' Grace said.

'Well you can share if you like, but I was thinking more about right now?' she said, holding up the bag.

'Oh, I'll have the same,' Grace responded. She'd never eaten a pecan Danish in her life, but what the hell.

'Sure.' Drew put in a second Pecan Danish and handed over the bag.

Grace pulled out her wallet and waited.

'It's on me,' Drew said, and smiled.

Grace responded to the gesture with a smile that felt tighter and more restrained than the one she had received. 'Thanks, I'll let Harriet know,' she said.

'You have a great day.'

'You too.'

Grace was aware of being watched until she was out of view of the café. She wandered back to the house, pondering her feelings towards Drew. She shouldn't feel jealous after the night she had just shared with Harriet. Harriet was certainly attracted to her, even if she hadn't made any open declaration of love. Grace had sensed it, really sensed it. It was perfectly natural for Drew to know a lot about Harriet, of course. They had known each other all their lives, spent a lot of time with each other, and understood each other, well. Fuck! Harriet had made love to her though, and she had made love to Harriet, and

204

right now that was what mattered. The rest would come with time.

Flo bounded towards Grace as she approached the cottage. 'Hello girl,' she said, bracing herself, and ruffled the dog's neck, dropping the letter in the process.

Flo accepted the attention and then ran back into Harriet's and she picked up the mail and was still trying to juggle with it, the sugar, and the pastries, as she entered the kitchen.

'Here goes,' Grace said, landing the sugar and pastries on the table.

Harriet looked up from the sink. 'A letter,' she said.

'Yes. I'll open it later, probably work, or mum,' Grace said, hating the white lie that slipped effortlessly from her lips.

Harriet poured Grace a coffee and sat at the kitchen table.

Grace sat and dived hungrily into the Danish. 'This is good,' she said.

'Always,' Harriet said.

'Yes, Drew said it was your favourite.'

'Good,' Harriet said and sipped her coffee, her attention on Grace. 'Do you want to go to the barbeque later? If not, we can just go and collect Winnie this morning?'

Grace shrugged as she chewed. 'What would you like to do?'

'Spend time with you,' Harriet said.

Grace felt her mouth dry and the pastry was suddenly hard to swallow. She sipped at the coffee. 'Me too,' she said and smiled. 'I'll finish this and get changed and then we can decide.' The thought of time alone with Harriet filtered through to a mischievous grin and a sparkle in the eyes that rested flagrantly on Harriet's breasts. Harriet was blushing and Grace, head resting at an angle, grinned encouragingly.

'I'll be in the greenhouse,' Harriet said. She rose from the table and the dogs chased out the door. Moving to Grace's side she lifted her chin and kissed her with lingering tenderness. 'I feel the same way,' she said and walked out the door.

Grace finished her pastry and coffee slowly, picked up the letter and wandered across the driveway. When she opened the door, it was almost as if she were entering the house for the first time. Harriet's cottage felt far more familiar, and way more intimate.

Anticipation bubbled inside her and she ripped open the envelope and pulled out its contents as she climbed the stairs and entered the bedroom. Focusing on the large print, the headline seemed to take a long time to register. She stumbled towards the bed and sat, abandoning the letter beside her, the eruption inside flowing freely to her hands and down her legs.

'You've got to be fucking kidding me.'

In all her years working in business, any letter that began with the phrase 'Without Prejudice', had trouble written all over it. Her eyes moved directly to the bottom of the page. Stephanie's fucking signature! Where was the text, the email? And then she realised she hadn't looked at her phone in the last twenty-four hours. 'Shit, fucking, fuck.' She started from the top of the page, painstakingly reading every word.

In the light of the new evidence, it began. What fucking new evidence? She read further.

Sandra Floss has agreed to withdraw the allegation of sexual harassment she has lodged against you, and thus the company… That was progress. Providing that, what? No, No, No! No way am I giving up my fucking company for Sandra fucking Floss. No fucking way! Grace stood, picked up the letter and paced the room. Settlement? She read further. Two hundred thousand pounds and share options forfeited. There has got to be some mistake. The shares alone are worth over two million. What the fuck! No, No, No! This is not happening.

Grace continued to read. Sandra fucking Floss was willing to withdraw the allegation for a compensation payment and essentially evidence of the annihilation of Grace's career. Failure to agree the terms would result in a civil case of sexual assault being brought against her, which would not only be detrimental to her position and reputation but would also seriously damage the company's share price. In the Board's considered view, Grace would be advised to accept the terms as stated and walk away with her reputation intact.

The Board had been made privy to an audio file from an interaction between Grace and Ms Floss, which had taken place following the post-event party in April. Apparently, Ms Floss's version of events had been corroborated. Two employees had independently stated that Grace had bought Ms Floss drinks at the party and that the two women had been clearly seen touching each other and making eye contact, which the witnesses considered to be of a sensual nature. Witnesses! The word coercion had been used by the same witnesses, which was of great concern to the Board. Furthermore, an ex-employee had also come forward, claiming they were sexually harassed by Grace Pinkerton during their time with the company and stated it had been their main reason for leaving their employment. Whilst the Board were not inclined to confirm or support the allegations made by the ex-employee, they did feel there was enough cause for concern and that there might be a case to be answered. It had been agreed that if publicity of this nature could be avoided it would be better for all parties concerned. Of course, Grace should seek legal advice before confirming her acceptance of the terms set out in the enclosed agreement, but again the Board strongly recommended...

Grace dropped the letter onto the bed and picked up the paperwork that accompanied the letter. Her hands were still trembling as she scanned the compromise agreement with small, yellow tags attached to several pages, indicating where she needed to sign. Fuck that! She needed to speak to

Stephanie. This wasn't supposed to happen. Best interests my arse!

Grace went downstairs and grabbed her mobile from the kitchen surface. Fuck, no battery. She went back to the bedroom, connected it to the charger, sat on the bed and flipped open her laptop. The damn thing wouldn't fire up quickly enough and her instinct was to launch it across the room. She waited, her knees bouncing underneath the machine, her stomach turning in knots. Finally! She opened her email and Stephanie's name popped up. The message was brief, confirming the letter had been sent and needed signing asap, and ideally within seven working days, apologising for the delay and reaffirming the fact that the contents of the letter and associated documentation contained the Board's recommended course of action. Stephanie would be out of reach over the weekend, but in the office and could take a call on Monday should there be anything Grace might wish to discuss.

Grace slammed the lid down and threw the laptop across the bed. Fuck! She stood, paced the room and stopped at the window. As she stared out across the valley, she became aware of the vibration consuming her. She held out her hands to observe them shaking, the energy draining out of her and leaving her feeling weak, confused, and isolated. Harriet! She couldn't tell Harriet. How do you explain to the person you are in love with that you've been accused of a sexual offence? And worst still, that from the victim's and the Board's perspective there was a genuine case to answer.

It didn't matter that hurting Sandra Floss hadn't been Grace's intention. She would never wish that sort of harm on anyone, but she could see how her behaviour might have been wrongly construed as predatory and sexually aggressive. The witnesses hadn't seen the looks across the boardroom, the seductive smiles and innuendo that had passed from Sandra to her. She hadn't been making it up. Sandra Floss had been coming on to her for weeks before the event. Was it all planned? Grace held her head in her hands and slumped to the bed. It was twisted, perverse, and unjust on every level, and she couldn't help but feel set up. She didn't have an answer, but every person on her Board would know she wasn't capable of this alleged assault and she was dismayed that they hadn't defended her case with more vigour.

Grace's mind started to spin. Shit, was this about power? With her out of the way, the Board, and Stephanie, would be able to follow the more aggressive growth plans she had fought so hard against. Yes, she had been a thorn in their side at times, but she had made the right choices for the company. They were too greedy and too willing to take unnecessary risks, but to go this far? Surely not! Stephanie wouldn't do this to her, would she? The Board's focus on increasing shareholder value had been driven by short-sightedness and she had told them so. Was that what this was all about? She had no proof; it was just a hunch. She needed to speak to Stephanie. Fucking, Monday!

Her hands were still shaking and she felt sick. She sat, controlling her breathing, trying to guide her attention back to Harriet and the time they had spent together, but even those thoughts just left a dark empty feeling and a pain that seemed to cut through her. She stood and went to the shower.

Grace washed and dressed slowly, all the while processing the situation, raw anger filling her in waves and urging her desire to fight back, to defend her position. She stood at the window and gazed down at Buzz and Fizz, the dogs sniffing around in the grass, chewing something, and Harriet just doing what she always did. Harriet held her attention and emptiness filled her and then the emptiness moved through her in waves and tears rolled onto her cheeks. Oh my God, what would she say to Harriet? They had shared the most intimate times Grace had ever experienced; she trusted Harriet and Harriet had put trust in her too. This would break Harriet. She wiped the tears from her cheeks and tried to breathe deeply. There was nothing she could do about anything until Monday. Then, she would speak to Stephanie and come up with a plan.

Grace tried to bring her mind to the present and collecting Winnie. Perhaps a barbeque with strangers would take her mind off things? Every ounce of her being wanted to be alone, but that wouldn't be fair to Harriet either. She needed to put on a brave face and make sure Harriet didn't sense a problem. She took in a deep breath and blew out hard, controlling the shaking that still vibrated through her. If she stayed in the bedroom, she would just oscillate between anger and sadness. She needed her CEO head on, the one that had to step onto the podium no matter what and perform for the audience. Right, let's do this, she said and puffed out a few times before heading down the stairs and across the drive.

'Hmm!' Harriet said, undressing Grace with her eyes as Grace approached. 'You look good, smell good too,' Harriet said, her cheeks rosy, her smile inviting. And then she looked at Grace. 'What's wrong?' she said.

Shit, Grace was clearly out of practise on the performing front!

'Nothing,' Grace said, putting on her bravest smile. Harriet was still staring at her as if confirming her suspicions. Grace hoped she wouldn't push the topic further.

'Do you fancy barbeque or quiet day?' Harriet said.

Quiet day flew into Grace's mind. 'Barbeque will be great,' she said, with a firm commitment to distracting herself by being around people.

Harriet tilted her head, seeking Grace's evasive eyes, and Grace felt the discomfort drowning her.

'I honestly don't mind,' Harriet said.

Grace shrugged and looked towards the cottage.

'You sure nothing's wrong?' Harriet said.

Grace cleared her throat and looked back to Harriet. 'It's just business; it's nothing to worry about,' she said.

'You look worried,' Harriet said.

Fuck, fuck. This wasn't going to be easy.

'I,' Grace started and then stopped.

Harriet was frowning, leaning towards Grace, waiting for more. 'What?' she said.

'I need to speak to my Board on Monday about something, that's all,' Grace said and felt the pain shift inside her.

Harriet smiled and seemed to relax. 'Okay,' she said. She reached out and cupped Grace's cheek. 'You had me really worried for a moment. I thought there was something seriously wrong,' Harriet said.

Grace felt the touch burn right through her, enflame the lie that was seeking the deepest, darkest cavern in her mind in which to hide. No, she couldn't tell Harriet. She just needed to find some way of dealing with this and make it all go away. Harriet stepped towards her and when the soft, tender kiss landed, it damn near swept the feet from beneath her. In the absence of Harriet's lips, the tingling continued to resonate and merged to create a cocktail of confusion and agony. 'You feel good,' Grace said.

'I have an idea,' Harriet said and she took Grace's hand and led her into the house. The dogs chased into the living room and Harriet shut the front door.

Grace was aware of her racing heart, but instead of the thrill that had butterflies dancing at the thought of making love to Harriet, she felt anxious and guilty. Harriet walked past the stairs and opened another door and Grace released a long breath and followed her.

'Come on.' Harriet insisted. 'I promised to show you how to develop film and print photos,' she said.

'Oh!' That hadn't been on Grace's mind, at all, but she was relieved.

'If I'm feeling out of sorts, I'll come down here,' Harriet said. 'There's something cathartic about developing photographs,' she said.

Grace nodded and followed Harriet into the darkroom.

Grace gazed around the dimly lit space and then her eyes fixed on Harriet and there was only one thought on her mind. Sandra fucking Floss!

Grace's smile must have revealed that thought because Harriet reached up and cupped her cheek.

'You can talk to me, Grace,' Harriet said.

No, I can't.

Grace nodded and gave her attention to the workbench.

20.

Grace studied her phone; the minute's ticked by too slowly for her nerves to settle. The weekend had passed with her oscillating from pure joy to intense distress, with more time in distressed mode than joy. Harriet hadn't pressed her any further about work, which had been a good thing, but she had noticed her quizzical gaze from time to time and been overwhelmed with guilt, and sadness. Her heart thumped as she watched another minute tick past. She would feel less nervous presenting to a prestigious group of business executives, royalty even, than she did at the idea of picking up the phone and making this call to Stephanie.

Winnie pottered in from the garden and lay on the cool tiled floor of the hunting room. Flo was sniffing around the bushes, occupying herself. She seemed to enjoy the fact that Winnie was back. Grace felt relieved to see the old dog in better health. She seemed more active and interested, younger even than she had in the previous days. Kelly had said she might have had a low-grade infection for a few days before it blew up and, with hindsight, that seemed to fit Grace's memory of Winnie's behaviour.

She looked at the time again, her heart skipping a beat. It was after 9 am. She poured a coffee, stirred in an extra spoon of sugar, and sipped with hands shaking. She found Stephanie's contact details on her mobile as she went to the living room, picked up the house's landline phone, and dialled the number. She took in a deep breath and puffed out and then the line went silent, and then Stephanie spoke and Grace felt a wave of relief at the familiarity of her voice.

'Hey Stephanie, it's Grace.'
'Grace, how are you?'

Grace picked up the uncharacteristic formality in Stephanie's tone and felt the heckles rise. 'How do you think I am?' she said defensively, the distance between them causing the anger to flare. This wasn't going well.

'Grace, I'm really sorry that it has to be this way,' Stephanie said.

'Stephanie, I'm fucking innocent. What do you mean, has to be this way?'

'Grace?'

The line went silent.

'Grace, we, the Board have considered this unfortunate situation in great detail. God knows we've sought legal counsel, the works. Yes, you can fight it, if you really want, and you could end up in a civil court defending the more serious allegation. Is that what you want?'

'You think I want to defend a charge of sexual assault?' Grace shouted. 'The woman's a fucking nutcase.'

'Well, she's presented evidence, Grace. There's no question that you were the other party involved and no doubting that she said no to your advances,' she said. 'If you can get a witness, an ex-girlfriend, or several, to say that this is out of character for you, then maybe it would give us something else to go on,' Stephanie said, and Grace picked up more than a hint of sarcasm in her voice.

Grace looked to the ceiling. Stephanie knew Grace couldn't approach any ex-girlfriend; for a start, no one Grace had been with qualified as such. Asking for a character witness from any of her lovers was simply rubbing salt in a raw wound. She wanted to scream down the line at Stephanie but released a silent breath and controlled her tone. 'I don't have anyone I can ask to be a character witness for me, as well you know, Stephanie,' she said calmly.

Stephanie damn near sniggered down the line. 'That doesn't help either of us, Grace.'

214

'I know, but surely there's someone who can talk sense into Sandra fucking Floss?'

Harriet stood, frozen in the foyer, the words Sandra fucking Floss and sexual assault, ringing in her ears and causing her head to spin.

'Stephanie, the woman's fucking mad.'

Grace blaming?

'No, I didn't take things too far. You can't tell me a woman hasn't said 'no' to you in a moment of passion, and you've...' Grace stopped talking and bit on her lip to silence herself.

Sandra Floss said no?

'No, I'm not accusing you of anything, Stephanie, of course, I'm not. I'm just saying.' Grace stopped talking. She didn't know what she was trying to say but whatever words she used didn't seem to be helping her case. 'We were both drunk,' she said.

Harriet's hand clasped her mouth to prevent the gasp escaping and alerting Grace as to her presence.

'I don't know anything about these other allegations.'

There are others! Harriet ran out the door and across the drive.

'I'm being set up, Stephanie. This is a fucking set up and you know it,' Grace said.

'Grace. It's all in the letter. Statements confirming that you plied her with alcohol, coerced her and touched her inappropriately during the evening and then left with her at the end of the night.'

'I didn't ply her with drinks,' Grace shouted.

'Did you buy her a drink and take it to her, while she was with a group of colleagues?'

'Yes.'

'Did you buy anyone else in that group a drink, Grace?'

Grace paused and looked to the ceiling again. 'They were already breaking up for the night when I went across to them,' she said.

'Were you taking them all a drink or just Sandra Floss?' Stephanie persisted.

'Stephanie, I know how this looks.'

Stephanie interrupted her. 'Grace, in this business, how things look is all that matters.'

She was right, and Grace fucking knew it.

'Tell me, Stephanie, does any of this have anything to do with my relationship to the Board?'

Silence came back at her.

'No, Grace, it doesn't. Your,' she paused. 'Your relationship to the Board has been a little fractious at times and that's accepted as a given, but that has had no bearing on this decision. We are trying to save your company and your reputation, Grace.'

'It won't be my fucking company though will it, Stephanie?'

Silence.

'You're asking me to forfeit my rights to my shares and accept a payoff that is worth ten times less than my shareholding is worth.'

'You know the company doesn't have two million to pay out, Grace. This is a fair offer under the circumstances. The company also needs to make a significant payment to Ms Floss to make all this go away, Grace. Or, there's a civil case in court that will be hanging over all our heads Grace. It's that simple.'

Grace slumped into the sofa and stared at the deer. She related to his position, hung out, dried, and pinned to the wall. 'Fuck you, Stephanie, fuck you,' she said and slammed the handset onto the receiver. She sat staring at the dark-brown eyes, the deer staring back at her. 'I know how you feel, mate,' she said and closed her eyes.

*

Harriet stood with her back pressed firmly against the inside of the cottage front door, her hands shaking, her legs weak and struggling to hold her upright. The thoughts wouldn't relent and she sunk to the floor. And then tears flowed down her cheeks and she sobbed. Who was this woman? She thought she had come to know Grace well, that they had something special, something that might last. Oh my God. How wrong could she be? Was Grace Pinkerton just a self-obsessed, arrogant, egotistical bitch who could swan in and charm people into falling in love with her. Christ, there wasn't a person in the village who hadn't fallen for Grace. Was she that duplicitous? Clearly, Vera didn't know her niece very well at all! Vera wouldn't do this to her. Vera wouldn't expose her in this way. Vera was as much a mother figure to her as her own mother.

Maybe she had misheard, misunderstood? She went over the scene again. Grace was angry, clearly in conversation with someone called Stephanie. But she wasn't talking about this Sandra Floss woman as if it were a case in relation to another colleague. The sudden sabbatical and lack of explanation for her motivation in taking it, and the avoidance of any real discussion about Grace's work now made sense. She had been under investigation, and from the sound of it, she was guilty of sexually assaulting another woman. Grace was a predator of the worst kind.

Harriet covered her mouth with her hand, reminded of the first time they had kissed. Grace had kissed her, and it had felt wrong and Harriet had pushed her away because of it. Oh God, no! The sobs continued, Archie nuzzling at her leg and wanting to play. She couldn't face Grace. Her chest ached with the pain that now swamped every cell in her body. There was no escaping the truth and even though she hadn't been able to bring herself to say the words, she had fallen head over heels in

217

love with Grace, and now? She couldn't even think about now. Now was a pack of lies carefully packaged to effectively deceive and seduce her. She held her head in her hands, hoping she was on the outside of a very bad dream that she would wake up from at any moment. She waited, and the nightmare persisted. Sobs turned to silence and the silence became consumed by emptiness. She felt numb.

Harriet slowly stood, walked to the sink and splashed her face with cold water. Nothing made sense anymore. Even looking out at the horses, Archie at her side, the vegetable plots, the greenhouses, the orchards, none of it – it all felt so oddly distant.

She had immersed herself in the smallholding after Annabel had left and it had been the source of much comfort. Looking out the window now, the only feeling was that of profound hurt. She picked up her mobile and wallet, put Archie on the lead, and headed out the door. She walked straight to the main road, without glancing in the direction of Duckton House. Grace was as good as dead to her. She didn't turn towards town; she went towards the hills. She needed space first, and then, maybe, she would go to the coffee shop and speak to Drew. Drew she could always trust.

*

'You need to talk to Harriet, Grace.'

The voice came again and Grace blinked, opened her eyes. The white-haired lady stood with her back to Grace, staring into the fireplace, the end of the lead swinging freely from her right hand. Grace froze, closed her eyes and opened them again. The vision had disappeared and she found she could turn her head, but not her body. She must have been dreaming. She closed her eyes again, aware that her heart thundered as if trying to break free.

'You need to talk to Harriet, Grace. Explain to her.'

Grace opened her eyes sharply and the woman was walking out the living room door and heading through the foyer.

Grace gulped air into her dry mouth. She blinked several times and the image disappeared again. The deer stared at her and she stared back. 'What are you looking at?' she said.

Finding her feet, she approached the door and scanned the foyer. Nothing. She walked tentatively into the kitchen; both dogs were laid out on their beds in the hunting room. Winnie was snoring. 'Come on, let's go and find Harriet,' she said, compelled not by the words of some figment of her imagination, but the reality that there were chores to be done and she could do with the distraction. She needed a space to think and work out what to do about the offer on the table. Even considering it made her feel powerless and that was irritating. Flo got up and followed her out the door. Winnie made it to the front door and watched as they crossed the driveway.

Grace tried to open the cottage door, finding it locked. Strange! She banged and waited. Nothing. She walked around to the garden, no sign of Harriet or Archie. Archie would have come running by now. She went back to the door and banged harder. She glanced around unable to spot anything that might tell her Harriet was about. She couldn't recall Harriet saying she was going out. On the contrary, they had planned to work together. Maybe, Harriet was in the darkroom. She banged again, even louder, and waited. Flo whined at her and yawned. 'I don't think they're in,' she said.

Flo whined again and let out a single bark.

'Come on,' she said and walked back to the house, Flo bounding excitedly. She stood in the kitchen for a long time, wondering what to do next, and it dawned on her how much a part of her life Harriet had become. It was as if Harriet had always existed, and in her absence, something significant and wonderful had been stolen from her. Fuck London fuck the business and fuck Sandra fucking Floss. None of them compared to Harriet. Not even close. Where was Harriet? Sod it! She reached for the blue bottle and poured a large gin and tonic. And who gives a fuck that it's only 11 am. She needed to think.

*

Harriet walked into the coffee shop and slumped into the seat and Archie immediately laid out on the cool tiled floor by her feet.

'Hey Harriet, what?' Drew looked up from the counter and immediately stopped talking. She walked over to Harriet and sat next to her. Watching the tears spill onto Harriet's cheeks, she got up, switched the sign to closed and locked the door. 'Come on,' she said, taking Harriet by the hand and leading her through the back and up the stairs to the flat above the café.

Archie lifted his head watched them leave then resumed his position on the floor releasing a puff of air as he settled.

'Sit,' Drew ordered, and Harriet sat. Drew reached into the fridge and took out an unlabelled green bottle. She poured two glasses and sat next to Harriet, handing her a glass. 'It's your mum's special,' she said and managed a hint of a smile, though her gaze remained sombre. She took a large slug of the substance and declared, 'Not bad. That's got a better taste to it.' She looked at Harriet. 'Right, what's happened? You look God awful.'

Tears flowed onto Harriet's cheeks and she wiped them away as fast as they came. She sipped at the drink, the flavour not registering, and stared at the wall opposite her. 'Grace isn't who I thought she was,' she said.

Drew frowned. 'What do you mean?'

'I thought she was honourable, honest, kind.'

'What makes you think she isn't?'

Harriet swallowed. She felt bad enough for spying on Grace, let alone confessing that much to Drew. 'I overheard a conversation she was having with a work colleague this morning.'

'And?'

Harriet turned to face Drew. 'She sexually assaulted another woman, more than one by the sound of it,' Harriet said.

Drew frowned and started shaking her head. 'That doesn't make sense. Why would Vera and your mum try and set you two up if Grace was like that?'

Harriet held her head in her hands. 'I knew they were up to something,' she said.

'No matter about that, you were both getting on really well together despite their interference.'

'Vera obviously doesn't know about this.'

'No.' Drew pondered, sipping from the glass. 'Are you absolutely sure?'

'I heard her talking, Drew. Saying the woman was mad, needing to have someone talking some sense into her. The woman said no, Drew, and Grace still had sex with her.'

'Fuck! That sounds serious. Has Grace said anything to you?'

Harriet looked away. 'I haven't seen her today. I couldn't. I can't be with another woman like that, Drew, I can't do it.'

'Whoa, I know. I know.' Drew put her arm around Harriet and pulled her closer.

Harriet moved out of the hold and stared at Drew. 'She got a letter in the post on Saturday and has been strange ever since,' Harriet said. 'It must be related to the conversation.'

'What are you going to do?'

'I need her to leave.'

'What about the dogs?'

'I'll look after them,' Harriet said. 'That was the original idea anyway, until those two concocted some hideous plan to get me together with a psycho bunny boiler,' Harriet said. Saying the words hurt.

'How are you going to get Grace to leave?'

Harriet held Drew's gaze.

'You want me to go talk to her?'

'Would you?'

Drew held her head in her hands. Fuck! She took in a deep breath. It all sounded very odd, but she wasn't in Harriet's position, so who was she to offer sound advice? She looked into the red, puffy, pleading eyes. 'For you, yes,' she said softly.

Harriet nodded, wiped at streaming tears. 'I feel so betrayed,' she said.

'Come here,' Drew said and hugged Harriet.

Fuck!

21.

'It's all gone tits, Vera!' Jenny slurred. She'd already supped more than half a bottle of home brew. Delia sat at the table nodding her head as Jenny spoke, having supped the remainder of the bottle and just started on the next.

'What do you mean, it's all gone tits?'

'Upside down justice – dishonesty,' Delia slurred. As if that would make more sense to Vera.

'Harriet and Grace.' Jenny said.

'They were getting married, last we spoke.' Vera said.

Jenny paused before speaking. 'I might have been mistaken,' she said. 'What are we going to do?'

'What do you mean, dishonesty?' Vera said, her tone shifting to concern. 'Jenny, what's happened?

'Grace has gone.' Jenny said.

'What do you mean gone,' Vera said, with increasing alarm. 'For God's sake, Jenny, have you been on the hooch?'

'She upped and left for London this morning,' Jenny said.

'What the hell happened?'

Nell had come to stand by Vera's side and held her concerned gaze with her own, equally perturbed look.

'Eight of cups,' Delia chirped up. 'Walking away.'

'Shut the fuck up, Delia,' Jenny blurted.

Delia mumbled inaudibly and poured them both another drink.

'Apparently, the reason she's off work is that she was under investigation,' Jenny said.

Nell gasped.

'Investigation for what? Fraud? What?'

Jenny braced herself, paused, took in a deep breath and spoke quietly. 'She sexually assaulted another woman.'

'What?' Vera and Nell chorused.

'No way,' Nell said. 'No way, that's not Grace at all. She may not have found the right one yet, but she's got boundaries. She wouldn't do that,' Nell insisted.

'That doesn't sound right at all?' Vera said, shaking her head.

'What did Grace say about it?'

The line went quiet.

'Jen, what did Grace have to say?'

'Well.'

'Well, what?'

'Harriet couldn't face Grace after she overheard the conversation and Drew went to the house and asked Grace to leave. No one saw Grace before she left.'

'Oh, for fuck sake, Jen. So, no one has actually asked Grace?'

Jenny couldn't speak.

'How is Harriet?' Vera asked.

'Devastated. She's not talking to me. Says it's my fault for interfering in the first place. She's got the dogs with her.' Jenny added.

'We need to do something. We need to talk to Grace.' Vera said.

'I'll call Grace,' Nell said.

'Jenny, listen to me carefully. We need an intervention.' Vera said.

Delia started shuffling the cards.

'What kind of intervention?' Jenny slurred. 'Bryan has already told me to keep away and stop interfering. Said, Harriet told him to tell me that,' she said.

'Pah!' Vera retorted. 'That was until this little turn of events. Things just got serious, Jen,' she said. 'We're not staying out of this, now. The girls need our help.'

Delia turned three cards: The Knight of Cups, the Ten of Swords reversed and the Star. 'Ooh, that's looking up,' she said.

'What's that?' Vera said, unable to make out what was happening at the other end of the line.

'Delia's doing the cards,' Jenny said.

'What do they say?'

'Following the heart and it can't get any worse,' Delia said.

'Well that's fucking reassuring,' Vera said and Jenny sensed the sarcasm.

'And there's hope, faith and rejuvenation,' Delia added.

'Hmm!' Vera mumbled. 'I bloody hope so. There's no way Grace is involved in anything like this. No way at all.'

'You sound certain,' Jenny said.

'Of course, I'm bloody certain,' Vera shouted. 'Run the bloody cards on it, Delia.'

Delia seemed to wander into a trance, and then turned over the top card. 'Justice,' she said and beamed a smile.

'What the fuck does that mean? Justice came up last time; I remember it,' Jenny said.

'That was reversed,' Delia said. 'So, it could mean that there has been an injustice and that the truth will come out,' she said.

'You mean she didn't do it?' Jenny pondered. 'Hang on, you said the Justice reversed was about dishonesty, last time,' she said to Delia.

Delia's cheeks darkened. 'Well, it can be about unfairness too,' she admitted. 'It's not always easy to tell.'

Jenny groaned. 'So, Grace didn't do anything wrong?'

'Not according to the cards,' Delia confirmed. 'More likely she's on the receiving end of an injustice. That the truth will come out.'

'We need an intervention,' Jenny confirmed.

'Nell and I will talk to Grace. Jenny, you and Delia need to convince Harriet.' Vera said.

'Good plan,' Jenny said.

Delia turned the Wheel of Fortune. It was inevitable, fate.

*

Grace looked at the ringing phone and pressed the decline button. There was no way she was going to speak to her mother. She would delete the answerphone message without listening to it, as she had done all week.

'Leave me alone,' she mumbled.

She picked up her glass and sipped, re-reading the contract from the top for the third time. She wasn't expecting to see anything different. It was just some vain attempt to adjust to the fact that she needed to sign and return it before the day was over or run the risk of ending up in court with a more extreme charge hanging over her head.

Something really didn't sit right. Yes, she had made a poor, and stupid decision. She'd been seduced by a good-looking woman. She had succumbed to the thrill of achievement, her inhibitions suppressed by the free flow of alcohol and charmed by the flirtatious banter. She had been duped. But why would Sandra Floss do this to her? She hadn't struck Grace as the vindictive kind, and Grace had always been a good judge of character. It didn't stack up.

She leaned back in the chair, the warmth of the sun on her face, and images of Harriet came to her. The tightness in her chest increased and emptiness filled her. Tears made their way through closed eyes and slid down her cheeks.

Drew had tried to be tactful, but she too had been angry at Grace and there had been no chance to explain her perspective. Grace had felt more alone at that moment than in any other in her life. The realisation that she would never see Harriet again had landed like a lead weight and drained the essence of life from her. Bryan had been kind enough to drop her at the station, and he seemed to be empathic when Grace had denied the allegation, but he was a man of the village and Harriet was his daughter.

Travelling back to London had happened in a fog of disbelief and when she had opened the door to her flat the chill had taken hold of her. It still hadn't lifted. The emptiness hadn't shifted all week; she hadn't expected that it would. It would never lift. Her life was worthless, and hope was a word without meaning. Anything that meant something to her was in a village a long way from London, a place that was out of reach to her physically, but the thought of what might have been would continue to torture her. She now knew what it felt like to have someone get inside her soul and then rip it up and stamp all over it. She sipped at the drink and stared once again at the paperwork.

She had tried to arrange to go into work to speak to Stephanie, but she had been wrapped up with important meetings all week and could only speak briefly on the phone. She'd had nothing to add to the points in the letter and reminded Grace that the Board needed a decision before the deadline.

That day had arrived. Grace wiped away the tears and felt the familiar surge of anger flood her. She suppressed a scream and slugged at the drink, running her fingers vigorously through her hair. She leafed the sheets of the contract. This is what fifteen-years of hard fucking graft looked like.

Two hundred thousand pounds!

It wasn't about the money, though. The thing that she valued didn't have a pound sign against it. She had decided, before Drew had asked her to leave, that she would give everything up for Harriet; for a chance to create a life with

Harriet. Harriet with her micro-farm; Harriet with her photography. Harriet with the dogs, the walks, the time spent gazing out over acres of green, and the hills, the stream, the picnic, and the horses. Christ, even the meetings and pub quiz. She had enjoyed the riding lessons, especially the last one, Harriet coaching Luce and then Luce coaching Grace as they both walked the horses around the yard. It was as close as she had ever felt to being part of a family, and then within twenty-four hours, that family had been ripped from her. That was a wound that would never heal.

She finished the drink, poured another one and finished that quickly too. She scrawled her signature and initialled all the highlighted pages as per the contract instructions then picked up her mobile. The courier arrived an hour later and took the envelope. She sat back in the chair and gazed around the room. Off-white walls, clean lines, a single vase for decorative purposes, on the window ledge absent of flowers, and a single framed image on the wall. She studied the picture but it didn't touch her. The ambience was different here. It was clinical, a reflection of her lifeless existence in the shallow world of transactions, prestige, and profits.

She had to find a way of getting back to Harriet. She needed to talk to her, explain her side of the story. She was innocent, and surely Harriet would sense that. She needed evidence! Police sirens, car engines, horns beeping, filtered from the outside, and then in a moment of near silence, birdsong reminding her of standing at the landing window of Duckton House and looking out across the fields, and watching Harriet as she tended to the horses.

Another hour passed and Grace sighed. Stephanie would have the documents in her hand now. It was over. Her heart felt heavier and her world had just become smaller, but the absence of any threat brought with it a sense of calm, and then relief flooded her and she sobbed.

*

'Harriet!'

Harriet looked up from the pew she had slid into. She struggled to find her voice. 'Hello Vicar,' she said in almost a whisper.

Elvis sat beside her and they both looked to the large wooden cross on the wall behind the altar. 'How are you, Harriet?' he asked, his voice conveying compassion.

Harriet's eyes glassed over. 'Not good, to be honest,' she said in a whisper.

Elvis nodded. 'If there's anything I can do to help?' he said.

'I can't believe it, Vicar,' she said.

'The world works in mysterious ways,' Elvis said.

Harriet studied the old man. His eyes still sparkled. 'Why do you believe in God?' she said.

Elvis considered the question. 'Because it suits me,' he said.

Harriet frowned.

'I have come to realise that we believe what we want to believe, Harriet. Some people say there is no tangible evidence for God, but that doesn't mean God doesn't exist, and that leaves people free to make their own choices. There are those who would move heaven and hell to try to disprove God's existence of course, and I would just say to them for what purpose? All that would happen is, it would bring down the foundation of other people's existence and in doing so create a world of pain where none needs to exist. Some people just like to prove others wrong and themselves right, Harriet. It's part of the human nature. To blame and accuse can provide the illusion of power and strength, when in truth it is often a sign of insecurity and weakness.'

Harriet considered his words.

Elvis took her hand. 'Sometimes, I think, in people searching long and hard to find evidence for what they want to see, they are missing the point! It is easy to misrepresent our experiences to fit our perspective, Harriet. And that doesn't come from any theories of God; that's just good old science. Communication isn't easy, but confusion is.'

'Do you think Grace is guilty?' Harriet said.

'That's not for me to say,' Elvis said.

Harriet sighed.

'Grace didn't strike me as someone who would wish to hurt anyone, Harriet. But I have nothing substantive to base my judgement on, and frankly, I don't need it. You had a tough time with Annabel. And sometimes it can be difficult to see things clearly when the lens through which we look has been scratched and tarnished. You're a photographer so you of all people know how the aspect changes from day to day. It's easy to see that change when it's on the outside. It's more of a challenge when the lens itself is faulty, everything and everyone is coloured by it.'

Harriet allowed the tears to slide onto her cheeks. 'Do you think I've made a mistake?' she asked.

'Nothing that can't be rectified, Harriet, but the question you need to ask yourself is, will you be able to believe Grace if she tells you she didn't do it? We aren't talking about hard-evidence, Harriet. We're talking about faith. Do you have faith enough to trust her? For you to be able to open your heart to her?'

'I never closed my heart,' Harriet admitted. 'I couldn't. I was angry and scared, and I reacted badly. Now, I think maybe I should have given her a chance to explain,' she said.

'Good!' Elvis said. He stood and straightened his shirt.

'What will I do now?' Harriet said looking to Elvis, and he smiled warmly.

'I'm sure the answer will come to you, Harriet. It's lovely to see you here,' he said.

Harriet nodded. 'Thank you, Vicar,' she said.

Elvis smiled. 'God bless you, Harriet,' he said.

22.

Grace stood gazing out over the busy street, sipping coffee. Even though the sun shone, the world had lost its vibrant colour and zest. But she had had time to think and that had left her more determined than ever. She picked up her mobile and brought up the contact details she needed. She tapped out the message and pressed send before reconsidering the plan. Stephanie had confirmed receipt of the paperwork and she had complied with the instructions not to contact Sandra Floss during the process. But the process was now complete. Sandra Floss had a choice whether she responded to the text or not. Grace wanted to apologise, and, more importantly, she needed to know the truth.

The knocking at her front door took her by surprise. The estate agents weren't scheduled until later. She put down the cup and went to the door, the banging coming again. 'All right,' she shouted and opened the door.

Vera marched past Grace, followed closely by Nell.

Grace stared at Vera. 'What are you doing here? I thought you were on a cruise.' She looked at Nell. 'Mum!' she said.

'And I thought you were looking after my two dogs,' Vera said.

Grace straightened at the jibe. 'I'm sorry I had to leave. I'm sure you've heard already.'

Vera presented a feisty palm. 'I've heard a load of codswallop, is what I've heard. And, from what I can gather, you've walked away from the best thing that's happened in your life,' she said.

Grace rolled her eyes.

'Don't you go rolling your eyes at me, young lady. Your mother and I have been so worried about you.'

Grace hadn't known that.

'Harriet is perfect for you, and you are perfect for her. So, what are you doing down here while she's up there?' Vera said.

Grace sighed. 'It's complicated,' she said.

'It's as bloody complicated as you want to make it. Did you not speak to Harriet, explain yourself, woman?'

'Drew made it clear that Harriet didn't want to speak to me,' Grace said.

'I'm sure she did. She's very protective of Harriet and that's an admirable quality in a good friend, but you didn't do anything wrong, so why wouldn't you go and tell Harriet that?'

'I can't prove it, Vera. It's this woman's word against mine, and the Board have taken the view that.' She stopped. 'It doesn't matter. I've quit my job, I've handed over the company, and the whole thing is in the past.'

Vera frowned. 'What do you mean, you've handed over the company?'

'It was part of the deal.'

'What deal?'

'Look, I don't want to get into this, thanks. I appreciate your coming all this way. Anyway, why aren't you on a cruise.'

'I was never on a bloody cruise,' Vera blurted.

Grace stared at her aunt; eyebrows raised.

'We thought it would be an idea to get you and Harriet together,' Nell admitted.

Grace rubbed her head in her hands. 'So, it was all a ruse to get us together?'

'Not exactly. We knew you two would be good together. It was in the cards, and the cards never lie. It was just a matter of finding an opportunity and with you taking time off from work, well, it all seemed to come together,' Vera said.

Grace started to roll her eyes and then stopped. 'I was suspended from work,' she said. The distinction was important.

Nell reached out and squeezed Grace's arm. 'I'm sorry darling; I didn't know.'

'That was my fault,' Grace said. 'I thought it was going to go away. The Board needed to work through a process but there was no substance behind the claim as far as I was concerned, so being off work was just an inconvenience I had to tolerate. And then, being in Duckton, and meeting Harriet changed a lot of things. We had fun together, and.' She stopped talking and drifted with the intimate memories she didn't feel inclined to share.

Vera studied her niece carefully and when she spoke the fire in her tone had dissipated. 'You're in love with her,' she said.

Grace struggled to hold back the tears at the loss that transfixed her. 'Yes, I fell in love with her,' she said softly.

Grace's phone pinged. Sandra Floss had agreed to meet.

'Well, that's it then.' Vera said. 'You need to go and get her back. What are you waiting for?' she said.

'I need to prove my innocence,' Grace said. 'Harriet deserves that at least. I should have been honest with her from the start, but I really didn't see it coming to this.'

'How are you going to do that?' Vera said.

Grace held up her phone. 'Sandra, the woman who made the allegation, has agreed to meet with me,' she said.

'Why?' Nell said.

Grace shrugged. 'I said I wanted to apologise to her face-to-face. She has her money now, so she has nothing to lose,' Grace said. 'I was planning to record an admission from her on my phone,' she added.

Vera looked to Nell and shook her head with a frown. 'I've got a better plan,' she said.

*

Harriet walked into the coffee shop and up to the counter.

'Coffee?' Drew said.

'Hot chocolate, please.'

'You okay?'

'Not really.'

Drew nodded. 'Take a seat. I'll be over,' she said and went about making the drink.

Harriet sat and stared vacantly.

The days had passed in a blur since speaking to Elvis, each day bringing with it a deeper feeling of loneliness, a greater sense of loss, and the emptiness was like nothing she had experienced before. She hadn't realised how much Grace had got under her skin until she wasn't there anymore. The place seemed ghostly quiet, and yet it was as it had been before Grace arrived. An image of Grace flat on her back on that first day, Flo pinning her to the ground and licking her neck came to mind and she felt the flicker of a glow inside. She had been so embarrassed but had known from the first moment of laying eyes on Grace, the way her heart raced and her stomach tingled, that she was attracted to her. She hadn't expected Grace to be so interesting, either. Reserved, a little, but that all made sense now. She had enjoyed hearing about Grace's travels around the world, the places she had seen and the people she had met. She had enjoyed spending time with Grace, no matter what they were doing.

'Here,' Drew said. She placed a large cream-laden hot chocolate drink and piece of flapjack in front of Harriet. 'Sugar always makes things better,' she said and smiled.

And then the door clanged open and Delia and Jenny entered. They walked straight up to the table and sat.

'We'll have one of those please,' Delia said to Drew.

Drew smiled at Harriet and winked at the two older women. 'Coming right up,' she said.

'Harriet,' Jenny said.

'Mum!'

'I've spoken to our Vera.'

Harriet rolled her eyes. 'How's the cruise going?' she said.

'She's going to speak to Grace,' Jenny said.

Harriet puffed out air.

'In fact, she'll be at Grace's flat.' She looked at her watch. 'About now,' she said.

Harriet frowned. 'What are you talking about?'

'Vera's been staying at Nell's. Anyway, Delia and I aren't here to get into that, we're here to stop you making the daftest decision of your life,' Jenny said.

'Mum!' Harriet started.

'Don't you mum me,' Jenny said.

'I've seen you wither away these last years. You're in your prime and life is passing you by.'

'Oh, for God's sake, mum!'

'I mean it. You're a beautiful, intelligent, sexy woman.'

Harriet winced.

'You are. And, what's more, so is Grace. Very intelligent; very sexy in fact.'

'Mum, seriously!'

'What your mum is trying to say is, you and Grace were right together. You complemented each other, like Ying and Yang,' Delia said. 'It's fate, Harriet, you and Grace. Fate. You were meant to be together. It's written in the cards, and they're never wrong.'

Harriet doubted the last point, but she couldn't argue with the rest of it.

'Here goes,' Drew said, and loaded the table with hot chocolate and a selection of cakes.

'She didn't do anything wrong, Harriet,' Jenny said.

Harriet looked away from the two women who were staring at her intently.

'She didn't. She's been set up; Vera and Nell are sure of it.'

They don't have evidence though, do they? Harriet sighed, and Elvis's words of wisdom came to her. 'I just don't know,' she said.

'Are you or are you not in love with Grace?' Jenny said.

Harriet blushed. She hadn't even admitted that fact to Grace. She picked up the hot chocolate and sipped, hoping the heat would expand her oesophagus. It didn't, it just burned and she started to cough.

'You are, I can tell. It's a mother's instinct,' Jenny said, nodding her head. 'In fact, I would go so far as to say you didn't feel as strongly about Abigail.'

'Annabel,' Harriet corrected.

'As you do about Grace,' Jenny finished.

Harriet felt the heat sitting in her cheeks and continued to hide behind the mug of hot chocolate.

'What if she didn't do it?' Jenny was trying a new tack. 'Let's just say, for argument's sake, Grace can't prove it. What if, this other woman has set her up and Grace is the victim in all of this, and you haven't even given her a chance to tell you her side of the story? What then?'

Harriet sighed.

'What if you let go of the best thing that's happened to you in forever?' Jenny said.

'She's got a good point,' Drew said from the other side of the counter.

Harriet glared at Drew.

Drew smiled at her warmly.

Harriet looked from one woman to another and sighed. 'I'm scared,' she said.

Jenny reached out and held Harriet's hand. 'Of course, you are darling, that's only natural. I just want you to be happy, and Grace made you happy. I've never seen you as at ease with someone.'

Harriet nodded. It was true. She had been happy with Grace around. And, she'd been lonely since Grace had left. And no, she hadn't given Grace the chance to explain, she'd felt too hurt, too let down, and betrayed by the apparent deception. And, yes, that might just be the lens of the past reflected on the present. She gazed to the café window, the street beyond. 'I should have let her speak,' she said.

'It's not too late,' Jenny said, squeezing her daughter's hand with enthusiasm.

'It's fate,' Delia said and dived into a cream slice.

Harriet felt lifted by the resolution and, ignoring the flapjack, opted for the round, iced bun with a cherry on the top. Her choice didn't go unnoticed by the three women smiling at her.

'That's my girl,' Jenny said and tucked into a jam doughnut, spilling the red sauce onto her chin.

23.

Grace checked the time. She pulled on her Moschino jacket and stepped into the street. She wasn't entirely convinced of the plan, but in the absence of a better alternative had gone along with Vera's suggestion. 6 pm in the Carpenter's Arms, at the back of the pub, the first booth on the right. Those had been Sandra Floss's instructions. They had all sat in the same booth for management-team drinks a few months ago and Sandra had caught her attention. The memory was a bitter one. At least the booth would be marginally quieter at that time of day.

As she approached the pub, her heart pounded with the thought that Sandra Floss might believe she had been assaulted. But she had agreed to meet and if that were the case Grace could at least apologise in person, rather than try and communicate through the impersonal, destructive, litigious process that had already taken place. She stepped up to the bar, ordered a gin and tonic and sought out the booth.

'Are you in position?' the whispered voice came from behind her, from inside the attached booth.

Grace rolled her eyes. 'SSShhhh!' she said and silence came in response. She sipped from the drink and waited. Five past six came and then a quarter past. By half-past six, there was still no sign of Sandra Floss. She checked her phone. No message either. But then, Sandra Floss didn't need to send her a message if she had changed her mind. Sandra Floss was under no obligation to speak to her. Grace closed her eyes and waited.

'What's happening?' Nell whispered as Vera peaked out from the booth and looked around the pub.

'I can't see anyone coming this way.' Vera said. She sat back in her seat. 'I need another drink,' she said and got up.

'You're fidgeting, V,' Nell remarked.

'You want another drink?'

'Yes, please.'

'Then I'm not fidgeting, I'm going to get drinks,' Vera said and stomped towards the bar.

'Are you still there?' Nell said to Grace.

Grace opened her eyes; the feeling of anticipation having drained from her. 'I don't think she's going to show up,' she said.

Nell remained silent.

Vera returned, handed a gin to Grace as she passed the booth and sat facing Nell. 'I can't see this Sandra woman,' she said.

'V, you don't know what she looks like,' Nell said.

'That's not the point. I would know her if I saw her. It's an instinct. Her kind of people have an aura about them, an unpleasant one,' she said.

'Ssshhh!' Grace said and sipped at her drink. She's not going to show. The emptiness swelled inside her, drawing her into a well of darkness. It was hopeless. She picked up her phone and studied it. Her heart ached, Harriet's beautiful, innocent, face in her mind's eye.

'Is that her?' Vera announced, drawing Grace's attention.

'No,' Grace responded. She looked at her phone again. No messages and it was seven-thirty. 'I'll text her,' Grace said.

'Wait!' Vera said, and pondered. 'What if she's playing you? Texting her gives her power,' she said. 'Don't do it, she's not worth it, Grace. That mother-fucking.'

'Vera!' Nell exclaimed.

'Well, I am livid.'

Grace stood. 'You're probably right,' she said, and calmly finished her drink.

Nell put a soothing hand on Vera's shoulder. It didn't relax her.

'I need another gin,' Vera said. 'Make it a double.'

'I need to go home,' Grace said, full of resignation.

'What will you do?' Nell said, reaching for Grace's arm.

Grace paid for the drinks. 'I don't know,' she said. 'The most important thing is that you know the truth. That Harriet knows the truth,' she said. 'And, I can't get that if Sandra fucking Floss isn't willing to talk to me.

'A no-show is a sure sign of guilt in my book,' Vera said.

'Yes, I agree,' Nell said. And then paused. 'We have no doubt you didn't do anything wrong, Grace.'

Grace looked at both women and smiled weakly. 'I'm not entirely without blame, mum, but I did not sexually harass or assault Sandra Floss. I would never do that.'

Nell's smile was a little tight. 'I'm sure,' she said.

'I genuinely thought she wanted to be with me.'

'We don't need to know the details, darling. I trust you,' Nell said, looking around the bar.

'I need you both to know,' Grace said. 'She had been coming on to me for weeks, flirting in the office when no one was around. I was flattered and surprised at first, and then she made her intentions very clear during the party. She suggested going to my room and I fell for it. Yes, we were both very drunk. But when we started.'

'Yes, darling,' Nell interrupted, unable to hold eye contact with her daughter, acutely aware that people around them might be snooping.

'She said no and I stopped. Then she ran out of the room. Next thing I know, she has filed a complaint and I'm suspended by the Board.'

Nell put an arm around Grace, pulled her close and kissed the top of her head. 'It all sounds quite horrific, darling. I am so sorry. Why didn't you tell me?'

Grace pinched the bridge of her nose to stop from crying. 'I honestly thought it would all go away because it wasn't true. I think she had planned the whole thing. Made a point of recording us and got others to say that I had plied her with drink and made a pass at her. I didn't do that. I was stupid and made a dumb drunken decision on the euphoria of an exceptionally successful event. But, I would never.'

'Sshh, I know, darling. I know.'

'It's a bloody good job she hasn't shown up,' Vera said. 'I'd have her guts for garters.'

Grace eased out from her mother's embrace. 'What am I going to do about Harriet?' she said.

'You're going to go and talk to her,' Vera said. 'She's not naïve and she will understand. She got badly hurt, Grace, and I'm sure that's why she reacted as she did. Jenny and Delia have been talking to her. She's in love with you as much as you are with her, and it doesn't take a rocket scientist to work out that you both belong together. She misses you, and I'm sure when you get to talk to her, she will believe you,' Vera said.

'I wanted proof,' Grace said.

'I know. That makes it easier, but sometimes you must take a leap of faith and trust. It's tough, but you'll both know it in here,' Vera said, putting her hand to her heart.

Nell smiled at her sister, and it occurred to her that Vera spoke from experience. Had Vera taken a leap of faith in the past, and been burned too? She became painfully aware that she didn't know a great deal about her older sister's life, and that, she vowed, needed to change. 'She's right,' Nell said.

Grace nodded.

'Anyone hungry?' Vera said. 'I've built up quite an appetite.'

'V,' Nell admonished, aware that Grace looked a million miles away from having a desire to eat.

'Come on Grace, food is a necessary evil sometimes, lifts the spirits,' she said and hooked an arm through Grace's.

'I know just the place,' Grace said.

'Is it good comfort food?' Vera said.

'It is mine,' Grace said. She felt lifted by their unwavering support and as she plotted her next move, and Harriet's beautiful smile, she too smiled.

'That's good,' Nell said.

*

Vera studied the meze with a look of disdain. 'Bloody food, my arse,' she said.

'Oh, don't you worry. You'll be stuffed before you get to the main course,' Grace said, and draped a piece of flatbread enthusiastically through the spicy hummus dip, fuelled by her resolution to go to Harriet and explain everything.

'It's been quite a day,' Nell said.

'You need to get a life, sister,' Vera said. 'Devon's one step short of the bloody grave.'

'It is not, Vera. We have a wonderful life down there,' Nell defended.

'Everyone's different, Vera,' Grace said.

Vera huffed and bit into a stuffed vine leaf. 'Hmm, this taste's good,' she said.

'It's the best in town,' Grace said.

Nell studied her daughter, feeling overwhelmed with emotion. 'What are you going to do?' she said.

'I'm selling my flat and going to speak to Harriet,' Grace said.

Nell and Vera smiled.

Grace took a sip of wine. 'And, I thought, if things work out, I might look for a place in a village called Upper Duckton,' she said.

'Over my dead body!' Vera exclaimed.

Grace laughed. 'What?'

'No relation of mine is going to settle in Upper fucking Duckton,' she said.

'Doug says it's the place to be,' Grace teased.

'Doug Pettigrew is delusional,' Vera said. 'I know just the place, though,' she added and drifted in thought.

Grace looked at her. 'I am not living in a bloody haunted house,' she said.

'And, I'm not selling that there haunted house,' Vera retorted. 'Good God no! Old Hilda Spencer and I are good friends. Has she been looking out for you?' she said.

Grace choked on the taramasalata, the fishy paste lingering in her throat and preventing her from speaking.

'The other side of the village, there's a three-bed cottage, with a smallholding and a pretty stream that runs along the bottom of the fields. I thought about buying it myself, but I can't leave Hilda all alone in that big old house. Looks out over the valley, and down into Lower Duckton. Beautiful aspect,' Vera said.

It felt too far away from Harriet's cottage. 'I'll see,' Grace said.

'Anyway, first things first, you need to speak to Harriet,' Vera said.

Grace's stomach flipped. Yes, she did. She wanted to call Harriet there and then, but she needed to speak to her face-to-face, to be able to look into her eyes and hold her close. 'I need to sort a few things out here first,' she said. 'Might take a few days.'

'I've got an idea,' Vera said as if talking to herself.

'Oh dear!' Nell remarked.

Nell and Grace looked at Vera, waiting for more information.

Vera looked at them. 'I'm stuffed,' she said and shoved an olive into her mouth.

Was Vera talking to herself? 'That was the first starter course,' Grace said and chuckled.

'I'll live,' Vera said. 'Bring it on! Don't get food like this in Devon. Fish and chips if you're lucky and never on a Monday.'

'Stop yourself, Vera Thistlethwaite. You've had the time of your life rocking with your little sister this last fortnight. You'll miss it, you know you will.'

Vera flushed. 'We should make it an annual event,' she said with genuine affection.

Nell looked at her and smiled. 'Deal,' she said. 'And I'll come to you for a week too.'

'I'll need to okay that with Hilda,' Vera said, and Grace started laughing.

'She's serious,' Nell said.

Grace stopped laughing and looked from Nell to Grace. 'I know,' she said. 'Hilda spoke to me.'

Vera smiled. 'Did she now?' she said, with more than an echo of surprise in her tone. 'Well, I never did.'

Grace couldn't resist any longer. She picked up her phone and texted Harriet.

I need to talk to you.

The response pinged back immediately.

I want to talk to you too.

Face to face? Grace responded.

Yes. I'll come to London.

I'm planning to come back to Duckton. I'll confirm when I know. Give me a couple of days. Grace replied.

I love you.

Grace's heart skipped a beat and she grinned, heat infusing her cheeks.

I love you.

She put the phone down and swallowed, suddenly aware that two pairs of eyes were smiling at her.

'All good?' Vera said.

'All good,' Grace said. She was shaking with relief and anticipation.

'That's good,' Nell said and squeezed Grace's hand.

24.

Grace closed the front door to her flat and handed the keys to the estate agent. She looked up at the Georgian building with its original sash windows and smiled. At a point in time, she had thought of it as pretty. It wasn't that the flat had changed in any way; it was just that she had discovered something even more beautiful.

'You've got a fantastic property, it won't take long to sell,' the man said enthusiastically, for the millionth time of not being asked.

Grace smiled politely. 'You've got my contact details,' she said.

He nodded. 'We'll be in touch with regular updates,' he said.

'Sure,' she responded and smiled again. She picked up the last of her suitcases and walked to the old, two-tone VW camper van with its four-way flashing lights, and a note she had put in the window that read, loading this vehicle, please do not ticket. She placed the case inside the van, climbed into the driver's side and turned the engine. She turned to the passenger seat and smiled. 'You ready?' she said.

'Hell yes! I've never taken a ride in a camper van,' Vera said.

'All strapped in?'

'Drive on, James,' Vera said and waved her hand in the air like royalty.

Grace chuckled. Vera reminded her of herself in a lot of ways. 'Got the flask of coffee?'

Vera tapped the bag at her feet. 'And thirty-five bottles of gin,' Vera said, tilting her head to the rear of the van. 'What a brilliant idea to have a gin tent at the summer fete; you are genius Grace Pinkerton, just like your aunt Vera. Genius!'

Grace chuckled. She picked up the note from the dashboard screwed it into a ball and threw it in the door's side pocket, found first gear, and pulled away from the kerb.

Grace had never owned a camper van and the choice had been made on the back of having had two random thoughts. The first, that it would give her a place to stay, parked on Vera's driveway if necessary, while she sorted out something more permanent. That was the worst excuse. The second more enticing thought had to do with Harriet and what she might like to do with Harriet in the camper van. The idea of spending time in an undisturbed location of their choosing had appealed. Then her mind drifted to making love in the confined space and then she hadn't been able to shift the thought – so she had been compelled to buy the van. She grinned, amused by what Harriet might think of her plan. She couldn't get to Duckton-by-Dale quickly enough, though the camper van had a leisurely pace of its own.

'Did you choose bright pink, or was it the only option available?' Vera said, nosing at the bonnet through the windscreen and then putting on her sunglasses. 'Damn near blinding me.'

Grace laughed. 'Are you going to moan all the way?' she said. She couldn't even see the bonnet that well on the virtually flat fronted vehicle.

'Only as far as Nottingham,' Vera said. 'Then I'll snore the rest of the way.' She chuckled, reached across and patted Grace on the leg. 'You're a good kid,' she said.

Grace flushed. 'You got the map?'

'Fuck that! Stick the satnav on, will you? I'll get travel sick looking down.'

'I thought you wanted to do this the old-fashioned way?' Grace said. 'I bought a map specifically.'

'I draw the line,' Vera said. 'And can we get a McDonalds' on the way up? Your mother hasn't let me eat junk food the whole holiday. Should have gone on that cruise,' she mumbled.

'I like pink,' Grace said, and beeped the horn and waved at a group of tourists who were eagerly pointing cameras at the vehicle as she drove past.

The vehicle spluttered and Vera looked at Grace. 'Is it going to get us there?'.

'It better had,' Grace said and smiled.

*

Harriet cradled the framed image, her gaze following the line of Grace in profile, the highlights tinting her hair and the glow in her cheeks. The fine lines that appeared as she squinted slightly with the brightness of the sun, betraying the depth of experience that otherwise remained hidden behind youthful skin and a tender smile. Her heart raced and butterflies danced frantically in her stomach. She looked at the clock. It would be hours before Grace arrived, and it already felt as though hours had passed since she woke. Time seemed to be standing still exactly when she wanted it to speed up. She had motored through the gardening, boxed up the plants and vegetables for the Friday market and tended to the horses. She wondered about going into town, having a coffee and long lunch, occupying time with Drew, but she felt too on edge to sit and make conversation. She placed the framed image onto the mantelpiece and walked into the kitchen.

'Come on,' she said and Archie leapt from his bed, closely followed by Flo, Winnie coming a close third. 'Let's go for a walk,' she said. At the sound of the word, all three dogs either whined, nudged or leapt and scraped at her legs. She picked up the leads from the hook on the wall and all three dogs sat patiently, until Flo started whining and bopped Archie with a playful paw, and then yawned. She secured each dog in turn and stepped out the door. A couple of hours would pass the time of day and she could get some photographs up towards Cariscarn, and overlooking Upper Duckton. Grace would recognise the Duckton Arms from the shots. She stopped in her tracks, suddenly aware of the white-haired lady heading to the rear of Vera's house. She blinked, stood staring reconciling the vision with reality, and came up with confusion. Surely not! She didn't recall seeing a lead, and there definitely wasn't sheep or dog in sight. She stepped towards the house and jumped when the flash of white moved across the window, the vision heading from the kitchen through the foyer and into the living room. She made her way to the kitchen door and looked through the window. Nothing. She continued, through a second gate and around the back of the house, past the old coal house, and continued around to the front door. Nothing.

Then she heard a rumble and clatter coming from the back of the house and followed the noise. She leapt as Terence jumped from the top of the coal house roof and cursed him. And then the coal house door flung open, and the vision in white hair stood before her.

'Mother!' Harriet screamed.

'Ahh!' Jenny screamed, clinging at her chest. 'Harriet, what are you trying to do to me?'

Harriet stood, mouth wide-open, eyes on stalks. 'What are you doing, mum?' she said, assessing her. Her hair didn't look quite as white as it had done from the cottage and she frowned, shaking her head.

'We're airing the place before Vera gets back,' Jenny said. She stepped back through the coal house and into an internal narrow corridor.

Harriet followed her, dogs in tow. 'I thought this was blocked up years ago,' Grace said, studying the dark cold space. She shivered.

Jenny went through another door and entered the living room, ignoring Harriet's statement.

'Does the gin go back in this cupboard?' Delia said, appearing from the upstairs carrying a box of six bottles. 'Oh, hello Harriet,' she added.

'Yes, please,' Jenny said, ignoring Delia's flushed state.

'It was you?' Harriet said.

'What's that, dear?' Jenny said, distracting herself with a feather duster.

'Hilda Spencer, moving things around?' she said. 'It was you two?'

Jenny looked at her blankly. 'Good heavens no! We're just here to spring clean. Are you going for a walk?' she said.

Harriet squinted at her.

'Delia, can you put the linen on the line, I think the wash just finished,' she shouted.

'Yes,' Harriet said.

'Good, good, they'll be here soon enough,' Jenny said with a beaming grin.

Harriet stood, gazing oddly at her mother, her mother staring back at her refusing to give any additional information.

'I need to get on, dear, unless there's anything else?' Jenny said.

'Right, yes, no!' Harriet said and led the dogs out the front door. God, she needed a long walk.

*

Harriet spotted the pink and white camper van before she crossed the main road, a beacon blotting the otherwise aesthetic view. 'Good God! What is that?'

Flo barked enthusiastically in response and stood at her waist.

Her racing heart answered the rhetorical question and she took a sharp intake of breath, feeling the impact through to the weakness that rocked her. She started to chuckle, with a flurry of excitement, and Flo tugged on the lead.

As she approached the house, she allowed Flo and Winnie off the lead and Flo bounded down the driveway, whining and barking towards the familiar figure.

Grace smiled at the dog as it approached. And then it became apparent that Flo had no intention of stopping and Grace's expression shifted. Unable to brace herself in time, the thrust of the dog's welcome landed her on her back, and she lay there laughing, Flo's paws pinning her in place, Flo's tongue licking and nuzzling her neck. 'Well hello to you,' she said.

Vera appeared from the front door of Duckton House and Winnie sprinted as fast as her short stubby legs would take her. Vera picked her up and received a verbal wet greeting. 'Hello, my lovely, did you miss your Mumma then?' Vera said. 'Of course, you did,' she continued, carrying the dog to the house. 'Mumma's got you some treats,' Vera was heard saying as she disappeared through the front door.

Grace had managed to pull herself from Flo's clutches and stood, dusting her jeans down and wiping at her neck with the cuff of her sleeve. She held Harriet's gaze.

Archie took a step toward Grace and growled and Harriet tugged his lead.

Grace smiled. 'Hello Archie,' she said. She bent down and ruffled his neck. 'Good to see you too.' She stood facing Harriet and Harriet's smile turned to a chuckle and Grace couldn't stop staring at her. 'Hey,' she croaked.

'Hey,' Harriet said.

'You look good.'

Harriet smiled. She reached down and let Archie off the lead. 'Go play,' she said, and he ran off with Flo into the field. She stepped up to Grace. 'I missed you,' she said.

Grace could feel the fire in her cheeks, the pounding in her chest. 'I missed you, too,' she whispered.

'Would you like a cup of tea?'

'Sounds perfect.' Grace smiled, held out her hand and Harriet took it.

'What on earth is that abomination to the eye doing on my driveway?' Harriet said as they passed the VW camper van.

Grace hadn't expected that response. 'Is it the colour? We can paint it,' she said.

Harriet stopped and studied the vehicle with a bemused gaze. 'Hmm! I guess that would be a start,' she said, and smiled.

It was the sweetest smile Grace had ever seen.

'I've got a plan,' Grace said.

And Harriet laughed. 'You fit in so well here,' she said and cupped Grace's cheek with tenderness.

The touch was brief but Grace's skin still stung as she stood watching Harriet making tea, entranced by the well-practised movements, enjoying the familiar shape of her, the way she tucked her hair around her ear, toyed with the spoon while waiting for the water to boil.

'I'm so sorry,' Harriet said in a quiet voice, and when she turned Grace saw the damp sheen covering her eyes.

'I'm sorry too, I should have talked to you.'

'I should have let you,' Harriet said.

'Hey,' Grace said, softly. She moved to Harriet and opened her arms. Harriet leant into the embrace and Grace held her tightly. 'I need to explain,' Grace said.

Harriet eased back and gazed into Grace's eyes. 'I know you didn't do it,' she said.

Grace's smile was tight. 'Vera?'

'No, the cards,' Harriet said, and for a moment Grace couldn't tell whether she was joking. 'And, the fact that you've been nothing but honourable since the day I met you. People who do that sort of thing aren't,' she said.

253

Grace nodded. 'I'm pretty sure I was setup,' she said.

'Why?'

'I can't prove it, but I don't think Sandra would have done this of her own volition, though. I think Stephanie was behind it. She's the chair of the Board, and the Board are greedy, and.' She paused. 'Stephanie knew my weak spot and exploited it.'

Harriet stared at Grace.

'You know I said I wasn't good with relationships?'

Harriet nodded.

'I've never been in a long-term relationship, Harriet. I've probably spent no more than a long weekend living with someone. It's just not something I've ever done. And, I'm sure I've broken a few hearts along the way. Not intentionally, more as a function of the lifestyle we were all living, I guess. I'm not making an excuse, Harriet. And, I'm not proud of it either.'

Harriet nodded, turned and poured hot water into the mugs.

'Stephanie and I had a very brief affair. It was years ago, and a long time before she became chair of the Board. We've worked together for years, and I never ever.' She paused again, finding the words difficult to say. 'I've never harassed or assaulted anyone in my life, Harriet. I made a huge fucking mistake going anywhere near Sandra Floss and I have since wondered whether Stephanie was behind this all along. But I don't have any answers.'

Harriet stirred the tea, then turned to face Grace.

'I tried to meet Sandra face-to-face to apologise, and I wanted her to tell me that nothing had happened between us so I could prove it to you. I sent her a message and then she didn't show up. I just wanted you to know the truth, Harriet. I don't care about the business. I don't care about Sandra or Stephanie. I'm not a vindictive person.' She paused, took in a deep breath. 'I'm in love with you Harriet, and I've never been in love before, and it scares the shit out of me, but...'

Harriet closed the space between them and took Grace's breath away with a hungry kiss. When she eased back, both women had tears wetting their cheeks. 'I know you didn't do it, Grace. I should have let you explain. I'm sorry I overheard your call and got confused. I was so stupid.'

Harriet turned her head and Grace ran an index finger tenderly down her cheek, tucked the hair behind her ear and drew Harriet's attention to her again. She leaned closer and kissed Harriet on the forehead, then her eyelids and then she found her lips and held her in a lingering kiss, her arms wrapped around Harriet and pressing their bodies together. She moaned and eased out of the kiss, maintaining the eye contact between them. 'Can we try and leave the past in the past?' she said.

Harriet nodded. 'Yes,' she said and smiled. She continued to look at Grace. 'Thank you for coming back,' she said.

'I'm here to stay if you'll have me?'

Harriet smiled.

'I'll sleep in the van until I find a place,' she said, looking out the window at the pink and white blot on the landscape.

Harriet started laughing. 'You'll do no such thing. There's a spare bed here if you feel you need to be on your own,' she said and studied Grace. 'And that monstrosity.' She looked to the van. 'That, I've no idea what to do with,' she said.

'It needs a bit of work, but the engine's kind of sound. I thought we might go camping sometime,' Grace said.

Harriet laughed. 'Is that your plan?' she said. She reached out, traced a finger down Grace's jawline, down her neck, her collarbone and the centre of her chest. 'I've got a much better idea,' she said. Abandoning the tea, she took Grace by the hand and led her up the stairs.

25.

'One, two, three, and lift. Right a bit, towards me, and slowly, down. Great,' Grace said. 'Right let's get this one up next,' she said. She looked to the blue sky, the sun bright even at this early hour.

Doug, Drew and Bryan started fitting the tent-poles together and put the frame into position.

'I don't think we need the partition between the tents,' Grace said. 'The beer tent and gin bar should be connected.'

'Agreed,' Doug said and helped position the adjoining tent.

They stood back and admired their work. The two white tents sat side by side, the separating flaps removed.

'That's better. Tables next,' Grace said, wiping the sweat from her brow.

'We'll get them,' Doug said, indicating for Drew to help him.

'We'll get the other gazebos up,' Grace said and moved to the next slot on the field.

'Where are we putting the Wellie tossing?' Neville said. He already had his tape measure in hand and was eyeing up the field.

'It goes here,' the tall, handsome man said, as he walked up.

'It was agreed to move it further down the field, Neville,' Doris said and eyed the young man with disdain.

'It was entirely my fault last year, Mrs Akeman. I'd like to help Neville manage the wellie tossing this year, make sure there isn't an incident.' He smiled broadly. 'I won't be throwing the wellies, I promise,' he added, holding his palms up.

'Well, I don't know about,' Doris started.

Neville cut Doris off before she could go any further. 'Of course, you can, Jonny. That will be very helpful, thank you.'

Jonny 'Wilkinson' Jones beamed. 'Right, shall we rope off the area a bit further over that way, then the café should be well out of reach?' he said. 'I'll stand out there and field any wild throws that might get close. Could do without any cakes flying eh? Or heart attacks!'

'Good idea,' Neville said and reached for the tape. 'Here you go, son. So, how's uni going? Your mum must be happy you're home for the holidays.'

Doris marched off towards the stage under construction.

Grace smiled at Harriet as she walked past carrying another crate of plants heading for the horticultural tent. 'You want anything?' she said, unpacking a bottle of gin and setting it on the table. Harriet's eyebrows lifted highlighting seductively dark eyes and Grace felt it in the weight of the t-shirt pressing against her nipples. 'A drink?' she clarified.

'It's only half-eight,' Harriet remarked.

'I was thinking coffee, and a bacon sandwich,' Grace said, indicating to the café that was already fully functioning, the aromas drifting around the field.

Harriet continued to undress Grace with her eyes and a smile that ripped through Grace. 'Count me in,' Harriet said, and disappeared into the horticultural tent, leaving Grace weak at the knees.

Grace gazed around the field. Kev and Luke were constructing a makeshift fence along the bottom of the field to host the sheep races, and Rex lay in the grass watching them both. Kelly and Vera were chatting, pointing and roping off an area in the centre of the field for the dog show, taking care to avoid the cricket crease. Little use a few bits of string would be if a dog decided to make a run for it! Another team were pushing the cricket net to its rightful spot to host the coconut shy and

Sheila seemed to be in control of loading the crockery onto the dresser for the plate smashing. Grace pondered the precision and diligence with which Shelia approached the task, aligning the plates in perfect symmetry and ensuring the cups sat with their patterns to the front. Had she grasped the fact that they would be smashed to smithereens within an hour? The stage was about ready and Drew seemed to be running at full steam, serving breakfast for the hungry helpers.

Elvis, Doug and Bryan had the beer running on tap and had several plastic half-filled cups lined up on the bar. For testing purposes, Doug had insisted and Grace had laughed. It was a beautiful sight, the slow steady construction, everyone playing a part in the well-oiled machine. Grace turned her attention to the figure walking towards her and smiled.

'You watching or helping?' Harriet said, and smiled.

Grace's steely eyes held Harriet's attention and both women flushed. 'Definitely watching,' Grace said, her voice slightly broken.

'Big lorry just showed up,' Doug said, disturbing Grace's concentration.

She smiled at him. 'That'll be the band,' she said.

'What are they called again?' he asked.

'Rocking 60s. They're a sixties tribute band, Doug.'

'Right. You know Elvis can't stand rock and roll, right?' Doug said.

'No, I didn't.' Grace grinned. 'You're kidding, right?'

'Nope, he's a mod through and through,' Doug said and walked off.

Fuck!

'Is that right, Elvis doesn't do rock music?' Grace said to Harriet.

'Yep, he's a mod, through and through,' she said, heading towards the café.

Grace walked with her. 'How did he get the name, Elvis?'

'His parents were big fans.' Harriet chuckled.

'Fuck! I'll need to see if they can throw in some soul and R&B or something,' she said.

Harriet laughed. 'I wouldn't worry, the rest of the village love a bit of rock and roll and since he bans it on the jukebox, he can suffer for his loyal flock today,' she said.

Grace laughed. She gazed at Harriet drinking her coffee and devoured the bacon sandwich. 'I needed that, what's next,' she said.

'We need to get the Tarot tent up, and there's the veggie display to set out, and I need to get Fizz settled over by the fence.'

'Okay, I'll go and speak to the band and then meet you at the horticultural tent,' Grace said. She looked up, blue sky and bright sunshine. 'It's going to be hot,' she said.

'Hmm, already is!' Harriet said, her eyes never leaving Grace. 'Very hot,' she mumbled.

'Come on you love birds, you've got work to do,' Drew said and ushered them out of the café.

Grace felt the distance as she and Harriet headed in opposite directions. She sighed, looked at her watch, feeling slightly edgy as she returned from talking to the band, although relieved that they were able to cater for a wide range of music tastes.

'Morning Grace,' Delia said, arriving with a suitcase in hand.

'Morning Grace,' Jenny said, a pace behind her, carrying a cold bag.

'I'll need to put your gazebo up,' Grace said and followed the two women to the table that was already in position.

259

'Looks to be coming together,' Jenny said and waved in Vera's direction. Vera and Kelly waved back.

'Can you grab that end and hold it down until I say?' Grace said, pointing to the spot she needed Jenny to secure.

Jenny followed the instructions, and then Grace removed her hand. Jenny hadn't anticipated the sudden force. Her hand slipped and then whoosh! The gazebo flew open, slapping Grace square in the face and slamming her onto her back. She groaned.

'Ooh, that was quick,' Jenny said, unaware of the blood oozing from Grace's nose.

'Good heavens,' Delia remarked, spotting the injury and immediately reaching into her bag.

Grace moaned, pinched her nose and remained seated on the grass. 'I've got stars floating in front of my eyes,' she said, the stinging sensation bringing tears.

'Ooh, that'll be a sign,' Delia remarked and dived into the suitcase and took out, *The Energy of Astronomy: A users guide to the meaning of star patterns and their relationship to health and wellbeing.*

'It's a bloody sign alright. A sign that Jenny let go of the bloody gazebo,' Grace said, pinching her nose.

'Oh my God,' Harriet screamed, running towards them. She threw herself to her knees and wrapped Grace in her arms. 'Oh, my God, are you okay?' She cupped Grace's cheeks, took the offered scented cloth from Delia and held it to Grace's nose.

Grace wiped the water from her eyes and started to chuckle. 'Jeez, that hurt,' she said.

Harriet studied Grace and brushed her cheeks tenderly, and Jenny nudged Delia and smiled.

'I'm really sorry, Grace. I didn't know it was going to ping open like that,' Jenny said.

Grace nodded and smiled. 'You two really are that determined to get Harriet and me together,' she said and chuckled.

Jenny flushed and Delia glared at her. 'Good God no! That was an accident, I swear.'

Harriet laughed at the look of horror on her mother's face. She turned to Grace and inspected the damage. 'You might end up with a black eye,' she said and then she kissed Grace.

'My ears are ringing,' Grace said. 'And no, that's not another sign, Delia.'

'Come on,' Harriet said, holding out a hand and pulling Grace to her feet. 'Let's get the doc to check you over?' she said.

Grace's attention was distracted by the arrival of the horsebox in the carpark. 'I'll be fine,' she said. 'I need to deal with this,' and with that, she kissed Harriet and headed towards the carpark.

'I honestly didn't mean to let go.' Jenny said to Harriet. She looked devastated.

'It's okay mum, I know. You might want to peg that tent down though before it blows away,' she said, pointing to the gazebo that had started to slide across the grass. She walked back to the horticultural tent.

Grace walked back from the carpark and the horsebox set off down the road.

Vera approached Grace and introduced herself to the jet-black pony with a white stripe running the length of its nose. 'She's a fine-looking animal,' she said.

Grace was grinning, her heart racing.

Vera looked towards the horticultural tent. 'Good luck,' she said.

Grace walked the pony across the field, watched by the whole village. As she approached the tent, Harriet emerged.

'Grace!' she exclaimed.

'She's for you,' Grace said. 'I thought we could.'

261

Harriet's mouth claimed Grace's stopping any further words and her arms wrapped firmly around Grace's neck.

A cheer went up and then Harriet stood back and studied Grace intently.

'I thought we might start up the riding lessons again,' Grace said. Harriet continued to stare at her and for a moment Grace wondered if she'd been too presumptuous. The gaze felt excruciating, and then a smile grew on Harriet's face and she felt the weight of concern slide from her shoulders.

'I love you, Grace Pinkerton,' Harriet said. She caressed the horse's head, smoothed down her neck and patted along her length. 'She's beautiful.'

'I'm glad you like her,' Grace said. 'I thought two ponies for the rides today would be helpful,' she added.

'So, you weren't just watching then?' Harriet teased. She slipped a hand around Grace's waist and pulled her into her body.

'Flo was my second option, she's almost the size of a Shetland pony but clearly lacks the discipline and patience needed for a novice, screaming, rider,' Harriet teased.

Harriet shut her up with another kiss.

Weakness moved through Grace in a wave, and when Harriet placed a tender kiss on her sore nose, the urge to escape the fete and hide out in the camper van came to her.

Harriet studied the pony again. 'Let's introduce her to Fizz,' she said. 'Does she have a name?'

'Midnight,' Grace said.

'Come on Midnight,' Harriet said and led the horse to the fence.

*

The band struck up *The House of the Rising Sun*, and much to everyone's surprise Elvis was spotted singing along.

262

When *I Can't Get No Satisfaction* followed, Doug was heard to shout out, 'Ain't that a fact,' and got an elbow in the ribs from Esther, who had already sampled five different flavours of gin and was now insistent on exploring the rhubarb and ginger liqueur.

'How's your nose?' Harriet asked as they walked the ponies' side by side for the last ride of the session.

'Better.'

'Delia's potion always works,' Harriet said and chuckled. She studied Grace. 'You've got a black eye,' she said. 'It's adorable, but will need some attention later,' she said, and Grace melted at the thought.

'All seems to be going well?' Grace said.

'Very smoothly,' Harriet said. 'Colin's cucumber won, so he's ecstatic.'

Grace turned to face Harriet. 'Are you happy?'

Harriet held Grace's eyes with such intensity that it took her breath away. 'Yes, I am now,' she said.

'Me too,' Grace said.

'Yes,' Harriet agreed. She had noticed.

The Morris dancers kicked off, and Grace's eyes tracked down the tinkling bells and tambourine noises to the side of the stage. Oh my God, the average age of the six men must have been sixty-five and one of them looked to be under fifty! And then one of the men stumbled and fear shot through Grace; she hadn't put them on the bloody risk assessment. Harriet was laughing at the display and then Grace saw Jarid standing closer cheering the men along with the crowd that had gathered, and she felt somewhat more reassured that the antics were all a part of the act.

The Morris dancers came to an end and a line of children marched across the grass and gathered around the tall Maypole. Grace couldn't see that well, as spectators and proud family members surrounded them clapping and cheering, but from what she could tell, they seemed to spend more time untangling the coloured ribbons hanging from the pole than they did dancing around the pole. One of the younger boys seemed insistent on going in the opposite direction to the rest of the dancers.

Harriet laughed. 'That's Jonny's youngest brother,' she said. 'Jonny used to do exactly the same thing.'

Grace observed Harriet in profile and at that moment she didn't give a shit about the Maypole dancers, cute though they might be. 'So, how about a camping weekend?' she said.

Harriet turned to face her. 'Not on your life,' she said and started laughing. 'I may be a country bumpkin, but I like my home comforts, you know.'

'I'll make you comfy,' Grace said and wiggled her eyebrows.

Bringing the ponies to a stop and dismounting two chirpy children, 'Fancy a drink?' Harriet said.

'Gin?'

'Hell yes!'

They walked towards the gin tent.

'Duuuccckkkkton!' The voice screamed across the field, grabbing Grace's attention a split second before the wellie scooted past her right ear.

'Jeez, it's like a bloody battle zone here,' she said and started laughing. 'I didn't have that one down on the risk assessment either,' she said. 'I thought it was the café under threat last year,' she joked.

'We'll add it in for next year,' Harriet said, and linked arms with Grace and dragged her out of the firing zone.

'Right,' Jenny said, leaning back in the chair and refilling her glass again from the unlabelled green bottle. She seemed to be staring across the field at the activities around the café and gin tent. 'We need a plan,' she slurred to Delia.

Overhearing the statement as he approached, Kelly on his arm. 'Oh no you don't,' Jarid said. 'You leave well alone mum,' he said. Delia was nodding in agreement. They looked relaxed and Kelly had a healthy glow about her. 'You've caught the sun,' she said.

'It's a beautiful day,' Kelly said.

'Come on, Delia, you can do a reading for me,' Jarid said.

'Ooh, that will be fun,' Delia said and started shuffling the cards. 'Put your hand on the top of the pack and imagine the next year,' she said.

Jarid followed the instructions and closed his eyes.

Delia cut the pack and turned over the top card. 'The Empress,' she said.

'What does that mean?'

'Fertility,' Kelly said.

Delia looked at her daughter and smiled.

Jarid went pale and gazed from Kelly to her mother and back again. 'No! Seriously?'

Kelly cupped his cheek and held his dazed look. 'The cards never lie,' she said and kissed him on the lips.

A grin slowly formed on Jarid's face and his cheeks darkened with the realisation. 'I'm going to be a dad?' he said.

'It seems so.' Kelly said and winked at the older women.

Delia squealed, 'I'm going to be a grandmother,' she announced. 'I need a drink to celebrate,' she added and filled her glass from Jenny's bottle.

Jarid and Kelly walked away from the Tarot tent, him muttering about being a father and directing them towards the beer tent. A cheer came back to Delia and Jenny as they sat drinking hooch, watching.

'That went down better than the Mayor last year,' Jenny said.

Vera wandered over and Jenny handed her a glass of hooch. The three women sat watching from a distance and then

265

Esther tottered towards them carrying a bottle half-filled with a blood-red-looking drink. 'Raspberry gin liqueur,' she said. 'It's bloody marvellous,' she slurred. 'Try it?'

The three women emptied their glasses and presented them to Esther, who had to give a lot of attention to the pouring of the drinks. She managed to achieve the task and then sat on the grass next to them.

'We need a plan,' Delia said again.

'Hmm, this is good,' Vera said, waving towards the bottom of the field.

'Who are you waving at?' Esther slurred.

'It's just Hilda, with Brambles,' Vera said, and Jenny looked up and waved.

'Why can't I see her?' Delia said.

'Probably, the raspberry gin,' Jenny said.

'I think the girls are doing just fine,' Vera said, gazing towards the gin tent. The band started up an Elvis song and everyone cheered, joining in at the chorus. *I Can't Help Falling in Love With You*, echoed around the field and Vera took Jenny's hand and smiled at her with deep affection.

'No, I mean a plan for Drew,' Jenny said.

'Ooh, now there's a good idea,' Delia said and started shuffling the cards.

Esther lay on the grass, hugging the raspberry gin bottle to her chest, snoring.

*

'I'm exhausted,' Grace said, slumping into the living room chair. 'I ache from nose to foot,' she said.

Harriet climbed on top of her and sat astride her legs.

'Oh my God, and now a deadweight in my lap,' Grace added, chuckling.

Harriet wriggled in her lap and Grace moaned. She stared intently at the dark eyes as they approached, and when Harriet's lips met hers, sparks shot through her, warming her from the inside.

Harriet eased off Grace's lap and held out her hand. 'Come on,' she said. 'I need a bath, and so do you.'

'You say the nicest things, Harriet Haversham,' Grace said allowing herself to be pulled to her aching feet. She stopped, and noted the framed picture on the mantelpiece, not for the first time, and felt her heart ache with love for the photographer who had captured the shot. She took a deep breath and released it slowly, pulling Harriet into her arms. 'I love you so much,' she said and breathed in the essence of her.

'I'm in love with you Grace Pinkerton, and I know I always will be,' Harriet said.

Grace cupped Harriet's cheeks, placed a tender kiss on her lips, and then held her gaze with unwavering certainty. 'You know it's fate?' she whispered.

Harriet's chuckle became a moan as Grace's lips came to her and caressed her with a lingering kiss. 'I'll give you fate,' she said and studied the bruising that had formed under Grace's right eye. 'I need to tend to that nose of yours,' she said and gently kissed the sore spot.

Grace chuckled. 'I've got something way more in need of attention,' she said taking Harriet by the hand and leading her up the stairs. 'Now, about that camper van holiday,' she added.

'No chance,' Harriet said but her smile said otherwise.

About Emma Nichols

Emma Nichols lives in Buckinghamshire with her partner and two children. She served for 12 years in the British Army, studied Psychology, and published several non-fiction books under another name, before dipping her toes into the world of lesbian fiction.

You can contact Emma through her website and social media:

www.emmanicholsauthor.com
www.facebook.com/EmmaNicholsAuthor
www.twitter.com/ENichols_Author

And do please leave a review if you enjoyed this book. Reviews really help independent authors to promote their work. Thank you.

Other Books by Emma Nichols

Visit **getbook.at/TheVincentiSeries** to discover The Vincenti Series: Finding You, Remember Us and The Hangover.

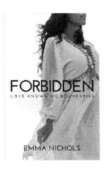  

Visit **getbook.at/ForbiddenBook** to start reading **Forbidden**

Visit **getbook.at/Ariana** to delve into the bestselling summer lesbian romance Ariana.

Visit **viewbook.at/Madeleine** to be transported to post-WW2 France and a timeless lesbian romance.

Thanks for reading and supporting!

61161890R00155

Made in the USA
Middletown, DE
17 August 2019